AN UNPARALLELED LOOK INTO THE SE-
CRET HEART OF ONE OF THE GREAT
FIGURES IN TWENTIETH-CENTURY LIT-
ERATURE . . . A ROMANTIC NOVEL OF
BREATHTAKING EMOTIONAL FORCE.

Julian sprang up; he caught her by the wrist,—
"Gipsy!"

"Come with the gipsy?" she whispered.

Her scented hair blew near him, and her face was upturned, with its soft, sweet mouth.

"Away from Aphros?" he said, losing his head.

"All over the world!"

He was suddenly swept away by the full force of her
wild, irresponsible seduction.

"Anywhere you choose, Eve."

She triumphed, close to him, and wanton.

"You'd sacrifice Aphros to me?"

"Anything you asked for," he said desperately.

She laughed, and danced away, stretching out her hands
towards him,—

"Join in the saraband, Julian?"

Avon Books by
Vita Sackville-West

THE EDWARDIANS   22731 $1.50

CHALLENGE

Vita Sackville-West

AVON
PUBLISHERS OF BARD, CAMELOT, DISCUS, EQUINOX AND FLARE BOOKS

AVON BOOKS
A division of
The Hearst Corporation
959 Eighth Avenue
New York, New York 10019

Foreword Copyright © 1974 by Nigel Nicolson.
Published by arrangement with The Executors
of the Estate of Mrs. Harold Nicolson.

ISBN: 0-380-00359-7

First Avon Printing, June, 1975.

AVON TRADEMARK REG. U.S. PAT. OFF. AND
FOREIGN COUNTRIES, REGISTERED TRADEMARK—
MARCA REGISTRADA, HECHO EN CHICAGO, U.S.A.

Printed in the U.S.A.

DEDICATION

ACABA EMBEO SIN TIRO, MEN CHUAJANI;
LIRENAS, BERJARAS TIRI OCHI BUSNE,
CHANGERI, TA ARMENSALLE

Foreword

CHALLENGE was Vita Sackville-West's second novel. She
wrote it between May 1918 and November 1919, and it
was published by George H. Doran Company, New York,
in 1924. It has never hitherto been published in England.
Some explanation is required why a young writer, who
had already gained a reputation for her poetry and whose
first novel *Heritage* (1919) had met with unusual acclaim,
should at the last moment, when *Challenge* was actually
printed and ready for binding, have decided to cancel publication in this country. It was not because she thought it
bad. 'I don't care what you say,' she wrote to Harold Nicolson, 'it is *damned good*. So there. Now you can think
me conceited if you like. I am pleased with it, really
pleased.' She cancelled it because family and friends
feared a scandal.

The novel is about her lover Violet Keppel (Trefusis). I
have described in *Portrait of a Marriage* how Vita and Violet, childhood friends since 1904 when Vita was twelve
and Violet ten, felt for each other a physical and intellectual attraction which suddenly, in 1918, burst into a flame
which burnt brilliantly and disastrously for the next three
years. Both were married (Vita in 1913, Violet in 1919),
but no family affections were strong enough to quench
their love. For months on end they played truant at
Monte Carlo, and in February 1920 made up their minds
to abandon everything, everyone, to spend the rest of their
lives together. They eloped to France. Their husbands
caught up with them at Amiens, and after an appalling exchange of reproach and counter-reproach the runaways
were recalled to sanity, and their affair gradually fizzled
out.

The proofs of *Challenge* reached Vita when she was
recovering from this ordeal in Paris. Much of the novel

had been written in Monte Carlo at the height of the affair, and the agony of revising her work threw her into a new emotional turmoil. *Challenge* was her declaration of defiance, an apologia for her conduct. She wished to publish it as a memorial to what she had endured, as her statement of what love could and should be. She first called the book *Rebellion*, then *Enchantment*, then *Vanity*. She finally settled on *Challenge*, as a summing-up of everything she wished to convey.

She was persuaded to cancel publication by her mother, Lady Sackville, by Violet's mother, Alice Keppel, and by their unexpected ally, Mrs Belloc Lowndes. 'Go to see Mrs Belloc Lowndes,' wrote Vita in her diary for 15 March 1920. 'She wants me to cancel the publication of *Challenge*. She says that if Violet were dead, would I publish it? That hit me. Gossip I don't care a damn about. So I give it up. I hope Mama [Lady Sackville] is pleased. She has beaten me.' And in Lady Sackville's diary: 'Vita is plucky about her bitter disappointment when Mrs Lowndes told her about the scandal it would create.' Violet was even more disappointed than Vita. 'You can't seriously mean it,' she wrote when she heard the news. 'It would be idiotic. The book is quite admirable. Ten times better than *Heritage*. Don't relent, sigh or soften. It's absurd, disloyal to me, and useless.'

By 'useless' she meant that the book's publication would add nothing to the gossip with which London already hummed: on the contrary, it would explain to the cynics how profound, how noble, their love for each other had been. To those who knew nothing of the real circumstances it would be a simple love-story with no overtones or undercurrents. Not one in a thousand readers would recognise Violet in the character of Eve, nor Vita herself in Julian. But Vita felt the risk to be too great. At the last moment she yielded, not to shame, but to reticence. She told her publishers, Collins, that she had changed her mind, giving as her false reason her disappointment with its literary quality. Lady Sackville, on her behalf, paid Collins £150 in compensation for cancelling publication, since the book had already been advertised as forthcoming. Four years later Vita agreed to its publication in America, making one change only: for the phrase 'Dedicated with gratitude for much excellent copy to the original of Eve' she substituted three lines of a Turkish love-poem which nobody was expected to understand.

The novel can now do no conceivable harm to anyone, and it is fitting that it should be reborn under the imprint of the same publisher from whom it was snatched at the font more than half a century ago.

There is much autobiography in the book, as in all Vita's novels. The scene, it is true, is set in Greece where she had never been, and its plot was derived solely from her imagination. But she knew other parts of the Mediterranean well—Italy, Spain, southern France—and the landscape, seascape and townscape, the climate and vegetation, the throbbing life of the quays and villages, are taken from Monte Carlo and attributed to her fictional Herakleion. One can discover in her contemporary diaries and letters the originals of many incidents and minor characters in the story. Fireworks in Monte Carlo one day become fireworks in Herakleion the next. From an earlier period in her life, when she spent six months in Constantinople as the newly married wife of the Third Secretary at the British Embassy, she drew material for her satirical picture of diplomatic life, mocking at its pettiness and self-importance, its 'coy platitudes', scorning the social conventions of which she had been a victim, but understanding far better than Harold Nicolson had realised the subtleties of diplomatic intrigue. The professional relationships between the representatives of the different countries at Herakleion, and between the ambassadors and their staffs, are acutely observed, as is the power-game played by the Greek politicians. Some readers may find the plot slightly improbable. A young Byronic Englishman is not likely to have seduced the loyalty of a bunch of Greek islanders from their parent state, nor be accepted by them as their rebel President. But given that the novel was intended as a romantic adventure story, the detail is well worked out, and the characterisation is convincing.

It is a love story, written in the presence of the beloved, inspired by her, corrected by her (for Vita each evening would read to Violet the pages she had written during the day), and embellished by her with words and whole sentences written into the manuscript. Eve is a portrait of Violet as exact as Vita could make it, having her model al-

9

ways at her side. Physically Eve resembled Violet precisely. 'She could not be called beautiful; her mouth was too large and too red.' But she was charming, malicious, vain, witty, her eyes 'deep-set, slanting slightly upwards, so ironical sometimes, and sometimes so inexplicably sad . . . Whatever she touched she lit.' Nor could Eve be called wicked. She was too adventurous for that, too brave. But she was selfish, with a jealous selfishness, which Vita not only excused but admired, since it was an animal quality, half-kitten, half-monkey, admirable because it could be cruel. The subtlety of *Challenge* is that an odious girl is made convincingly lovable. Eve, like Violet, is a creature who combined aristocratic *hauteur* with the vulnerability of a waif, a seductress who risked time and again her victim's love by indifference, insult, and finally by betrayal. Eve is the portrait of a clever, infuriating, infinitely charming witch.

Vita herself is Julian—not exactly, for she has given him qualities of disdain and leadership which she did not possess herself, and except in moments of reckless abandon she was gentler. She admired the rare Julians of this world, finding them in history more than in her contemporary world. He is an Elizabethan, the type of Sir Philip Sidney, a poet, an adventurer, a charmer when he wished to charm, arrogant when he was bored, the son whom Vita wished to have and never had, the man she would have wanted to be if she had been born a boy (and not to have been born a boy was her lifelong regret).

There is no triviality nor squalor in the love of Eve and Julian, as there was none in the love of Vita and Violet. A fierce flame rose between them, as likely to consume both of them as other people who got in the way. This was Vita's declaration of her understanding of love: it should be lit by magnesium, clouded by pain. Hers was a romantic, rebellious nature softened by tenderness. Seldom can a novelist have expressed so clearly, in the differing characters of her hero and heroine, her conception of the capacity of the human spirit.

The literary merits of the book are strong. Vita was an instinctive novelist. She could express easily anything which her mind conceived. The manuscript (which I have at Sissinghurst) is written almost without correction, often pencilled in short bursts, as if an idea which had occurred to her in her bath must be scribbled down before dinner, lest she forget it. The narrative and dialogue are sharp and percipient, and the characters are people whom one could immediately identify in a crowd. No wonder that she was pleased with the book. She would be glad to know that this edition has saved her passionate story from disappearing irrevocably down the literary sluice.

NIGEL NICOLSON

Sissinghurst Castle, Kent
October 1973

PART I
Julian

One

On Sunday, after the races were over, the diplomatic, indigenous, and cosmopolitan society of Herakleion, by virtue of a custom they never sought to dispute, streamed through the turnstiles of the race-course to regain their carriages and to drive for an hour in the ilex avenue consecrated to that purpose outside the suburbs of the town. Like the angels on Jacob's ladder, the carriages went up one side and down the other, at a slow walk, the procession invariably headed by the barouche of the French Legation, containing M. Lafarge, chief of the mission, his beard spread fan-like over his frock-coat, but so disposed as to reveal the rosette in his buttonhole, peeping with a coy red eye at the passing world; Madame Lafarge, sitting erect and bowing stiffly from her unassailable position as dictator to social Herakleion; and, on the *strapontin*, Julie Lafarge, repressed, sallow-faced daughter of the emissaries of France. Streaming after the barouche came mere humanity, some in victorias, some in open cabs, all going at a walk, and down the centre rode the young men of the place, and down the centre Alexander Christopoulos, who dared all and to whom all was forgiven, drove his light buggy and American trotter at a rattling pace and in a cloud of dust.

The diplomatic carriages were distinguished by the presence of a chasseur on the box, though none so gorgeous as the huge scarlet-coated chasseur of the French Legation. It was commonly said that the Danish Minister and his wife, who were poor, denied themselves food in order to maintain their carriage for the Sunday drive. The rich Greeks, on the other hand, from generation to generation, inherited the family brake, which was habitually driven by the head of the clan on the box, his wife beside him, and his sons and unmarried daughters sitting two by

15

two, on the six remaining seats behind. There had been a rush of scandal when Alexander Christopoulos had appeared for the first time alone in his buggy, his seat in the family brake conspicuously empty. There remained, however, his four sisters, the Virgins of Herakleion, whose ages ranged from thirty-five to forty, and whose batteries were unfailingly directed against the latest arrival. The fifth sister had married a banker in Frankfort, and was not often mentioned. There were, besides the brakes of the rich Greeks, the wagonettes of the English Davenants, who always had English coachmen, and frequently absented themselves from the Sunday drive to remind Herakleion that, although resident, they were neither diplomatic, indigenous, nor cosmopolitan, but unalterably English. They were too numerous and too influential to be disregarded, but when the name of Davenant was mentioned in their absence, a murmur was certain to make itself heard, discreet, unvindictive, but none the less remorseless, 'Ah yes, the English Levantines.'

Sunshades were lowered in the ilex avenue, for the shadows of the ancient trees fell cool and heavy across the white dust. Through the ilexes, the sea glimmered on a lower level, washing idly on the shore; vainly blue, for Herakleion had no eyes for the sea. The sea was always there, always blue, just as Mount Mylassa was always there, behind the town, monotonous and immovable. The sea was made for the transport of merchandise and to provide man with fish. No one had ever discovered a purpose in Mount Mylassa.

When the French barouche had reached the end of the avenue, it turned gravely in a wide circle and took its place at the head of the descending carriages. When it had reached its starting-point, the entrance to the avenue, it detached itself from the procession and continued on its way towards the town. The procession did not follow it. Another turn up and down the avenue remained for the procession, and the laughter became perceptibly brighter, the smiles of greeting more cordial, with the removal of Madame Lafarge's influence. It was known that the barouche would pass the race-course at its former dignified walk, but that, once out of sight, Madame Lafarge would say, 'Grigora, Vassili!' to the chasseur, that the horses would be urged into a shambling trot and that the ladies

16

in the carriage would open their sunshades to keep off the glare of the sun which beat down from heaven and reverberated from the pavements and the white walls of the houses as they drove through the streets of the deserted town.

Deserted, for that part of the population which was not within doors strolled in the ilex avenue, looking at the carriages. A few lean dogs slept on door-steps where the shadow of the portico fell sharply dividing the step into a dark and a sunny half. The barouche rolled along the wide quay, where here and there the parapet was broken by a flight of steps descending to the water; passed the casino, white, with palms and cacti growing hideously in the forecourt; rolled across the square *platia*, where a group of men stood lounging within the cool and cavernous passage-way of the club.

Madame Lafarge stopped the barouche.

A young man detached himself from the group with a slightly bored and supercilious expression. He was tall beyond the ordinary run of Frenchmen; had dark eyes under meeting eyebrows in an ivory face, and an immensely high, flat, white brow, from which the black wavy hair grew straight back, smoothed to the polish of a black greyhound. 'Our Persian miniature,' the fat American wife of the Danish Minister, called him, establishing herself as the wit of Herakleion where anyone with sufficient presumption could establish him or herself in any chosen rôle. The young man had accepted the title languidly, but had taken care that it should not die forgotten.

Madame Lafarge said to him in a tone which conveyed a command rather than proffered a favour, 'If you like, we can drive you to the Legation.'

She spoke in a booming voice that burst surprisingly out of the compression of a generously furnished bust. The young man, accepting the offer, seated himself beside Julie on the *strapontin* opposite his chief, who sat silent and majestically bearded. The immense chasseur stood stiffly by the side of the carriage, his eyes gazing unblinkingly across the *platia*, and the tips of his long drooping whiskers obscuring the braid of his scarlet collar. Madame Lafarge addressed herself to the group of men,—

'I did not see you at the races?'

Her graciousness did not conceal the rebuke. She continued,—

'I shall hope to welcome you presently at the Legation.'

With a bow worthy of Theodora, whom she had once been told that she resembled, she gave the order to drive on. The loaded barouche, with the splendid red figure on the box, rolled away across the dazzling square. The French Legation stood back behind a grille in the main street of the town, built of white stucco like the majority of the houses. Inside, it was cool and dark, the Venetian blinds were drawn, and the lighted candles in the sconces on the walls reflected pleasantly, and with a curious effect of freshening night, in the polished floors. Gilt chairs were arranged in circles, and little tables stood about, glitteringly laden with tall tumblers and bottles of coloured sirops. Madame Lafarge surveyed these things as she had surveyed them every Sunday evening since Julie could remember. The young man danced attendance in his languid way.

'The chandeliers may be lighted,' her Excellency said to the chasseur, who had followed.

The three stood watching while the candles sprang into little spears of light under the touch of the taper, Madame Lafarge contrasting displeasedly the lemon sallowness of her daughter's complexion with the warm magnolia-like pallor of the secretary's face. The contrast caused her to speak sharply,—

'Julie, you had better go now and take off your hat.'

When her submissive daughter had gone, she said,—

'Julie is looking ill. The summer does not suit her. But what is to be done? I cannot leave Herakleion.'

'Obviously,' murmured the secretary, 'Herakleion would fall all to pieces. Your Sunday evenings,' he continued, 'the races . . . your picnics . . .'

'Impossible,' she cried with determination. 'One owes a duty to the country one represents, and I have always said that, whereas politics are the affairs of men, the woman's social obligation is no less urgent. It is a great career, Armand, and to such a career one must be prepared to sacrifice one's personal convenience.'

'And one's health . . . the health of one's children,' he added, looking down at his almond nails.

'If need be,' she replied, with a sigh and, fanning herself, repeated, 'If need be.'

The rooms began to fill. A little middle-aged Greek, his wrinkled saffron face curiously emphasised by the beautiful whiteness of his hair and moustaches, took his stand near Madame Lafarge, who in speaking to him looked down on the top of his head over the broad plateau of her bust.

'These cool rooms of yours,' he murmured, as he kissed her hand. 'One cannot believe in the heat of the sun outside.'

He made this remark every other Sunday.

Lafarge came up and took the little Greek banker by the arm.

'I hear,' he said, 'that there is fresh trouble in the Islands.'

'We can leave it to the Davenants,' said Christopoulos with an unpleasant smile.

'But that is exactly what I have always urged you not to do,' said the French Minister, drawing the little Greek into a corner. 'You know the proverbial reputation of the English: you do not see them coming, but they insinuate themselves until one day you open your eyes to the fact that they are there. You will be making a very great mistake, my dear friend, if you allow the Davenants to settle disputes in the Islands. Have you forgotten that in the last generation a Davenant caused himself to be elected President?'

'Considering that they are virtually kings, I do not see that the nominal title of President can make a vast difference.'

Lafarge sent his eyes round the room and through the doorway into the room beyond; he saw the familiar, daily faces and returned to the charge.

'You are pleased to be sarcastic, I know. Nevertheless allow me to offer you my advice. It is not a question of Kingship or Presidency. It is a question of a complete break on the part of the Islands. They are small, but their strategic value is self-evident. Remember Italy has her eye upon them. . . . The Davenants are democrats, and have always preached liberty to the islanders. The Davenant wealth supports them. Can you calmly contemplate the existence of an independent archipelago a few miles from your shore?'

A dull red crept under the banker's yellow skin, giving him a suffused appearance.

'You are very emphatic.'

'The occasion surely warrants emphasis.'

The rooms were by now quite full. Little centres of laughter had formed themselves and were distinguishable. Alexander Christopoulos had once boasted that he could, merely by looking round a room and arguing from the juxtaposition of conversationalists, give a fairly accurate *résumé* of what every one was saying. He also claimed to tell from the expression of the Danish Excellency whether she was or was not arriving primed with a new epigram. He was now at the side of the Danish Excellency, fat, fair, and foolish, but good-natured, and having a fund of veritable humanity which was lacking in most of her colleagues. The careful English of Alexander reached his father's ears through the babel,—

'The Empress Eugénie set the fashion of wearing *décolleté* in the shape the water in your bath makes round your shoulders . . .'

Lafarge went on,—

'The Davenants are sly; they keep apart; they mix with us, but they do not mingle. They are like oil upon water. Where is William Davenant now, do you know?'

'He is just arriving,' said Christopoulos.

Lafarge saw him then, bowing over his hostess's hand, polite, but with absent eyes that perpetually strayed from the person he was talking to. Behind him came a tall, loose-limbed boy, untidy, graceful; he glanced at the various groups, and the women looked at him with interest. A single leap might carry him at any moment out of the room in which his presence seemed so incongruous.

The tall mirrors on the walls sent back the reflection of the many candles, and in them the same spectral company came and went that moved and chattered in the rooms.

'At least he is not on the Islands,' said Christopoulos.

'After all,' said Lafarge, with a sudden weariness, 'perhaps I am inclined to exaggerate the importance of the Islands. It is difficult to keep a true sense of proportion. Herakleion is a little place. One forgets that one is not at the centre of the world.'

He could not have tracked his lassitude to its origin, but as his eyes rested again on the free, generous limbs of the Davenant boy, he felt a slight revolt against the babble, the coloured sirops, and the artificially lighted rooms from which the sun was so carefully excluded. The yellow skin of little Christopoulos gave him the appearance of a plant which has been deprived of light. His snowy hair, too, soft and billowy, looked as though it had been deliberately and consistently bleached.

He murmured a gentle protest to the Minister's words,—

'Surely not, dear Excellency, surely you do not exaggerate the importance of the Islands. We could not, as you say, tolerate the existence of an independent archipelago a few miles from our shores. Do not allow my sarcasm to lead you into the belief that I under-estimate either their importance, or the value, the compliment of your interest in the politics of our country. The friendship of France . . .'

His voice died away into suave nothings. The French Minister emerged with an effort from his mood of temporary discontent, endeavouring to recapture the habitual serenity of his life.

'And you will remember my hint about the Davenants?'

Christopoulos looked again at William Davenant, who, perfectly courteous but incorrigibly absent-minded, was still listening to Madame Lafarge.

'It is a scandal,' she was saying, resuming her conversation in the intervals of interruption occasioned by newly-arriving guests, 'a scandal that the Museum should remain without a catalogue . . .'

'I will remember,' said Christopoulos. 'I will tell Alexander to distract that youth's attention; one Davenant the less, you follow me, to give us any trouble.'

'Pooh! a schoolboy,' interjected the Minister.

Christopoulos pursed his lips and moved his snowy head portentously up and down.

'A schoolboy, but nevertheless he probably shares the enthusiasms of his age. The Islands are sufficiently romantic to appeal to his imagination. Remember, his grandfather ruled there for a year.'

'His grandfather? *un farceur!*' said Lafarge.

Christopoulos assented, and the two men, smiling

tolerantly, continued to look across at the unconscious boy though their minds were already occupied by other things. Madame Lafarge, catching sight of them, was annoyed by her husband's aloofness from the social aspect of her weekly reception. It pleased her—in fact, she exacted—that a certain political atmosphere should pervade any gathering in her drawing-rooms, but at the same time she resented a political interview which deprived, at once, her guests of a host and herself of a *cavalier servente*. She accordingly stared at Christopoulos while continuing her conversation with William Davenant, until the little Greek became aware of her gaze, and crossed the room obediently to the unspoken summons.

William Davenant moved away in relief; he knew his duty to Madame Lafarge, but performed it wearily and without pleasure. It was now over for a month, he thought, deciding that he would not be expected to attend the three succeeding Sundays. He paused beside his son, who had been captured by two of the sisters Christopoulos and who, with two Russian secretaries, was being forced to join in a round game. The sisters gave little shrieks and peals of laughter; it was their idea of merriment. They sat one on each side of Julian Davenant, on a small gilt sofa covered with imitation tapestry. Near by, listening to the game with a gentle and languorous smile upon his lips, stood the Persian Minister, who understood very little French, his fine Oriental figure buttoned into the traditional frock-coat, and a black lamb's-wool fez upon his head. He was not very popular in Herakleion; he did not know enough French to amuse the women, so, as at present, he silently haunted the circles of the younger generation, with mingled humility and dignity.

William Davenant paused there for a moment, met his son's eyes with a gleam of sympathy, then passed on to pay his monthly duty to influence and fashion. The Danish Excellency whispered behind her fan to Alexander Christopoulos as he passed, and the young man screwed in his eyeglass to examine the retreating back of the Englishman. The red-coated chasseur came round, gravely offering sandwiches on a tray.

'Uneatable,' said Alexander Christopoulos, taking one and hiding it beneath his chair.

The courage of the young man! the insolence!

'Julie will see you,' giggled the Danish Excellency.

'And what if she does?' he retorted.

'You have no respect, no veneration,' she chided him.

'For *maman* Lafarge? *la bonne bourgeoise!*' he exclaimed, but not very loudly.

'Alexander!' she said, but her tone said, 'I adore you.'

'One must be something,' the young Christopoulos had once told himself; 'I will be insolent and contemptuous; I will impose myself upon Herakleion; my surroundings shall accept me with admiration and without protest.'

He consequently went to Oxford, affected to speak Greek with difficulty, interlarded his English with American slang, instituted a polo club, and drove an American trotter. He was entirely successful. Unlike many a greater man, he had achieved his ambition. He knew, moreover, that Madame Lafarge would give him her daughter for the asking.

'Shall I make Julie sing?' he said suddenly to the Danish Excellency, searching among the moving groups for the victim of this classic joke of Herakleion.

'Alexander, you are too cruel,' she murmured.

He was flattered; he felt himself an irresistible autocrat and breaker of hearts. He tolerated the Danish Excellency, as he had often said in the club, because she had no other thought than of him. She, on the other hand, boasted in her fat, good-humoured way to her intimates,—

'I may be a fool, but no woman is completely a fool who has realised the depths of man's vanity.'

Julie Lafarge, who was always given to understand that one day she would marry the insolent Alexander, was too efficiently repressed to be jealous of the Danish Excellency. Under the mischievous influence of her friend, Eve Davenant, she would occasionally make an attempt to attract the young man; a pitiable, grotesque attempt, prompted by the desire to compel his homage, to hear herself called beautiful—which she was not. So far she did not delude herself that she had succeeded, but she did delude herself that it gave him pleasure to hear her sing. She stood now beside a little table, dispensing sirops in tall tumblers, very sallow in her white muslin, with a locket on a short gold chain hanging between the bones of her neck. Her very thin brown arms, which were covered with small

23

black hairs, protruded ungracefully from the short sleeves of her dress.

Alexander presented himself before her; she had seen him coming in one of the mirrors on the walls. Madame Lafarge cherished an affection for these mirrors, because thanks to them her drawing-rooms always appeared twice as crowded as they really were.

Alexander uttered his request in a tone at once beseeching and compelling; she thought him irresistible. Nevertheless, she protested: there were too many people present, her singing would interrupt all conversation, her mother would be annoyed. But those standing near by seconded Alexander, and Madame Lafarge herself bore down majestically upon her daughter, so that all protest was at an end.

Julie stood beside the open piano with her hands loosely folded in a rehearsed and approved attitude while the room disposed itself to listen, and Alexander, who was to accompany her, let his fingers roam negligently over the keyboard. Chairs were turned to face the piano, people drifted in from the farther drawing-room, young men leaned in the doorways and against the walls. Lafarge folded his arms across his chest, freeing his imprisoned beard by an upward movement of his chin, and smiled encouragingly and benignly at his daughter. Speech dropped into whispers, whispers into silence. Alexander struck a few preliminary chords. Julie sang; she sang, quite execrably, romantic German music, and out of the roomful of people only three, herself, her father, and her mother, thought that she sang well. Despite this fact she was loudly applauded, congratulated, and pressed for more.

Julian Davenant, taking advantage of the diversion to escape from the sisters Christopoulos, slipped away to one of the window recesses where he could partly conceal himself behind the stiff, brocaded curtain. Horizontal strings of sunlight barred the Venetian blind, and by peeping between its joints he could see the tops of the palms in the Legation forecourt, the iron grille which gave on to the main street, and a victoria standing near the grille, in the shade, the horse covered over with a flimsy, dust-coloured sheet, and the driver asleep inside the carriage, a fly-whisk drooping limply in his hand. He could hear the shrill squeaking of the tram as it came round the corner, and the clang of its bell. He knew that the sea lay blue beyond the white town, and that, out in the sea, lay the Islands, where the little grapes were spread, drying into currants, in the sun. He returned to the darkened, candle-lit room, where Julie Lafarge was singing 'Im wunderschönen Monat Mai.'

Looking across the room to the door which opened on to the landing at the top of the stairs, he saw a little stir of arrival, which was suppressed in order to avoid any interruption to the music. He distinguished the new-comer, a short, broad, middle-aged woman, out of breath after mounting the stairs, curiously draped in soft copper-coloured garments, with gold bangles on her bare arms, and a wreath of gold leaves round her dark head. He knew this woman, a singer. He neither liked nor disliked her, but had always thought of her as possessing a strangely classical quality, all the stranger because of her squat, almost grotesque ugliness; although not a dwarf, her great breadth gave her the appearance of one; but at the same time she was for him the embodiment of the wealth of the country, a kind of Demeter of the Islands, though he thought of Demeter as having corn-coloured hair, like the crops over which she presided, and this woman had blue-black hair, like the purple of the grapes that grew on the Islands. He had often heard her sing, and hoped now that she was arriving in her professional capacity, which seemed probable, both from her dress, and from the unlikelihood that she, a singer and a woman of the native people, would enter Madame Lafarge's house as a guest, renowned though she was, and fêted, in the capitals of Europe. He saw Lafarge tiptoe out to receive her, saw Madame Lafarge follow, and noted the faintly patronising manner of the Minister's wife in shaking hands with the artist.

Applause broke out as Julie finished her song. The Greek singer was brought forward into the room amid a general movement and redistribution of groups. Alexander Christopoulos relinquished his place at the piano, and joined the Davenant boy by the window. He appeared bored and languid.

'It is really painful ... as well listen to a macaw singing,' he said. 'You are not musical, are you, Julian?

25

You can scarcely imagine what I endured. Have you heard this woman, Kato?'

Julian said that he had.

'Quite uneducated,' Christopoulos said loftily. 'Any woman in the fields sings as well. It was new to Paris, and Paris raved. You and I, my dear Julian, have heard the same thing a hundred times. Shall we escape?'

'I must wait for my father,' said Julian, who detested his present companion; 'he and I are going to dine with my uncle.'

'So am I', Christopoulos answered, and, leaning over to the English boy, he began to speak in a confidential voice.

'You know, my dear Julian, in this society of ours your father is not trusted. But, after all, what is this society? *un tas de rastas*. Do you think I shall remain here long? not I. *Je me fiche des Balcans*. And you? Are you going to bury yourself on those Islands of yours, growing grapes, ripening olives? What? That satisfied the old generations. What have I to do with a banking house in Herakleion, you with a few vineyards near the coast? I shall marry, and spend the rest of my life in Paris.'

'You're ambitious to-day,' Julian said mildly.

'Ambitious! shall I tell you why? Yesterday was my twenty-fifth birthday. I've done with Herakleion . . .'

'Conquered it, you mean,' said Julian, 'squeezed it dry.'

The other glanced at him suspiciously.

'Are you laughing at me? Confound your quiet manner, Julian, I believe my family is right to mistrust your family. Very well, then: conquered it. Believe me, it isn't worth conquering. Don't waste your youth on your vineyards, but come with me. Let the Islands go. They are always in trouble, and the trouble is getting more acute. They are untidy specks on the map. Don't you hear the call of Paris and the world?'

Julian, looking at him, and seeing the laughable intrigue, was mercifully saved from replying, for at that moment Madame Kato began to sing. She sang without accompaniment, songs of the people, in a curiously guttural voice with an occasionally nasal note, songs no different from those sung in the streets or, as Christopoulos had said, in the fields, different only in that, to this peasant music, half melancholy, half emotional, its cadence born of physical labour, she brought the genius of a great artist. As she stood there, singing, Julian reflected that her song emphasised the something classical, something massive, something monumental, about her, which overshadowed what might have been slightly grotesque in her appearance. She was, indeed, a Demeter of the vineyards. She should have stood singing in the sun, not beneath the pale mockery of the candles.

'Entirely uneducated,' Christopoulos said again, shifting his shoulders as he leaned against the wall. 'That is why Paris liked her: as a contrast. She was clever enough to know that. Contrasts are always artistically effective.'

He went off, pleased, to repeat his facile epigram to the Danish Excellency. Madame Lafarge was looking round to see whether the audience had approved of the innovation. The audience was waiting to hear the expression of an opinion which it might safely follow. Presently the word, 'Uneducated,' was on every lip. Julian remained at the window, chained there by his natural reserve and shyness; he looked up at the lighted chandeliers, and down at their reflection in the floors; he saw the faces of people turned towards him, and the back of their heads in the mirrors; he saw Armand, the French secretary, with the face of a Persian prince, offering red sirop to Madame Kato. He wished to go and speak to her, but his feet would not carry him forward. He felt himself apart from the talk and the easy laughter.

Presently Mlle Lafarge, seeing him there alone, came to him with her awkward and rather touching grace as a hostess.

'You know, I suppose,' she said to him, 'that Madame Kato is a friend of Eve's? Will you not come and speak to her?'

Released, he came. The singer was drinking her red sirop by the piano. The Persian Minister in the black fez was standing near, smiling gently at her with his usual mournful smile.

'You will not remember me, Julian Davenant,' the boy said in a low, shy voice. He spoke in Greek involuntarily, feeling that French would be an outrage in the presence of this so splendidly Hellenic woman. Armand had moved away, and they stood isolated, caressed by the vague smile of the Persian Minister.

Kato set down her glass of red sirop on the top of the

piano. She leaned against the piano talking to the English boy, her arms akimbo, as a peasant woman might lean in the doorway of her house gossiping in the cool of the evening, her little eyes keen and eager. The muscles of her arms and of her magnificent neck curved generously beneath her copper draperies, mocking the flimsy substance, and crying out for the labour of the vineyards. Her speech was tinged with the faint accent of the Islands, soft and slurring. It was more familiar to Julian Davenant than the harsher Greek of the town, for it was the speech of the women who had brought him up as a child, women of the Islands, his nurses in his father's big house in the *platia* of Herakleion. It murmured to him now in the rich voice of the singer beneath the chandelier.

'Eve; I have not seen her yet. You must tell her that I have returned and that she must come to my concert on Wednesday. Tell her that I will sing one song for her, but that all the other songs must be for my audience. I have brought back a new repertoire from Munich, which will please Herakleion better, I hope, than the common music it despises.'

She laughed a little.

'It has taken me thirty years to discover that mankind at large despises the art of its own country. Only the exotic catches the ear of fashion. But Eve has told me that you do not care for music?'

'I like your music,' he said.

'I will tell you why: because you are musically uneducated.'

He looked at her; she was smiling. He wondered whether she had overheard a whisper in the humming room.

'I speak without sarcasm,' she added; 'I envy you your early ignorance. In fact, I believe I have uttered a paradox, and that the words education and music are incompatible. Music is the emotional art, and where education steps in at the door emotion flies out at the window. We should keep education for literature, painting, architecture, and sculpture. Music is the medium to which we turn when these more intellectual mediums fail us.'

Julian listened with only half his brain. This peasant, this artist, spoke to him with the superficial ease of drawing-rooms; she employed words that matched ill with her appearance and with the accent of her speech. The native songs were right upon her lips, as the names of architecture and sculpture were wrong. He was offended in his sensitiveness. Demeter in analysis of the arts!

She was watching him.

'Ah, my young friend,' she said, 'you do not understand. I spoke to you as the cousin of Eve, who is a child, but who always understands. She is purely sentient, emotional.'

He protested,—

'I have always thought of Eve as exceptionally sophisticated.'

Kato said,—

'You are right. We are both right. Eve is childlike in many ways, but she is also wise beyond her years. She will grow, believe me, into a woman of exceptional attraction, and to such women existence is packed with danger. It is one of Providence's rare pieces of justice that they should be provided with a natural weapon of self-defence. To a lion his claws,' she said, smiling, 'and to the womanly woman the gift of penetration. Tell me, are you fond of Eve?'

Julian was surprised. He replied, naïf again and like a schoolboy,—

'She's my cousin. I haven't thought much about her. She's only a child. I haven't seen her yet either. I arrived from England this morning.'

They were more than ever isolated from the rest of the room. Madame Lafarge, talking to Don Rodrigo Valdez, the Spanish Minister, who had a birdlike head above his immensely high white collar, glanced now and then resentfully at the singer, but otherwise the room was indifferent. The sunlight between the cracks of the Venetian blinds had grown fainter, and the many candles were coming into their own. A few people had already taken their leave. An excited group of men had gathered round little Christopoulos, and the words 'local politics' shrieked from every gesture.

'I shall not be expected to sing again,' said Kato with a slight return to her ironical manner. 'Will you not come with Eve to my concert on Wednesday? Or, better, will you come to my house on Wednesday evening after the concert? I shall be alone, and I should like to talk to you.'

'To me?' broke from him, independently of his will.

'Remember,' she said, 'I am from the Islands. That is my country, and when my country is in trouble I am not indifferent. You are very young, Mr Davenant, and you are not very often in Herakleion, but your future, when you have done with Oxford and with England'—she made a large gesture—'lies in the Islands. You will hear a great deal about them; a little of this I should like you to hear from me. Will you come?'

The patriot beneath the artist! He would come, flattered, important; courted, at his nineteen years, by a singer of European reputation. Popularity was to him a new experience. He expanded beneath its warmth.

'I will come to the concert first with Eve.'

William Davenant, in search of his son, and light-hearted in his relief at the end of the monthly duty, was bowing to Madame Kato, whom he knew both as a singer and as a figure of some importance in the troubled politics of the tiny State. They had, in their lives, spent many an hour in confabulation, when his absent-minded manner left the man, and her acquired polish the woman. He deferred to her as a controlling agent in practical affairs, spoke of her to his brother with admiration.

'A remarkable woman, Robert, a true patriot; sexless, I believe, so far as her patriotism lies. Malteios, you say? well, I know; but, believe me, she uses him merely as a means to her end. Not a sexless means? Damn it, one picks up what weapons come to one's hand. She hasn't a thought for him, only for her wretched country. She is a force, I tell you, to be reckoned with. Forget her sex! Surely that is easy, with a woman who looks like a toad. You make the mistake of ignoring the people when it is with the people that you have to deal. Hear them speak about her: she is an inspiration, a local Joan of Arc. She works for them in Paris, in Berlin, and in London; she uses her sex, for them and for them alone. All her life is dedicated to them. She gives them her voice, and her genius.'

Madame Kato did not know that he said these things about her behind her back. Had she known, she would have been surprised neither at the opinions he expressed nor at the perception which enabled him to express them, for she had seen in him a shrewd, deliberate intellect that spoke little, listened gravely, and settled soberly down at length upon a much tested and corroborated opinion. Madame Lafarge, and the women to whom he paid his courtly, rather pompous duty in public, thought him dull and heavy, a true Englishman. The men mistrusted him in company with his brother Robert, silence, in the South, breeding mistrust as does volubility in the North.

The rooms were emptier now, and the candles, burning lower, showed long icicles of wax that overflowed on to the glass of the chandeliers. The tall tumblers had been set down, here and there, containing the dregs of the coloured sirops. Madame Lafarge looked hot and weary, drained of her early Sunday energy, and listening absently to the parting compliments of Christopoulos. From the other room, however, still came the laughter of the Christopoulos sisters, who were winding up their round game.

'Come, Julian,' said William Davenant, after he had spoken and made his farewells to Madame Kato.

Together they went down the stairs and out into the forecourt, where the hotter air of the day greeted them after the coolness of the house, though the heat was no longer that of the sun, but the closer, less glaring heat of the atmosphere absorbed during the grilling hours of the afternoon. The splendid chasseur handed them their hats, and they left the Legation and walked slowly down the crowded main street of the town.

Two

THE TOWN HOUSE of the Davenants stood in the *platia*, at
right angles to the club. On the death of old Mr
Davenant—'President Davenant,' as he was nick-named—
the town and the country properties had been divided between the two inheriting brothers; Herakleion said that the
brothers had drawn lots for the country house, but in point
of fact the matter had been settled by amicable arrangement. William Davenant, the elder of the brothers, wid-
owed, with an only son away for three-quarters of the year
at school in England, was more conveniently installed in
the town, within five minutes' reach of the central office,
than Robert, who, with a wife and a little girl, preferred
the distance of his country house and big garden. The two
establishments, as time went on, became practically inter-
changeable.

The rue Royale—Herakleion was so cosmopolitan as to
give to its principal thoroughfare a French name—was at
this hour crowded with the population that, imprisoned all
day behind closed shutters, sought in the evening what
freshness it could find in the cobbled streets between the
stucco houses. The street life of the town began between
five and six, and the Davenants, father and son, were jos-
tled as they walked slowly along the pavements, picking
their way amongst the small green tables set outside the
numerous cafés. At these tables sat the heterogeneous elements that composed the summer population of the place,
men of every nationality: old gamblers too disreputable
for Monte Carlo; young Levantines, natives, drinking
absinthe; Turks in their red fezzes; a few rakish South
Americans. The trams screamed discordantly in their iron
grooves, and the bells of the cinema tinkled unceasingly.
Between the tramlines and the kerb dawdled the hired vic-

torias, few empty at this time of day, but crowded with families of Levantines, the men in straw hats, the women for the most part in hot black, very stout, and constantly fanning their heavily powdered faces. Now and then a chasseur from some diplomatic house passed rapidly in a flaming livery.

Mr Davenant talked to his son as they made their way along.

'How terrible those parties are. I often wish I could dissociate myself altogether from that life, and God knows that I go merely to hear what people are saying. They know it, and of course they will never forgive me. Julian, in order to conciliate Herakleion, you will have to marry a Greek.'

'Alexander Christopoulos attacked me to-day,' Julian said. 'Wanted me to go to Paris with him and see the world.'

He did not note in his own mind that he refrained from saying that Madame Kato had also, so to speak, attacked him on the dangerous subject of the Islands.

They turned now, having reached the end of the rue Royale, into the *platia*, where the cavernous archway of the club stained the white front of the houses with a mouth of black. The houses of the *platia* were large, the hereditary residences of the local Greek families. The Christopoulos house stood next to the club, and next to that was the house of the Premier, His Excellency Platon Malteios, and next to that the Italian Consulate, with the arms of Italy on a painted hatchment over the door. The centre of the square was empty, cobbled in an elaborate pattern which gave the effect of a tessellated pavement; on the fourth side of the square were no houses, for here lay the wide quay which stretched right along above the sea from one end of the town to the other.

The Davenant house faced the sea, and from the balcony of his bedroom on the second floor Julian could see the Islands, yellow with little white houses on them; in the absolute stillness and limpidity of the air he could count the windows on Aphros, the biggest island, and the terraces on the slope of the hills. The first time he had arrived from school in England he had run up to his bedroom, out on to the balcony, to look across the *platia* with

33

its many gaudily striped sunblinds, at the blue sea and the little yellow stains a few miles out from the shore.

At the door of the Davenant house stood two horses ready saddled in the charge of the door-keeper, fat Aristotle, an islander, who wore the short bolero and pleated fustanelle, like a kilt, of his country. The door-keepers of the other houses had gathered round him, but as Mr Davenant came up they separated respectfully and melted away to their individual charges.

The way lay along the quays and down the now abandoned ilex avenue. The horses' hoofs padded softly in the thick dust. The road gleamed palely beneath the thick shadows of the trees, and the water, seen between the ancient trunks, was almost purple. The sun was gone, and only the last bars of the sunset lingered in the sky. At the tip of the pier of Herakleion twinkled already the single light of phosphorescent green that daily, at sunset, shone out, to reflect irregularly in the water.

They passed out of the avenue into the open country, the road still skirting the sea on their left, while on their right lay the strip of flat country crowded in between Mount Mylassa and the sea, carefully cultivated by the labourers of the Davenants, where the grapes hung on the festooned branches looped from pole to pole. William Davenant observed them critically, thinking to himself, 'A good harvest.' Julian Davenant, fresh from an English county, saw as with a new eye their beauty and their luxuriance. He rode loosely in the saddle, his long legs dangling, indisputably English, though born in one of the big painted rooms overlooking the *platia* of Herakleion, and reared in the country until the age of ten. He had always heard the vintage discussed since he could remember. He knew that his family for three generations had been the wealthiest in the little state, wealthier than the Greek banking-houses, and he knew that no move of the local politics was entirely free from the influence of his relations. His grandfather, indeed, having been refused a concession he wanted from the government, had roused his Islands to a declaration of independence under his own presidency—a state of affairs which, preposterous as it was, had profoundly alarmed the motley band that made up the Cabinet in Herakleion. What had been done once, could be repeated.... Granted his concession, Julian's grandfa-

34

ther had peaceably laid down the dignity of his new office, but who could say that his sons might not repeat the experiment?

These things had been always in the boy's scheme of life. He had not pondered them very deeply. He supposed that one day he would inherit his father's share in the concern, and would become one of the heads of the immense family which had spread like water over various districts of the Mediterranean coasts. Besides the Davenants of Herakleion, there were Davenants at Smyrna, Davenants at Salonica, Davenants at Constantinople. Colonies of Davenants. It was said that the Levant numbered about sixty families of Davenants. Julian was not acquainted with them all. He did not even know in what degree of relationship they stood to him.

Every time that he passed through London on his way to school, or, now, to Oxford, he was expected to visit his great-uncle, Sir Henry, who lived in an immense house in Belgrave Square, and had a business room downstairs where Julian was interviewed before luncheon. In this room hung framed plans of the various Davenant estates, and Julian, as he stood waiting for Sir Henry, would study the plan of Herakleion, tracing with his finger the line of the quays, the indent of the *platia*, the green of the racecourse, the square which indicated the country house; in a corner of this plan were the Islands, drawn each in separate detail. He became absorbed, and did not notice the entrance of Sir Henry till the old man's hand fell on his shoulder.

'Ha! Looking at the plan, are you? Familiar to you, what? So it is familiar to me, my boy. Never been there, you know. Yet I know it. I know my way about. Know it as though I had seen it.'

He didn't really know it, Julian thought—he didn't feel the sun hot on his hands, or see the dazzling, flapping sunblinds, or the advertisements written up in Greek characters in the streets.

Sir Henry went on with his sermon.

'You don't belong there, boy; don't you ever forget that. You belong here. You're English. Bend the riches of that country to your own purpose, that's all right, but don't identify yourself with it. Impose yourself. Make 'em adopt your methods. That's the strength of English colonisation.'

The old man, who was gouty, and leaned his hands on the top of a stick, clapped the back of one hand with the palm of the other and blew out his lips, looking at his great-nephew.

'Yes, yes, remember that. Impose yourself. On my soul, you're a well-grown boy. What are you? nineteen? Great overgrown colt. Get your hair cut. Foreign ways; don't approve of that. Big hands you've got; broad shoulders. Loosely put together. Hope you're not slack. Can you ride?'

'I ride all day out there,' said Julian softly, a little bewildered.

'Well, well. Come to luncheon. Keep a head on your shoulders. Your grandfather lost his once; very foolish man. Wonder he didn't lose it altogether. President indeed! stuff and nonsense. Not practical, sir, not practical.' Sir Henry blew very hard. 'Let's have no such rubbish from you, boy. What'll you drink? Here, I'll give you the best: Herakleion, 1895. Best year we ever had. Hope you appreciate good wine; you're a wine-merchant, you know.'

He cackled loudly at his joke. Julian drank the wine that had ripened on the slopes of Mount Mylassa, or possibly on the Islands, and wished that the old man had not so blatantly called him a wine-merchant. He liked Sir Henry, although after leaving him he always had the sensation of having been buffeted by spasmodic gusts of wind.

He was thinking about Sir Henry now as he rode along, and pitying the old man to whom those swags of fruit meant only a dusty bottle, a red or a blue seal, and a date stamped in gold numerals on a black label. The light was extraordinarily tender, and the air seemed almost tangible with the heavy, honeyed warmth that hung over the road. Julian took off his gray felt hat and hung it on the high peak of his saddle.

They passed through a little village, which was no more than a score of tumbledown houses sown carelessly on each side of the road; here, as in the rue Royale, the peasants sat drinking at round tables outside the café to the harsh music of a gramophone, with applause and noisy laughter. Near by, half a dozen men were playing at bowls. When they saw Mr Davenant, they came forward in a body and laid eager hands on the neck of his horse. He reined up.

Julian heard the tumult of words: some one had been arrested, it was Vassili's brother. Vassili, he knew, was the big chasseur at the French Legation. He heard his father soothing, promising he would look into the matter; he would, if need be, see the Premier on the morrow. A woman flung herself out of the café and clasped Julian by the knee. They had taken her lover. Would he, Julian, who was young, be merciful? Would he urge his father's interference? He promised also what was required of him, feeling a strange thrill of emotion and excitement. Ten days ago he had been at Oxford, and here, to-day, Kato had spoken to him as to a grown man, and here in the dusk a sobbing woman was clinging about his knee. This was a place in which anything, fantastic or preposterous, might come to pass.

As they rode on, side by side, his father spoke, thinking aloud. An absent-minded man, he gave his confidence soley in this, so to speak, unintentional manner. Long periods, extending sometimes over months, during which his mind lay fallow, had as their upshot an outbreak of this audible self-communion. Julian had inherited the trait; his mind progressed, not regularly, but by alternate stagnation and a forward bound.

'The mistake that we have made lies in the importation of whole families of islanders to the mainland. The Islands have always considered themselves as a thing apart, as, indeed, historically, they always were. A hundred years is not sufficient to make them an intrinsic part of the State of Herakleion. I cannot wonder that the authorities here dislike us. We have introduced a discontented population from the Islands to spread sedition among the hitherto contented population of the mainland. If we were wise, we should ship the whole lot back to the Islands they came from. Now, a man is arrested on the Islands by the authorities, and what happens? He is the brother of Vassili, an islander living in Herakleion. Vassili spreads the news, it flies up and down the town, and out into the country. It has greeted us out here already. In every café of the town at this moment the islanders are gathered together, muttering; some will get drunk, perhaps, and the municipal police will intervene; from a drunken row the affair will become political; some one will raise the cry of "Liberty!", heads will be broken, and to-morrow a score of islanders will be in jail. They will attribute their imprisonment to the general hostility to their nationality, rather than to the insignificant brawl. Vassili will come to me in Herakleion to-morrow. Will I exercise my influence with Malteios to get his brother released? I shall go, perhaps, to Malteios, who will listen to me suavely, evasively ... It has all happened a hundred times before. I say, we ought to ship the whole lot back to where they came from.'

'I suppose they are really treated with unfairness?' Julian said, more speculation than interest in his tone.

'I suppose a great many people would think so. The authorities are certainly severe, but they are constantly provoked. And, you know, your uncle and I make it up to the islanders in a number of private ways. Ninety per cent of the men on the Islands are employed by us, and it pays us to keep them devoted to us by more material bonds than mere sentiment; also it alleviates their discontent, and so obviates much friction with Herakleion.'

'But of course,' said Julian quickly, 'you don't allow Malteios to suspect this?'

'My dear boy! what do you suppose? Malteios is President of Herakleion. Of course, we don't mention such things. But he knows it all very well, and winks at it—perforce. Our understanding with Malteios is entirely satisfactory, entirely. He is on very wholesome terms of friendly respect to us.'

Julian rarely pronounced himself; he did so now.

'If I were an islander—that is, one of a subject race—I don't think I should be very well content to forgo my liberty in exchange for underhand compensation from an employer whose tactics it suited to conciliate my natural dissatisfaction.'

'What a ridiculous phrase. And what ridiculous sentiments you occasionally give vent to. No, no, the present arrangement is as satisfactory as we can hope to make it, always excepting that one flaw, that we ought not to allow islanders in large numbers to live upon the mainland.'

They turned in between the two white lodges of the country house, and rode up the drive between the tall, pungent, untidy trees of eucalyptus. The house, one-storied, low, and covered with wistaria and bougainvillaea, glimmered white in the uncertain light. The shutters were flung back and the open windows gaped, oblong and

38

black, at regular intervals on the upper floor. On the ground level, a broad veranda stretched right along the front of the house, and high French windows, opening on to this, yellow with light, gave access to the downstairs rooms.

'Holà!' Mr Davenant called in a loud voice.

'Malista, Kyrie,' a man's voice answered, and a servant in the white fustanelle of the Islands, with black puttees wound round his legs, and red shoes with turned-up toes and enormous rosettes on the tip, came running to hold the horses.

'They have taken Vassili's brother, Kyrie,' he said as Mr Davenant gave him the reins.

Julian was already in the drawing-room, among the chintz-covered sofas, loaded little tables, and ubiquitous gilt chairs. Four fat columns, painted to represent lapis-lazuli, divided the room into two halves, and from their Corinthian capitals issued flames made of red tinsel and painted gray smoke, which dispersed itself realistically over the ceiling.

He stood in the window, absently looking out into the garden across the veranda, where the dinner table was laid for six. Pots of oleander and agapanthus stood along the edge of the veranda, between the fat white columns, with gaps between them through which one might pass out into the garden, and beyond them in the garden proper the fruit gleamed on the lemon-trees, and, somewhere, the sea whispered in the dusk. The night was calm and hot with the serenity of established summer weather, the stars big and steady like sequins in the summer sky. The spirit of such serenity does not brood over England, where to-day's pretence of summer will be broken by the fresh laughter of to-morrow's shower. The rose must fall to pieces in the height of its beauty beneath the fingers of sudden and capricious storm. But here the lemons hung, swollen and heavily pendulous, among the metallic green of their leaves, awaiting the accomplished end of their existence, the deepening of their gold, the fuller curve of their ripened luxuriance, with the complacency of certainty; fruit, not for the whim of the elements, but progressing throughout the year steadfastly towards the hand and the basket of the picker. Here and there the overburdened stem would snap, and the oblong ball of greenish-gold would fall with a soft and melancholy thud, like a sigh of regret, upon the ground beneath the tree; would roll a little way, and then be still. The little grove stretched in ordered lines and spaces, from the veranda, where the windows of the house threw rectangles of yellow light on to the ground in the blackness, to the bottom of the garden, where the sea washed indolently against the rocks.

Presently he would see Eve, his eyes would meet her mocking eyes, and they would smile at one another out of the depths of their immemorial friendship. She was familiar to him, so familiar that he could not remember the time when, difficult, intractable, exasperating, subtle, incomprehensible, she had not formed part of his life. She was as familiar to him as the house in the *platia*, with its big, empty drawing-room, the walls frescoed with swinging monkeys, broken columns, and a romantic land and seascape; as the talk about the vintage; as the preposterous politics, always changing, yet always, monotonously, nauseatingly, pettishly, the same. She was not part of his life in England, the prosaic life; she was part of his life on the Greek seaboard, unreal and fantastic, where the most improbable happenings came along with an air of ingenuousness, romance walking in the garments of every day. After a week in Herakleion he could not disentangle the real from the unreal.

It was the more baffling because those around him, older and wiser than he, appeared to take the situation for granted and to treat it with a seriousness that sometimes led him, when, forgetful, he was off his guard, to believe that the country was a real country and that its statesmen, Platon Malteios, Gregori Stavridis, and the rest, were real statesmen working soberly towards a definite end. That its riots were revolutions; that its factions were political parties; that its discordant, abusive, wrangling Chamber was indeed a Senate. That its four hundred stout soldiers, who periodically paraded the *platia* under the command of a general in a uniform designed by a theatrical costumier in Buda-Pesth, were indeed an army. That the *platia* itself was a forum. That the society was brilliant; that its liaisons had the dignity of great passions. That his aunt, who talked weightily and contradicted every one, including herself—the only person who ever ventured to do such a thing—was indeed a political figure, an Egeria among the men in whose hands lay the direction of affairs. In his more forgetful moments, he was tempted to believe these things, when he saw his father and his Uncle Robert, both unbending, incisive, hard-headed business men, believing them. As a rule, preserving his nice sense of perspective, he saw them as a setting to Eve.

He was beginning to adjust himself again to the life which faded with so extraordinary a rapidity as the express or the steamer bore him away, three times a year, to England. It faded always then like a photographic proof when exposed to the light. The political jargon was the first to go—he knew the sequence—'civil war,' 'independent archipelago,' 'overthrow of the Cabinet,' 'a threat to the Malteios party,' 'intrigues of the Stavridists,' the well-known phrases that, through sheer force of reiteration, he accepted without analysis; then, after the political jargon, the familiar figures that he saw almost daily, Sharp, his father's chief clerk; Aristotle, the door-keeper, his tussore fustanelle hanging magisterially from the rotundity of his portentous figure; Madame Lafarge, erect, and upholstered like a sofa, driving in her barouche; the young men at the club, languid and insolent and licentious; then, after the familiar figures, the familiar scenes; and lastly Eve herself, till he could no longer recall the drowsy tones of her voice, or evoke her eyes, that, though alive with malice and mockery, were yet charged with a mystery to which he could give no name. He was sad when these things began to fade. He clung on to them, because they were dear, but they slipped through his fingers like running water. Their evanescence served only to convince him the more of their unreality.

Then, England, immutable, sagacious, balanced; Oxford, venerable and self-confident, turning the young men of the nation as by machinery out of her mould. Law-abiding England, where men worked their way upwards, attaining power and honour in the ripeness of years. London, where the houses were of stone. Where was Herakleion, stucco-built and tawdry, city of perpetually-clanging bells, revolutions, and Prime Ministers made and unmade in a day? Herakleion of the yellow islands, washed by too blue a sea. Where?

Eve had never been to England, nor could he see any place in England for her. She should continue to live as she had always lived, among the vines and the magnolias, attended by a fat old woman who, though English, had spent so many years of her life in Herakleion that her English speech was oddly tainted by the southern lisp of the native Greek she had never been able to master; old Nana, who had lost the familiarity of one tongue without acquiring that of another; the ideal duenna for Eve.

Then with a light step across the veranda a young Greek priest came into the room by one of the French windows, blinking and smiling in the light, dressed in a long black soutane and black cap, his red hair rolled up into a knob at the back of his head according to the fashion of his church. He tripped sometimes over his soutane as he walked, muscular and masculine inside that feminine garment, and when he did this he would gather it up impatiently with a hand on which grew a pelt of wiry red hairs. Father Paul had instituted himself as a kind of private chaplain to the Davenants. Eve encouraged him because she thought him picturesque. Mrs Robert Davenant found him invaluable as a lieutenant in her campaign of control over the peasants and villagers, over whom she exercised a despotic if benevolent authority. He was therefore free to come and go as he pleased.

The population, Julian thought, was flowing back into his recovered world.

England and Oxford were put aside; not forgotten, not indistinct, not faded like Herakleion was wont to fade, but merely put aside, laid away like winter garments in summer weather. He was once more in the kingdom of stucco and adventure. Eve was coming back to him, with her strange shadowy eyes and red mouth, and her frivolity beneath which lay some force which was not frivolous. There were women who were primarily pretty: women who were primarily motherly; women who, like Mrs Robert Davenant, were primarily efficient, commanding, successful, metallic; women who, like Kato, were consumed by a flame of purpose which broke, hot and scorching, from their speech and burned relentlessly in their eyes; women who were primarily vain and trifling; he found he could crowd Eve into no such category. He recalled her, spoilt, exquisite, witty, mettlesome, elusive, tantalising; detached from such practical considerations as punctuality, convenience, reliability. A creature that, from the age of three, had exacted homage and protection. . . .

He heard her indolent voice behind him in the room, and turned expectantly for their meeting.

Three

IT WAS, however, during his first visit to the singer's flat that he felt himself again completely a citizen of Herakleion; that he felt himself, in fact, closer than ever before to the beating heart of intrigue and aspiration. Kato received him alone, and her immediate comradely grasp of his hand dispelled the shyness which had been induced in him by the concert; her vigorous simplicity caused him to forget the applause and enthusiasm he had that afternoon seen lavished on her as a public figure; he found in her an almost masculine friendliness and keenness of intellect, which loosened his tongue, sharpened his wits, set him on the path of discovery and self-expression. Kato watched him with her little bright eyes, nodding her approval with quick grunts; he paced her room, talking.

'Does one come, ever, to a clear conception of one's ultimate ambitions? Not one's personal ambitions, of course; they don't count.' ('How young he is,' she thought.) 'But to conceive clearly. I mean, exactly what one sets out to create, and what to destroy. If not, one must surely spend the whole of life working in the dark? Laying in little bits of mosaic, without once stepping back to examine the whole scheme of the picture. . . . One instinctively opposes authority. One struggles for freedom. Why? Why? What's at the bottom of that instinct? Why are we, men, born the instinctive enemies of order and civilisation, when order and civilisation are the weapons and the shields we, men, have ourselves instituted for our own protection? It's illogical.

'Why do we, every one of us, refute the experience of others, preferring to gain our own? Why do we fight against government? Why do I want to be independent of my father? or the Islands independent of Herakleion? or Herakleion, independent of Greece? What's this instinct of

44

wanting to stand alone, to be oneself, isolated, free, individual? Why does instinct push us towards individualism, when the great well-being of mankind probably lies in solidarity? when the social system in its most elementary form starts with men clubbing together for comfort and greater safety? No sooner have we achieved our solidarity, our hierarchy, our social system, our civilisation, than we want to get away from it. A vicious circle; the wheel revolves, and brings us back to the same point from which we started.'

'Yes,' said Kato, 'there is certainly an obscure sympathy with the rebels, that lies somewhere dormant in the soul of the most platitudinous advocate of law and order.' She was amused by his generalisations, and was clever enough not to force him back too abruptly to the matter she had in mind. She thought him ludicrously, though rather touchingly, young, both in his ideas and his phraseology; but at the same time she shrewdly discerned the force which was in him and which she meant to use for her own ends. 'You,' she said to him, 'will argue in favour of society, yet you will spend your life, or at any rate your youth, in revolt against it. Youth dies, you see, when one ceases to rebel. Besides,' she added, scrutinising him, 'the time will very soon come when you cease to argue and begin to act. Believe me, one soon discards one's wider examinations, and learns to content oneself with the practical business of the moment. One's own bit of the mosaic, as you said.'

He felt wholesomely sobered, but not reproved; he liked Kato's penetration, her vivid, intelligent sympathy, and her point of view which was practical without being cynical.

'I have come to one real conclusion,' he said, 'which is, that pain alone is intrinsically evil, and that in the lightening or abolition of pain one is safe in going straight ahead; it is a bit of the mosaic worth doing. So in the Islands ...' he paused.

Kato repressed a smile; she was more and more touched and entertained by his youthful, dogmatic statements, which were delivered with a concentration and an ardour that utterly disarmed derision. She was flattered, too, by his unthinking confidence in her; for she knew him by report as morose and uncommunicative, with relapses into rough high spirits and a schoolboy sense of farce. Eve had described him as inaccessible. ...

'When you go, as you say, straight ahead,' he resumed, frowning, his eyes absent.

Kato began to dwell, very skilfully, upon the topic of the Islands. ...

Certain events which Madame Kato had then predicted to Julian followed with a suddenness, an unexpectedness, that perplexed the mind of the inquirer seeking, not only their origin, but their chronological sequence. They came like a summer storm sweeping briefly, boisterously across the land after the inadequate warning of distant rumbles and the flash of innocuous summer lightning. The thunder had rumbled so often, it might be said that it had rumbled daily, and the lightning had twitched so often in the sky, that men remained surprised and resentful long after the rough little tornado had passed away. They remained staring at one another, scratching their heads under their straw hats, or leaning against the parapet on the quays, exploring the recesses of their teeth with the omnipresent toothpick, and staring across the sea to those Islands whence the storm had surely come, as though by this intense, frowning contemplation they would finally provide themselves with enlightenment. Groups of men sat outside the cafés, their elbows on the tables, advancing in tones of whispered vehemence their individual positive theories and opinions, beating time to their own rhetoric and driving home each cherished point with the emphatic stab of a long cigar. In the casino itself, with the broken windows gaping jaggedly on to the forecourt, and the red curtains of the atrium hanging in rags from those same windows, men stood pointing in little knots. 'Here they stood still, and 'From here they threw the bomb,' and those who had been present on the day were listened to with a respect they never in their lives had commanded before and never would command again.

There was no sector of society in Herakleion that did not discuss the matter with avidity; more, with gratitude. Brigandage was brigandage, a picturesque but rather *opéra bouffe* form of crime, but at the same time an excitement was, indubitably, an excitement. The Ministers, in their despatches to their home governments, affected to treat the incident as the work of a fortuitous band rather than as an organised expedition with an underlying political significance, nevertheless they fastened upon it as a pretext for their wit in Herakleion, where no sardonic and departmental eye would regard them with superior tolerance much as a grown-up person regards the facile amusement of a child. At the diplomatic dinner parties very little else was talked of. At tea parties, women, drifting from house to house, passed on as their own the witticisms they had most recently heard, which became common property until reclaimed from general circulation by the indignant perpetrators. From the drawning-rooms of the French Legation, down to village cafés where the gramophone grated unheard and the bowls lay neglected on the bowling alley, one topic reigned supreme. What nobody knew, and what everybody wondered about, was the attitude adopted by the Davenants in the privacy of their country house. What spoken or unspoken understanding existed between the inscrutable brothers? What veiled references, or candid judgments, escaped from William Davenant's lips as he lay back in his chair after dinner, a glass of wine—wine of his own growing—between his fingers? What indiscretions, that would have fallen so delectably upon the inquisitive ears of Herakleion, did he utter, secure in the confederacy of his efficient and vigorous sister-in-law, of the more negligible Robert, the untidy and taciturn Julian, the indifferent Eve?

It was as universally taken for granted that the outrage proceeded from the islanders as it was ferociously regretted that the offenders could not, from lack of evidence, be brought to justice. They had, at the moment, no special grievance, only their perennial grievances, of which everybody was tired of hearing. The brother of Vassili, a quite unimportant labourer, had been released; Mr Lafarge had interested himself in his servant's brother, and had made representations to the Premier, which Malteios had met with his usual urbane courtesy. An hour later the fellow had been seen setting out in a rowing boat for Aphros. All, therefore, was for the best. Yet within twenty-four hours of this proof of leniency . . .

The élite were dining on the evening of these unexpected occurrences at the French Legation to meet two guests of honour, one a distinguished Albanian statesman who

47

could speak no language but his own, and the other an Englishman of irregular appearances and disappearances, an enthusiast on all matters connected with the Near East. In the countries he visited he was considered an expert who had the ear of the English Cabinet and House of Commons, but by these institutions he was considered merely a crank and a nuisance. His conversation was after the style of the more economical type of telegram, with all prepositions, most pronouns, and a good many verbs left out; it gained thereby in mystery what it lost in intelligibility, and added greatly to his reputation. He and the Albanian had stood apart in confabulation before dinner, the Englishman arguing, expounding, striking his open palm with the fingers of the other hand, shooting out his limbs in spasmodic and ungraceful gestures, the Albanian unable to put in a word, but appreciatively nodding his head and red fez.

Madame Lafarge sat between them both at dinner, listening to the Englishman as though she understood what he was saying to her, which she did not, and occasionally turning to the Albanian to whom she smiled and nodded in a friendly and regretful way. Whenever she did this he made her a profound bow and drank her health in the sweet champagne. Here their intercourse perforce ended.

Half-way through dinner a note was handed to M. Lafarge. He gave an exclamation which silenced all his end of the table, and the Englishman's voice was alone left talking in the sudden hush.

'Turkey!' he was saying. 'Another matter! Ah, ghost of Abdul Hamid!' and then, shaking his head mournfully, 'world-treachery—world-conspiracy . . .'

'Ah, yes,' said Madame Lafarge, rapt, 'how true that is, how right you are.'

She realised that no one else was speaking, and raised her head interrogatively.

Lafarge said,—

'Something has occurred at the casino, but there is no cause for alarm; nobody has been hurt. I am sending a messenger for further details. This note explicitly says'— he consulted it again—'that no one is injured. A mere question of robbery; an impudent and successful attempt. A bomb has been thrown,'—('*Mais ils sont donc tous apaches?*' cried Condesa Valdez. Lafarge went on)—'but they say the damage is all in the atrium, and is confined to broken windows, torn hangings, and mirrors cracked from top to bottom. Glass lies plentifully scattered about the floor. But I hope that before very long we may be in possession of a little more news.' He sent the smile of a host round the table, reassuring in the face of anxiety.

A little pause, punctuated by a few broken ejaculations, followed upon his announcement.

'How characteristic of Herakleion,' cried Alexander Christopoulos, who had been anxiously searching for something noteworthy and contemptuous to say, 'that even with the help of a bomb we can achieve only a disaster that tinkles.'

The Danish Excellency was heard to say tearfully,—

'A robbery! a bomb! and practically in broad daylight! What a place, what a place!'

'Those Islands again, for certain!' Madame Delahaye exclaimed, with entire absence of tact; her husband, the French Military Attaché, frowned at her across the table; and the diplomatists all looked down their noses.

Then the Englishman, seeing his opportunity, broke out,—

'Very significant! all of a piece—anarchy—intrigue—no strong hand—free peoples. Too many, too many. Small nationalities. Chips! Cut-throats, all. So?'—he drew his fingers with an expressive sibilant sound across his own throat. 'Asking for trouble. Yugo-Slavs—bah! Poles—pfui! Eastern empire, that's the thing. Turks the only people'— the Albanian, fortunately innocent of English, was smiling amiably as he stirred his champagne—'great people. Armenians, wash-out. Quite right too. Herakleion, worst of all. Not even a chip. Only the chip of a chip.'

'And the Islands,' said the Danish Excellency brightly, 'want to be the chip of a chip of a chip.'

'Yes, yes,' said Madame Lafarge, who had been getting a little anxious, trying to provoke a laugh, 'Fru Thyregod has hit it as usual—*elle a trouvé le mot juste*,' she added, thinking that if she turned the conversation back into French it might check the Englishman's truncated eloquence.

Out in the town, the quay was the centre of interest. A large crowd had collected there, noisy in the immense peace of the evening. Far, far out, a speck on the opal sea, could still be distinguished the little boat in which the three men, perpetrators of the outrage, had made good their escape. Beyond the little boat, even less distinct, the sea was dotted with tiny craft, the fleet of fishing-boats from the Islands. The green light gleamed at the end of the pier. On the quay, the crowd gesticulated, shouted, and pointed, as the water splashed under the ineffectual bullets from the carbines of the police. The Chief of Police was there, giving orders. The police motor-launch was to be got out immediately. The crowd set up a cheer; they did not know who the offenders were, but they would presently have the satisfaction of seeing them brought back in handcuffs.

It was at this point that the entire Lafarge dinner-party debouched upon the quay, the women wrapped in their light cloaks, tremulous and excited, the men affecting an amused superiority. They were joined by the Chief of Police, and by the Christopoulos, father and son. It was generally known, though never openly referred to, that the principal interest in the casino was held by them, a fact which explained the saffron-faced little banker's present agitation.

'The authorities must make better dispositions,' he kept saying to Madame Lafarge. 'With this example before them, half the blackguards of the country-side will be making similar attempts. It is too absurdly easy.'

He glared at the Chief of Police.

'Better dispositions,' he muttered, 'better dispositions.'

'This shooting is ridiculous,' Alexander said impatiently, 'the boat is at least three miles away. What do they hope to kill? a fish? Confound the dusk. How soon will the launch be ready?'

'It will be round to the steps at any moment now,' said the Chief of Police, and he gave an order in an irritable voice to his men, who had continued to let off their carbines aimlessly and spasmodically.

In spite of his assurance, the launch did not appear. The Englishman was heard discoursing at length to Madame Lafarge, who, at regular intervals, fervently agreed with what he had been saying, and the Danish Excellency whispered and tittered with young Christopoulos. Social distinctions were sharply marked: the diplomatic party stood away from the casual crowd, and the casual crowd stood away from the rabble. Over all the dusk deepened, one or two stars came out, and the little boat was no longer distinguishable from the fishing fleet with its triangular sails.

Finally, throbbing, fussing, important, the motor-launch came churning to a standstill at the foot of the steps. The Chief of Police jumped in, Alexander followed him, promising that he would come straight to the French Legation on his return and tell them exactly what had happened.

In the mirrored drawing-rooms, three hours later, he made his recital. The gilt chairs were drawn round in a circle, in the middle of which he stood, aware that the Danish Excellency was looking at him, enraptured, with her prominent blue eyes.

'Of course, in spite of the start they had had, we knew that they stood no chance against a motor-boat, no chance whatsoever. They could not hope to reach Aphros before we overtook them. We felt quite confident that it was only a question of minutes. We agreed that the men must have been mad to imagine that they could make good their escape in that way. Sterghiou and I sat in the stern, smoking and talking. What distressed us a little was that we could no longer see the boat we were after, but you know how quickly the darkness comes, so we paid very little attention to that.

'Presently we came up with the fishing smacks from Aphros, and they shouted to us to keep clear of their tackle—impudence. We shut off our engines while we made inquiries from them as to the rowing-boat. Rowing-boat? they looked blank. They had seen no rowing-boat—no boat of any sort, other than their own. The word was passed, shouting, from boat to boat of the fleet; no one had seen a rowing-boat. Of course they were lying; how could they not be lying? but the extraordinary fact remained'—he made an effective pause—'there was no sign of a rowing-boat anywhere on the sea.'

A movement of appreciative incredulity produced itself among his audience.

'Not a sign!' Alexander repeated luxuriously. 'The sea lay all round us without a ripple, and the fishing smacks, although they were under full sail, barely moved. It was so still that we could see their reflection unbroken in the water. There might have been twenty of them, dotted about—twenty crews of bland liars. We were, I may as well admit it, nonplussed. What can you do when you are surrounded by smiling and petticoated liars, leaning against their masts, and persisting in idiotic blankness to all your questions? Denial, denial, was all their stronghold. They had seen nothing. But they must be blind to have seen nothing? They were very sorry, they had seen nothing at all. Would the gentlemen look round for themselves, they would soon be satisfied that nothing was in sight.

'As for the idea that the boat had reached Aphros in the time at their disposal, it was absolutely out of the question.

'I could see that Sterghiou was getting very angry; I said nothing, but I think he was uncomfortable beneath my silent criticism. He and his police could regulate the traffic in the rue Royale, but they could not cope with an emergency of this sort. From the very first moment they had been at fault. And they had taken at least twenty minutes to get out the motor-launch. Sterghiou hated me, I feel sure, for having accompanied him and seen his discomfiture.

'Anyway, he felt he must take some sort of action, so he ordered his men to search all the fishing smacks in turn. We went the round, a short throbbing of the motors, and then silence as we drew alongside and the men went on board. Of course, they found nothing. I watched the faces of the islanders during this inspection; they sat on the sides of their boats, busy with their nets, and pretending not to notice the police that moved about, turing everything over in their inefficient way, but I guessed their covert grins, and I swear I caught two of them winking at one another. If I had told this to Sterghiou, I believe he would have arrested them on the spot, he was by then in such a state of exasperation, but you can't arrest a man on a wink, especially a wink when darkness has very nearly come.

'And there the matter remains. We had found nothing, and we were obliged to turn round and come back again, leaving that infernally impudent fleet of smacks in possession of the battle-ground. Oh, yes, there is no doubt that they got the best of it. Because, naturally, we have them to thank.'

'Have you a theory, Alexander?' some one asked, as they were intended to ask.

Alexander shrugged.

'It is so obvious. A knife through the bottom of the boat would very quickly send her to the bottom, and a shirt and a fustanelle will very quickly transform a respectable bank-thief into an ordinary islander. Who knows that the two ruffians I saw winking were not the very men we were after? A sufficiently ingenious scheme altogether—too ingenious for poor Sterghiou.'

Four

THESE THINGS came, made their stir, passed, and were forgotten, leaving only a quickened ripple upon the waters of Herakleion, of which Julian Davenant, undergraduate, aged nineteen, bordering upon twenty, was shortly made aware. He had arrived from England with no other thought in his mind than of his riding, hawking, and sailing, but found himself almost immediately netted in a tangle of affairs of which, hitherto, he had known only by the dim though persistent echoes which reached him through the veils of his deliberate indifference. He found now that his indifference was to be disregarded. Men clustered round him, shouting, and tearing with irascible hands at his unsubstantial covering. He was no longer permitted to remain a boy. The half-light of adolescence was peopled for him by a procession of figures, fortunately distinct by virtue of their life-long familiarity, figures that urged and upbraided him, some indignant, some plaintive, some reproachful, some vehement, some dissimulating and sly; many vociferous, all insistent; a crowd of human beings each playing his separate hand, each the expounder of his own theory, rooted in his own conviction; a succession of intrigues, men who took him by the arm, and, leading him aside, discoursed to him, a strange medley of names interlarding their discourse with concomitant abuse or praise; men who flattered him; men who sought merely his neutrality, speaking of his years in tones of gentle disparagement. Men who, above all, would not leave him alone. Who, by their persecution, even those who urged his youth as an argument in favour of his neutrality, demonstrated to him that he had, as a man, entered the arena.

For his part, badgered and astonished, he took refuge in a taciturnity which only tantalised his pursuers into a more zealous aggression. His opinions were unknown in the club where the men set upon him from the first moment of his appearance. He would sit with his legs thrown over the arm of a leather arm-chair, loose-limbed and gray-flannelled, his mournful eyes staring out of the nearest window, while Greek, diplomat, or foreigner argued at him with gesture and emphasis. They seemed to him, had they but known, surprisingly unreal for all their clamour, pompous and yet insignificant.

His father was aware of the attacks delivered on his son, but, saying nothing, allowed the natural and varied system of education to take its course. He saw him standing, grave and immovable, in the surging crowd of philosophies and nationalities, discarding the charlatan by some premature wisdom, and assimilating the rare crumbs of true worldly experience. He himself was ignorant of the thoughts passing in the boy's head. He had forgotten the visionary tumult of nineteen, when the storm of life flows first over the pleasant, easy meadows of youth. Himself now a sober man, he had forgotten, so completely that he had ceased to believe in, the facile succession of convictions, the uprooting of beliefs, the fanatical acceptance of newly proffered creeds. He scarcely considered, or he might perhaps not so readily have risked, the possible effect of the queer systems of diverse ideals picked up, unconsciously, and put together from the conversation of the mountebank administrators of that tiny state, the melodramatic champions of the oppressed poor, and the professional cynicism of dago adventurers. If, sometimes, he wondered what Julian made of the talk that had become a jargon, he dismissed his uneasiness, with a re-affirmation of confidence in his impenetrability.

'Broaden his mind,' he would say. 'It won't hurt him. It doesn't go deep. Foam breaking upon a rock.'

So might Sir Henry have spoken, to whom the swags of fruit were but the vintage of a particular year, put into a labelled bottle.

Julian had gone more than once out of a boyish curiosity to hear the wrangle of the parties in the Chamber. Sitting up in the gallery, and leaning his arms horizontally on the top of the brass railing, he had looked down on the long tables covered with red baize, whereon reposed, startlingly white, a square sheet of paper before the seat of each deputy, and a pencil, carefully sharpened, alongside.

He had seen the deputies assemble, correctly frock-coated, punctiliously shaking hands with one another, although they had probably spent the morning in one another's company at the club—the club was the natural meeting-place of the Greeks and the diplomats, while the foreigners, a doubtful lot, congregated either in the gambling-rooms or in the *jardin anglais* of the casino. He had watched them taking their places with a good deal of coughing, throat-clearing, and a certain amount of expectoration. He had seen the Premier come in amid a general hushing of voices, and take his seat in the magisterial arm-chair in the centre of the room, behind an enormous ink-pot, pulling up the knees of his trousers and smoothing his beard away from his rosy lips with the tips of his fingers as he did so. Julian's attention had strayed from the formalities attendant upon the opening of the session, and his eyes had wandered to the pictures hanging on the walls: Aristidi Patros, the first Premier, after the secession from Greece, b. 1760, d. 1831, Premier of the Republic of Herakleion from 1826 to 1830; Pericli Anghelis, general, 1774–1847; Constantine Stavridis, Premier from 1830 to 1835, and again from 1841 to 1846, when he died assassinated. The portraits of the other Premiers hung immediately below the gallery where Julian could not see them. At the end of the room, above the doors, hung a long and ambitious painting executed in 1840 and impregnated with the romanticism of that age, representing the Declaration of Independence in the *platia* of Herakleion on the 16th September—kept as an ever memorable and turbulent anniversary—1826. The Premier, Patros, occupied the foreground, declaiming from a scroll of parchment, and portrayed as a frock-coated young man of god-like beauty; behind him stood serried ranks of deputies, and in the left-hand corner a group of peasants, like an operatic chorus, tossed flowers from baskets on to the ground at his feet. The heads of women clustered at the windows of the familiar houses of the *platia*, beneath the fluttering flags with the colours of the new Republic, orange and green.

Julian always thought that a portrait of his grandfather, for twelve months President of the collective archipelago of Hagios Zacharie, should have been included among the notables.

He had tried to listen to the debates which followed upon the formal preliminaries; to the wrangle of opponents; to the clap-trap patriotism which so thinly veiled the desire of personal advancement; to the rodomontade of Panaïoannou, Commander-in-Chief of the army of four hundred men, whose sky-blue uniform and white breeches shone among all the black coats with a resplendency that gratified his histrionic vanity; to the bombastic eloquence which rolled out from the luxuriance of the Premier's beard, with a startling and deceptive dignity in the trappings of the ancient and classic tongue. Malteios used such long, such high-sounding words, and struck his fist upon the red baize table with such emphatic energy, that it was hard not to believe in the authenticity of his persuasion. Julian welcomed most the moments when, after a debate of an hour or more, tempers grew heated, and dignity—that is to say, the pretence of the sobriety of the gathering—was cast aside in childish petulance.

'The fur flew,' said Julian, who had enjoyed himself. 'Christopoulos called Panaïoannou a fire-eater, and Panaïoannou called Christopoulos a money-grubber. "Where would you be without my money?" "Where would you be without my army?" "Army! can the valiant general inform the Chamber how many of his troops collapsed from exhaustion on the *platia* last Independence Day, and had to be removed to the hospital?" And so on and so forth. They became so personal that I expected the general at any moment to ask Christopoulos how many unmarried daughters he had at home.'

Malteios himself, president of the little republic, most plausible and empiric of politicians, was not above the discussion of current affairs with the heir of the Davenants towards whom, it was suspected, the thoughts of the islanders were already turning. The President was among those who adopted the attitude of total discouragement. The interference of a headstrong and no doubt Quixotic schoolboy would be troublesome; might become disastrous. Having dined informally with the Davenant brothers at their country house, he crossed the drawing-room after dinner, genial, a long cigar protruding from his mouth, to the piano in the corner where Eve and Julian were turning over some sheets of music.

'May an old man,' he said with his deliberate but nevertheless charming suavity, 'intrude for a moment upon the young?'

He sat down, removing his cigar, and discoursed for a little upon the advantages of youth. He led the talk to Julian's Oxford career, and from there to his future in Herakleion.

'A knotty little problem, as you will some day find— not, I hope, for your own sake, until a very remote some day. Perhaps not until I and my friend and opponent Gregori Stavridis are figures of the past,' he said, puffing smoke and smiling at Julian; 'then perhaps you will take your place in Herakleion and bring your influence to bear upon your very difficult and contrary Islands. Oh, very difficult, I assure you,' he continued, shaking his head. 'I am a conciliatory man myself, and not unkindly, I think I may say; they would find Gregori Stavridis a harder taskmaster than I. They are the oldest cause of dispute, your Islands, between Gregori Stavridis and myself. Now see,' he went on, expanding, 'they lie like a belt of neutral territory, your discontented, your so terribly and unreasonably discontented Islands, between me and Stavridis. We may agree upon other points; upon that point we continually differ. He urges upon the Senate a policy of severity with which I cannot concur. I wish to compromise, to keep the peace, but he is, alas! perpetually aggressive. He invades the neutral zone, as it were, from the west—periodical forays—and I am obliged to invade it from the east; up till now we have avoided clashing in the centre.' Malteios, still smiling, sketched the imaginary lines of his illustration on his knee with the unlighted tip of his cigar. 'I would coax, and he would force, the islanders to content and friendliness.'

Julian listened, knowing well that Malteios and Stavridis, opponents from an incorrigible love of opposition for opposition's sake, rather than from any genuine diversity of conviction, had long since seized upon the Islands as a convenient pretext. Neither leader had any very definite conception of policy beyond the desire, respectively, to remain in, or to get himself into, power. Between them the unfortunate Islands, pulled like a rat between two terriers, were given ample cause for the discontent of which Malteios complained. Malteios, it was true, adopted the more clement attitude, but for this clemency, it was commonly said, the influence of Anastasia Kato was alone responsible.

Through the loud insistent voices of the men, Julian was to remember in after years the low music of that woman's voice, and to see, as in a vignette, the picture of himself in Kato's flat among the cushions of her divan, looking again in memory at the photographs and ornaments on the shelf that ran all round the four walls of the room, at the height of the top of a dado. These ornaments appeared to him the apotheosis of cosmopolitanism. There were small, square wooden figures from Russia, a few inches high, and brightly coloured; white and gray Danish china; little silver images from Spain; miniature plants of quartz and jade; Battersea snuff-boxes; photographs of an Austrian archduke in a white uniform and a leopard-skin, of a Mexican in a wide sombrero, mounted on a horse and holding a lasso, of Mounet-Sully as the blinded Œdipus. Every available inch of space in the singer's room was crowded with these and similar trophies, and the shelf had been added to take the overflow. Oriental embroideries, heavily silvered, were tacked up on the walls, and on them again were plates and brackets, the latter carrying more ornaments; high up in one corner was an ikon, and over the doors hung open-work linen curtains from the bazaars of Constantinople. Among the many ornaments the massive singer moved freely and spaciously, creating havoc as she moved, so that Julian's dominating impression remained one of setting erect again the diminutive objects she had knocked over. She would laugh good-humouredly at herself, and would give him unequalled Turkish coffee in little handleless cups, like egg-cups, off a tray of beaten brass set on a small octagonal table inlaid with mother-of-pearl, and all the while she would talk to him musically, earnestly, bending forward, and her restless fingers would turn the bangles round and round upon her arms.

He could not think Kato unreal, though many of the phrases upon her lips were the same as he heard from the men in the club; he could not think her unreal, when her voice broke over the words 'misery' and 'oppression,' and when her eyes burned their conviction into his. He began to believe in the call of the Islands, as he listened to the soft, slurring speech of their people in her voice, and discovered, listening to her words with only half his mind, the richness of the grapes in the loose coils of her dark hair, and the fulvous colouring of the Islands in the copper draperies she always affected. It seemed to Julian that, at whatever time of day he saw her, whether morning, afternoon, or evening, she was always wearing the same dress, but he supposed vaguely that this could not actually be so. Like his father, he maintained her as a woman of genuine patriotic ardour, dissociating her from Herakleion and its club and casino, and associating her with the Islands, where injustice and suffering, at least, were true things. He lavished his enthusiasm upon her, and his relations learned to refrain, in his presence, from making the usual obvious comments on her appearance. He looked upon her flat as a sanctuary and a shrine. He fled one day in disgust and disillusionment when the Premier appeared with his ingratiating smile in the doorway. Julain had known, of course, of the liaison, but was none the less distressed and nauseated when it materialised beneath his eyes.

He fled to nurse his soul-sickness in the country, lying on his back at full length under the olive-trees on the lower slopes of Mount Mylassa, his hands beneath his head, his horse moving near by and snuffing for pasture on the bare terraces. The sea, to-day of the profoundest indigo, sparkled in the sun below, and between the sea and the foot of the mountain, plainly, as in an embossed map, stretched the strip of flat cultivated land where he could distinguish first the dark ilex avenue, then the ribbon of road, then the village, finally the walled plantation which was his uncle's garden, and the roofs of the low house in the centre. The bougainvillaea climbing over the walls and roof of his uncle's house made a warm stain of magenta.

Herakleion was hidden from sight, on the other hand, by the curve of the hill, but the Islands were visible opposite, and, caring only for them, he gazed as he had done many times, but now their meaning and purport crystallised in his mind as never before. There was something symbolical in their detachment from the mainland—in their clean remoteness, their isolation; all the difference between the unfettered ideal and the tethered reality. An island! land that had slipped the leash of continents, forsworn solidarity, cut adrift from security and prudence!

One could readily believe that they made part of the divine, the universal discontent, that rare element, dynamic, life-giving, that here and there was to be met about the world, always fragmentary, yet always full and illuminating, even as the fragments of beauty.

This was a day which Julian remembered, marked as it were, with an asterisk in the calendar of his mind, by two notes which he found awaiting him on his return to the house in the *platia*. Aristotle handed them to him as he dismounted at the door.

The first he opened was from Eve.

'I am so angry with you, Julian. What have you done to my Kato? I found her in tears. She says you were with her when the Premier came, and that you vanished without a word.

'I know your *sauts de gazelle*; you are suddenly bored or annoyed, and you run away. Very naïf, very charming, very candid, very fawn-like—or is it, hideous suspicion, a pose?'

He was surprised and hurt by her taunt. One did not wish to remain, so one went away; it seemed to him very simple.

The second note was from Kato.

'Julian, forgive me,' it ran; 'I did not know he was coming. Forgive me. Send me a message to say when I shall see you. I did not know he was coming. Forgive me.'

He read these notes standing in the drawing-room with the palely-frescoed walls. He looked up from reading them, and encountered the grinning faces of the painted monkeys and the perspective of the romantic landscape. The colours were faint, and the rough grain of the plaster showed through in tiny lumps. Why should Kato apologise to him for the unexpected arrival of her lover? It was not his business. He sat down and wrote her a perfectly polite reply to say that he had nothing to forgive and had no intention of criticising her actions. The sense of unreality was strong within him.

It seemed that he could not escape the general determination to involve him, on one side or the other, in the local affairs. Besides the men at the club, Sharp, the head clerk at the office spoke to him—'The people look to you, Mr Julian; better keep clear of the Islands if you don't want a crowd of women hanging round kissing your hands,'— Vassili, the chasseur, murmured to him in the hall when he went to dine at the French Legation; Walters, the *Times* correspondent in Herakleion, winked to him with a man to man expression that flattered the boy.

'I know the Balkans inside out, mind you; nearly lost my head to the Bulgars and my property to the Serbs; I've been held to ransom by Albanian brigands, and shot at in the streets of Athens on December the second; I've had my rooms ransacked by the police, and I could have been a rich man now if I'd accepted half the bribes that I've had offered me. So you can have my advice, if you care to hear it, and that is, hold your tongue till you're sure you know your own mind.'

The women, following the lead, chattered to him. He had never known such popularity. It was hard, at times, to preserve his non-committal silence, yet he knew, ignorant and irresolute, that therein lay his only hope of safety. They must not perceive that they had taken him unawares, that he was hopelessly at sea in the mass of names, reminiscences, and prophecies that they showered upon him. They must not suspect that he really knew next to nothing about the situation. . . .

He felt his way cautiously and learnt, and felt his strength growing.

In despite of Sharp's warning, he went across to the Islands, taking with him Father Paul: Eve exclaimed that he took the priest solely from a sense of the suitability of a retinue, and Julian, though he denied the charge, did not do so very convincingly. He had certainly never before felt the need of a retinue. He had always spent at least a week of his holidays on Aphros, taking his favourite hawk with him, and living either in his father's house in the village, or staying with the peasants. When he returned, he was always uncommunicative as to how he had passed his time.

Because he felt the stirring of events in the air, and because he knew from signs and hints dropped to him that his coming was waited with an excited expectancy, he chose to provide himself with the dignity of an attendant. He had, characteristically, breathed no word of his suspicions, but moved coldly self-reliant in the midst of his uncertainties. Father Paul only thought him more than usually silent as he busied himself with the sail of his little boat and put out to sea from the pier of Herakleion. Aphros lay ahead, some seven or eight miles—a couple of hours' sailing in a good breeze.

His white sails were observed some way off by the villagers, who by chance were already assembled at the weekly market in the village square. They deserted the pens and stalls to cluster round the top of the steps that descended, steep as an upright ladder, and cut in the face of the rock, from the market place straight down to the sea, where the white foam broke round the foot of the cliff. Julian saw the coloured crowd from his boat; he distinguished faces as he drew nearer, and made out the flutter of handkerchiefs from the hands of the women. The village hung sheerly over the sea, the face of the white houses flat with the face of the brown rocks, the difference of colour alone betraying where the one began and the other ended, as though some giant carpenter had planed away all inequalities of surface from the eaves down to the washing water. The fleet of fishing-boats, their bare, graceful masts swaying a little from the perpendicular as the boats ranged gently at their moorings with the sigh of the almost imperceptible waves, lay like resting seagulls in the harbour.

'They are waiting to welcome you—feudal, too feudal,' growled Father Paul, who, though himself the creature and dependent of the Davenants, loudly upheld his democratic views for the rest of mankind.

'And why?' muttered Julian. 'This has never happened before. I have been away only four months.'

Three fishermen wearing the white kilted fustanelle and tasselled shoes were already on the jetty with hands outstretched to take his mooring-rope. Eager faces looked down from above, and a hum went through the little crowd as Julian sprang on to the jetty, the boat rocking as his weight released it—a hum that died slowly, like the note of an organ, fading harmoniously into a complete silence. Paul knew suddenly that the moment was significant. He saw Julian hesitate, faltering as it were between sea and land, his dark head and broad shoulders framed in an immensity of blue, the cynosure of the crowd above, still silent and intent upon his actions. He hesitated until his hesitation became apparent to all. Paul saw that his hands were shut and his face stern. The silence of the crowd was becoming oppressive, when a woman's voice rang out like a bell in the pellucid air,—

'Liberator!'

Clear, sudden, and resonant, the cry vibrated and hung upon echo, so that the mind followed it, when it was no more heard, round the island coast, where it ran up into the rocky creeks, and entered upon the breeze into the huts of goat-herds on the hill. Julian slowly raised his head as at a challenge. He looked up into the furnace of eyes bent upon him, lustrous eyes in the glow of faces tanned to a golden brown, finding in all the same query, the same expectancy, the same breathless and suspended confidence. For a long moment he gazed up, and they gazed down, challenge, acceptance, homage, loyalty, devotion, and covenant passing unspoken between them; then, his hesitation a dead and discarded thing, he moved forward and set his foot firmly upon the lowest step. The silence of the crowd was broken by a single collective murmur.

The crowd—which consisted of perhaps not more than fifty souls, men and women—parted at the top as his head and shoulders appeared on the level of the market-place. Paul followed, tripping over his soutane on the ladder-like stairs. He saw Julian's white shoes climbing, climbing the flight, until the boy stood deliberately upon the market-place. A few goats were penned up for sale between wattled hurdles, bleating for lost dams or kids; a clothes-stall displayed highly-coloured handkerchiefs, boleros for the men, silk sashes, puttees, tasselled caps, and kilted fustanelles; a fruit-stall, lined with bright blue paper, was stacked from floor to ceiling with oranges, figs, bunches of grapes, and scarlet tomatoes. An old woman, under an enormous green umbrella, sat hunched on the back of a tiny gray donkey.

Julian stood, grave and moody, surveying the people from under lowered brows. They were waiting for him to speak to them, but, as a contrast to the stifled volubility seething in their own breasts, his stillness, unexpected and surprising, impressed them more than any flow of eloquence. He seemed to have forgotten about them, though his eyes dwelt meditatively on their ranks; he seemed remote, preoccupied; faintly disdainful, though tolerant, of the allegiance they had already, mutely, laid at his feet, and were prepared to offer him in terms of emotional expression. He seemed content to take this for granted. He regarded them for a space, then turned to move in the direction of his father's house.

The people pressed forward after him, a whispering and rustling bodyguard, disconcerted but conquered and adoring. Their numbers had been increased since the news of his landing had run through the town. Fishermen, and labourers from olive-grove and vineyard, men whose lives were lived in the sun, their magnificent bare throats and arms glowed like nectarines in the white of the loose shirts they wore. Knotted handkerchiefs were about their heads, and many of them wore broad hats of rough straw over the handkerchief. Ancestrally more Italian than Greek, for the original population of the archipelago of Hagios Zacharie had, centuries before, been swamped by the settlements of colonising Genoese, they resembled the peasants of southern Italy.

The headman of the village walked with them, Tsantilas Tsigaridis, sailor and fisherman since he could remember, whose skin was drawn tightly over the fine bony structure of his face, and whose crisp white hair escaped in two bunches over his temples from under the red handkerchief he wore; he was dressed, incongruously enough, in a blue English jersey which Mrs Davenant had given him, and a coffee-coloured fustanelle. Behind the crowd, as though he were shepherding them, Nico Zapantiotis, overseer of the Davenant vineyards, walked with a long pole in his hand, a white sheepdog at his heels, and a striped blue and white shirt fluttering round his body, open at the throat, and revealing the swelling depth of his hairy chest. Between these two notables pressed the crowd, bronzed and coloured, eyes eager and attentive and full of fire, a gleam of silver ear-rings among the shiny black ringlets. Bare feet and heelless shoes shuffled alike over the cobbles.

At the end of the narrow street, where the children ran out as in the story of the Pied Piper to join in the progress, the doorway of the Davenant house faced them.

It was raised on three steps between two columns. The

monastery had been a Genoese building, but the Greek influence was unmistakable in the columns and the architrave over the portico. Julian strode forward as though unconscious of his following. Paul became anxious. He hurried alongside.

'You must speak to these people,' he whispered.

Julian mounted the steps and turned in the dark frame of the doorway. The people had come to a standstill, filling the narrow street. It was now they who looked up to Julian, and he who looked down upon them, considering them, still remote and preoccupied, conscious that here and now the seed sown in the clubrooms must bear its fruit, that life, grown impatient of waiting for a summons he did not give, had come to him of its own accord and ordered him to take the choice of peace or war within its folded cloak. If he had hoped to escape again to England with a decision still untaken, that hope was to be deluded. He was being forced and hustled out of his childhood into the responsibilities of a man. He could not plead the nebulousness of his mind; action called to him, loud and insistent. In vain he told himself, with the frown deepening between his brows, and the people who watched him torn with anxiety before that frown—in vain he told himself that the situation was fictitious, theatrical. He could not convince himself of this truth with the fire of the people's gaze directed upon him. He must speak to them; they were silent, expectant, waiting. The words broke from him impelled, as he thought, by his terror of his own helplessness and lack of control, but to his audience they came as a command, a threat, and an invitation.

'What is it you want of me?'

He stood on the highest of the three steps, alone, the back of his head pressed against the door, and a hand on each of the flanking columns. The black-robed priest had taken his place below him, to one side, on the ground level. Julian felt a sudden resentment against these waiting people, that had driven him to bay, the resentment of panic and isolation, but to them his attitude betraying nothing, he appeared infallible, dominating, and inaccessible.

Tsantilas Tsigaridis came forward as spokesman, a gold ring hanging in the lobe of one ear, and a heavy silver ring shining dully on the little finger of his brown, knotted hand.

'Kyrie,' he said, 'Angheliki Zapantiotis has hailed you. We are your own people. By the authorities we are persecuted as though we were Bulgars, we, their brothers in blood. Last week a score of police came in boats from Herakleion and raided our houses in search of weapons. Our women ran screaming to the vineyards. Such weapons as the police could find were but the pistols we carry for ornament on the feast-days of church, and these they removed, for the sake, as we know, not being blind, of the silver on the locks which they will use to their own advantage. By such persecutions we are harried. We may never know when a hand will not descend on one of our number, on a charge of sedition or conspiracy, and he be seen no more. We are not organised for resistance. We are blind beasts, leaderless.'

A woman in the crowd began to sob, burying her face in her scarlet apron. A man snarled his approval of the spokesman's words, and spat violently into the gutter.

'And you demand of me?' said Julian, again breaking his silence. 'Championship? leadership? You cannot say you are unjustly accused of sedition! What report of Aphros could I carry to Herakleion?'

He saw the people meek, submissive, beneath his young censure, and the knowledge of his power surged through him like a current through water.

'Kyrie,' said the old sailor, reproved, but with the same inflexible dignity, 'we know that we are at your mercy. But we are your own people. We have been the people of your people for four generations. The authorities have torn even the painting of your grandfather from the walls of our assembly room . . .'

'Small blame to them,' thought Julian; 'that shows their good sense.'

Tsantilas pursued,—

'. . . we are left neither public nor private liberty. We are already half-ruined by the port-dues which are directed against us islanders and us alone.' A crafty look came into his eyes. 'Here, Kyrie, you should be in sympathy.'

Julian's moment of panic had passed; he was now conscious only of his complete control. He gave way to the anger prompted by the mercenary trait of the Levantine that marred the man's natural and splendid dignity.

'What sympathy I may have,' he said loudly, 'is born of compassion, and not of avaricious interest.'

He could not have told what instinct urged him to rebuke these people to whose petition he was decided to yield. He observed that with each fresh reproof they cringed the more.

'Compassion, Kyrie, and proprietary benevolence,' Tsantilas rejoined, recognising his mistake. 'We know that in you we find a disinterested mediator. We pray to God that we may be allowed to live at peace with Herakleion. We pray that we may be allowed to place our difficulties and our sorrows in your hands for a peaceful settlement.'

Julian looked at him, majestic as an Arab and more cunning than a Jew, and a slightly ironical smile wavered on his lips.

'Old brigand,' he thought, 'the last thing he wants is to live at peace with Herakleion; he's spoiling for a stand-up fight. Men on horses, himself at their head, charging the police down this street, and defending our house like a beleaguered fort; rifles cracking from every window, and the more police corpses the better. May I be there to see it!'

His mind flew to Eve, whom he had last seen lying in a hammock, drowsy, dressed in white, and breathing the scent of the gardenia she held between her fingers. What part would she, the spoilt, the exquisite, play if there were to be bloodshed on Aphros?

All this while he was silent, scowling at the multitude, who waited breathless for his next words.

'Father will half kill me,' he thought.

At that moment Tsigaridis, overcome by his anxiety, stretched out his hands towards him, surrendering his dignity in a supreme appeal,—

'Kyrie? I have spoken.'

He dropped his hands to his sides, bowed his head, and fell back a pace.

Julian pressed his shoulders strongly against the door; it was solid enough. The sun, striking on his bare hand, was hot. The faces and necks and arms of the people below him were made of real flesh and blood. The tension, the anxiety in their eyes was genuine. He chased away the unreality.

'You have spoken,' he said, 'and I have accepted.'

The woman named Angheliki Zapantiotis, who had hailed him as liberator, cast herself forward on to the step at his feet, as a stir and a movement, that audibly expressed itself in the shifting of feet and the releasing of contained breaths, ruffled through the crowd. He lifted his hand to enjoin silence, and spoke with his hand raised high above the figure of the woman crouching on the step.

He told them that there could now be no going back, that, although the time of waiting might seem to them long and weary, they must have hopeful trust in him. He exacted from them trust, fidelity, and obedience. His voice rang sharply on the word, and his glance circled imperiously, challenging defiance. It encountered none. He told them that he would never give his sanction to violence save as a last resort. He became intoxicated with the unaccustomed wine of oratory.

'An island is our refuge; we are the garrison of a natural fortress, that we can hold against the assault of our enemies from the sea. We will never seek them out, we will be content to wait, restrained and patient, until they move with weapons in their hands against us. Let us swear that our only guilt of aggression shall be to preserve our coasts inviolate.'

A deep and savage growl answered him as he paused. He was flushed with the spirit of adventure, the prerogative of youth. The force of youth moved so strongly within him that every man present felt himself strangely ready and equipped for the calls of the enterprise. A mysterious alchemy had taken place. They, untutored, unorganised, scarcely knowing what they wanted, much less how to obtain it, had offered him the formless material of their blind and chaotic rebellion, and he, having blown upon it with the fire of his breath, was welding it now to an obedient, tempered weapon in his hands. He had taken control. He might disappear and the curtains of silence close together behind his exit; Paul, watching, knew that these people would henceforward wait patiently, and with confidence, for his return.

He dropped suddenly from his rhetoric into a lower key.

'In the meantime I lay upon you a charge of discretion. No one in Herakleion must get wind of this meeting; Father Paul and I will be silent, the rest lies with you. Until you hear of me again, I desire you to go peaceably about your ordinary occupations.'

'Better put that in,' he thought to himself.

'I know nothing, nor do I wish to know,' he continued, shrewdly examining their faces, 'of the part you played in the robbery at the casino. I only know that I will never countenance the repetition of any such attempt; you will have to choose between me and your brigandage.' He suddenly stamped his foot. 'Choose now! which is it to be?'

'Kyrie, Kyrie,' said Tsigaridis, 'you are our only hope.'

'Lift up your hands,' Julian said intolerantly.

His eyes searched among the bronzed arms that rose at his command like a forest of lances; he enjoyed forcing obedience upon the crowd and seeing their humiliation.

'Very well,' he said then, and the hands sank, 'see to it that you remember your promise. I have no more to say. Wait, trust, and hope.'

He carried his hand to his forehead and threw it out before him in a gesture of farewell and dismissal.

He suspected himself of having acted and spoken in a theatrical manner, but he knew also that through the chaos of his mind an unextinguishable light was dawning.

Five

JULIAN in the candour of his experience unquestioningly believed that the story would not reach Herakleoin. Before the week was out, however, he found himself curiously eyed in the streets, and by the end of the week, going to dinner at the French Legation, he was struck by the hush that fell as his name was announced in the mirrored drawing-rooms. Madame Lafarge said to him severely,—

'Jeune homme, vous avez été très indiscret,' but a smile lurked in her eyes beneath her severity.

An immense Serbian, almost a giant, named Grbits, with a flat, Mongolian face, loomed ominously over him.

'Young man, you have my sympathy. You have disquieted the Greeks. You may count at any time upon my friendship.'

His fingers were enveloped and crushed in Grbits' formidable handshake.

The older diplomatists greeted him with an assumption of censure that was not seriously intended to veil their tolerant amusement.

'Do you imagine that we have nothing to do,' Don Rodrigo Valdez said to him, 'that you set out to enliven the affairs of Herakleion?'

Fru Thyregod, the Danish Excellency, took him into a corner and tapped him on the arm with her fan with that half flirtatious, half friendly familiarity she adopted towards all men.

'You are a dark horse, my dark boy,' she said meaningly, and, as he pretended ignorance, raising his brows and shaking his head, added, 'I'm much indebted to you as a living proof of my perception. I always told them; I always said, "Carl, that boy is an adventurer," and Carl said, "Nonsense, Mabel, your head is full of romance," but I said, "Mark my words, Carl, that boy will flare up; he's quiet now, but you'll have to reckon with him." '

He realised the extent of the gratitude of social Herakleion. He had provided a flavour which was emphatically absent from the usual atmosphere of these gatherings. Every Legation in turn, during both the summer and the winter season, extended its hospitality to its colleagues with complete resignation as to the lack of all possibility of the unforeseen. The rules of the diplomatic precedence rigorously demanding a certain grouping, the Danish Excellency, for example, might sit before her mirror fluffing out her already fluffy fair hair with the complacent if not particularly pleasurable certainty that this evening, at the French Legation, she would be escorted in to dinner by the Roumanian Minister, and that on her other hand would sit the Italian Counsellor, while to-morrow, at the Spanish Legation, she would be escorted to dinner by the Italian Counsellor and would have upon her other hand the Roumanian Minister—unless, indeed, no other Minister's wife but Madame Lafarge was present, in which case she would be placed on the left hand of Don Rodrigo Valdez. She would have preferred to sit beside Julian Davenant, but he, of course, would be placed amongst the young men—secretaries, young Greeks, and what not—at the end of the table. These young men—'les petits jeunes gens du bout de la table,' as Alexander Christopoulos, including himself in their number, contemptuously called them—always ate mournfully through their dinner without speaking to one another. They did not enjoy themselves, nor did their host or hostess enjoy having them there, but it was customary to invite them . . . Fru Thyregod knew that she must not exhaust all her subjects of conversation with her two neighbours this evening, but must keep a provision against the morrow; therefore, true to her little science, she refrained from mentioning Julian's adventure on Aphros to the Roumanian, and discoursed on it behind her fan to the Italian only. Other people seemed to be doing the same. Julian heard whispers, and saw glances directed towards him. Distinctly, Herakleion and its hostesses would be grateful to him.

. He felt slightly exhilarated. He noticed that no Greeks were present, and thought that they had been omitted on his account. He reflected, not without a certain apprehensive pleasure, that if this roomful knew, as it evidently did, the story would not be long in reaching his father. Who had betrayed him? Not Paul, he was sure, nor Kato, to whom he had confided the story. (Tears had come into her eyes, she had clasped her hands, and she had kissed him, to his surprise, on his forehead.) He was glad on the whole that he had been betrayed. He had come home in a fever of exaltation and enthusiasm which had rendered concealment both damping and irksome. Little incidents, of significance to him alone, had punctuated his days by reminders of his incredible, preposterous, and penetrating secret; to-night, for instance, the chasseur in the hall, the big, scarlet-coated, chasseur, an islander, had covertly kissed his hand. . . .

His father took an unexpected view. Julian had been prepared for anger, in fact he had the countering phrases already in his mind as he mounted the stairs of the house in the *platia* on returning from the French Legation. His father was waiting, a candle in his hand, on the landing.

'I heard you come in. I want to ask you, Julian,' he said at once, 'whether the story I have heard in the club to-night is true? That you went to Aphros, and entered into heaven knows what absurd covenant with the people?'

Julian flushed at the reprimanding tone.

'I knew that you would not approve,' he said. 'But one must do something. Those miserable, bullied people, denied the right to live . . .'

'Tut,' said his father impatiently. 'Have they really taken you in? I thought you had more sense. I have had a good deal of trouble in explaining to Malteios that you are only a hot-headed boy, carried away by the excitement of the moment. You see, I am trying to make excuses for you, but I am annoyed, Julian, I am annoyed. I thought I could trust you. Paul, too. However, you bring your own punishment on your head, for you will have to keep away from Herakleion in the immediate future.'

'Keep away from Herakleion?' cried Julian.

'Malteios' hints were unmistakable,' his father said dryly. 'I am glad to see you are dismayed. You had better go to bed now, and I will speak to you to-morrow.'

Mr Davenant started to go upstairs, but turned again, and came down the two or three steps, still holding his candle in his hand.

'Come,' he said in a tone of remonstrance, 'if you really take the thing seriously, look at it at least for a moment with practical sense. What is the grievance of the Islands? That they want to be independent from Herakleion. If they must belong to anybody, they say, let them belong to Italy rather than to Greece or to Herakleion. And why? Because they speak an Italian rather than a Greek patois! Because a lot of piratical Genoese settled in them five hundred years ago! Well, what do you propose to do, my dear Julian? Hand the Islands over to Italy?'

'They want independence,' Julian muttered. 'They aren't even allowed to speak their own language,' he continued, raising his voice. 'You know it is forbidden in the schools. You know that the port-dues in Herakleion ruin them— and are intended to ruin them. You know they are oppressed in every petty as well as in every important way. You know that if they were independent they wouldn't trouble Herakleion.'

'Independent! independent!' said Mr Davenant, irritable and uneasy. 'Still, you haven't told me what you proposed to do. Did you mean to create a revolution?'

Julian hesitated. He did not know. He said boldly,—

'If need be.'

Mr Davenant snorted.

'Upon my word,' he cried sarcastically, 'you have caught the emotional tone of Aphros to perfection. I suppose you saw yourself holding Panaïoannou at bay? If these are your ideas, I shall certainly support Malteios in keeping you away. I am on the best of terms with Malteios, and I cannot afford to allow your Quixotism to upset the balance. I can obtain almost any concession from Malteios,' he added thoughtfully, narrowing his eyes and rubbing his hand across his chin.

Julian watched his father with distaste and antagonism.

'And that is all you consider?' he said then.

'What else is there to consider?' Mr Davenant replied. 'I am a practical man, and practical men don't run after chimeras. I hope I'm not more cynical than most. You know very well that at the bottom of my heart I sympathise with the Islands. Come,' he said, with a sudden assumption of frankness, seeing that he was creating an undesirable rift between himself and his son, 'I will even admit to you, in confidence, that the republic doesn't treat its

Islands as well as it might. You know, too, that I respect and admire Madame Kato; she comes from the Islands, and has every right to hold the views of an islander. But there's no reason why you should espouse those views, Julian. We are foreigners here, representatives of a great family business, and that business, when all's said and done, must always remain our first consideration.'

'Yet people here say,' Julian argued, still hoping for the best against the cold disillusionment creeping over him, 'that no political move can be made without allowing for your influence and Uncle Robert's. And my grandfather, after all . . .'

'Ah, your grandfather!' said Mr Davenant, 'your grandfather was an extremely sagacious man, the real founder of the family tradition, though I wouldn't like Malteois to hear me say so. He knew well enough that in the Islands he held a lever which gave him, if he chose to use it, absolute control over Herakleion. He only used it once, when he wanted something they refused to give him; they held out against him for a year, but ultimately they came to heel. A very sagacious man . . . Don't run away with the idea that he was inspired by anything other than a most practical grasp—though I don't say it wasn't a bold one—a most practical grasp of the situation. He gave the politicians of Herakleion a lesson they haven't yet forgotten.'

He paused, and, as Julian said nothing, added—

'We keep very quiet, your uncle Robert and I, but Malteios, and Stavridis himself, know that in reality we hold them on a rope. We give them a lot of play, but at any moment we choose, we can haul them in. A very satisfactory arrangement. Tacit agreements, to my mind, are always the most satisfactory. And so you see that I can't tolerate your absurd, uneducated interference. Why, there's no end to the harm you might do! Some day you will thank me.'

As Julian still said nothing, he looked at his son, who was standing, staring at the floor, a deep frown on his forehead, thunderous, unconvinced. Mr Davenant, being habitually uncommunicative, felt aggrieved that his explanatory condescension had not been received with a more attentive deference. He also felt uneasy. Julian's silences were always disquieting.

'You are very young still,' he said, in a more conciliatory tone, 'and I ought perhaps to blame myself for allowing you to go about so freely in this very unreal and bewildering place. Perhaps I ought not to have expected you to keep your head. Malteios is quite right: Herakleion is no place for a young man. Don't think me hard in sending you away. Some day you will come back with, I hope, a better understanding.'

He rested his hand kindly for a moment on Julian's shoulder, then turned away, and the light of his candle died as he passed the bend of the stairs.

On the following evening Julian, returning from the country-house where he had spent the day, was told that the Premier was with Mr Davenant and would be glad to see him.

He had ridden out to the country, regardless of the heat, turning instinctively to Eve in his strange and rebellious frame of mind. For some reason which he did not analyse, he identified her with Aphros—the Aphros of romance and glamour to which he so obstinately clung. To his surprise she listened unresponsive and sulky.

'You are not interested, Eve?'

Then the reason of her unreasonableness broke out.

'You have kept this from me for a whole week, and you confide in me now because you know the story is public property. You expect me to be interested. Grand merci!'

'But, Eve, I had pledged myself not to tell a soul.'

'Did you tell Kato?'

'Damn your intuition!' he said angrily.

She lashed at him then, making him feel guilty, miserable, ridiculous, though as he sat scowling over the sea—they were in their favourite place at the bottom of the garden, where under the pergola of gourds it was cool even at that time of the day—he appeared to her more than usually unmoved and forbidding.

After a long pause,—

'Julian, I am sorry.—I don't often apologise.—I said I was sorry.'

He looked coldly at her with his mournful eyes, that, green in respose, turned black in anger.

'Your vanity makes me ill.'

'You told Kato.'

'Jealousy!'

She began to protest; then, with a sudden change of front,—

'You know I am jealous. When I am jealous, I lie awake all night. I lose all sense of proportion. It's no joke, my jealousy; it's like an open wound. I put up a stockade round it to protect it. You are not considerate.'

'Can you never forget yourself? Do you care nothing for the Islands? Are you so self-centred, so empty-headed? Are all women, I wonder, as vain as you?'

They sat on the parapet, angry, inimical, with the coloured gourds hanging heavily over their heads.

Far out to sea the Islands lay, so pure and fair and delicate that Julian, beholding them, violently rejected the idea that in this possession of such disarming loveliness his grandfather had seen merely a lever for the coercion of recalcitrant politicians. They lay there as innocent and fragile as a lovely woman asleep, veiled by the haze of sunshine as the sleeper's limbs by a garment of lawn. Julian gazed till his eyes and his heart swam in the tenderness of passionate and protective ownership. He warmed towards his grandfather, the man whose generous ideals had been so cynically libelled by the succeeding generation. No man deserving the name could be guilty of so repulsive an act of prostitution. . . .

'They will see me here again,' he exclaimed, striking his fist on the parapet.

To the startled question in Eve's eyes he vouchsafed an explanation.

'Malteios is sending me away. But when his term of office is over, I shall come back. It will be a good opportunity. We will break with Herakleion over the change of government. Kato will restrain Malteios so long as he is in power, I can trust her; but I shall make my break with Stavridis.'

In his plans for the future he had again forgotten Eve.

'You are going away?'

'For a year or perhaps longer,' he said gloomily.

Her natural instinct of defiant secrecy kept the flood of protest back from her lips. Already in her surprisingly definite philosophy of life, self-concealment held a sacred and imperious position. Secrecy—and her secrecy, because disguised under a superficial show of expansiveness, was the more fundamental, the more dangerous—secrecy she recognised as being both a shield and a weapon. Therefore, already apprehending that existence in a world of men was a fight, a struggle, and a pursuit, she took refuge in her citadel. And, being possessed of a picturesque imagination, she had upon a certain solemn occasion carried a symbolic key to the steps which led down to the sea from the end of the pergola of gourds, and had flung it out as far as she was able into the guardianship of the waters.

She remembered this now as she sat on the parapet with Julian, and smiled to herself ironically. She looked at him with the eye of an artist, and thought how his limbs, fallen into their natural grace of relaxed muscularity, suggested the sculptural ease of stone far more than the flat surfaces of canvas. Sculptural, she thought, was undoubtedly the adjective which thrust itself upon one. In one of her spasmodic outbursts of activity she had modelled him, but, disdainful of her own talents, had left the clay to perish. Then she remembered acutely that she would not see him again.

'My mythological Julian . . .' she murmured, smiling.

A world of flattery lay in her tone.

'You odd little thing,' he said, 'why the adjective?'

She made an expressive gesture with her hands.

'Your indifference, your determination—you're so intractable, so contemptuous, so hard—and sometimes so inspired. You're so fatally well suited to the Islands. Prince of Aphros?' she launched at him insinuatingly.

She was skilful; he flushed. She was giving him what he had, half unconsciously, sought.

'Siren!' he said.

'Am I? Perhaps, after all, we are both equally well suited to the Islands,' she said lightly.

And for some reason their conversation dropped. Yet it sufficed to send him, stimulated, from her side, full of self-confidence; he had forgotten that she was barely seventeen, a child! and for him the smile of pride in her eyes had been the smile of Aphros.

In the house, on his way through, he met Father Paul.

'Everything is known,' said the priest, wringing his hand with his usual energy.

'What am I to do? Malteios wants me to leave Herak-

leion. Shall I refuse? I am glad to have met you,' said
Julian. 'I was on my way to find you.'

'Go, if Malteios wants you to go,' the priest replied, 'the
time is not ripe yet; but are you determined, in your own
mind, to throw in your lot with Hagios Zacharie? Remember, I cautioned you when we were still on Aphros: you
must be prepared for a complete estrangement from your
family. You will be running with the hare, no longer hunt-
ing with the hounds. Have you considered?'

'I am with the Islands.'

'Good,' said the priest, making a sign over him. 'Go, all
the same, if Malteios exacts it; you will be the more of a
man when you return. Malteios' party will surely fall at
the next elections. By then we shall be ready, and I will
see that you are summoned. God bless you.'

'Will you go out to Eve in the garden, father? She is under the pergola. Go and talk to her.'

'She is unhappy?' asked the priest, with a sharp look.

'A little, I think,' said Julian, 'will you go?'

'At once, at once,' said Paul, and he went quickly,
through the grove of lemon-trees, stumbling over his
soutane. . . .

Julian returned to Herakleion, where he found his father and Malteios in the big frescoed drawing-room,
standing in an embrasure of the windows. The Premier's
face as he turned was full of tolerant benignity.

'Ah, here is our young friend,' he began paternally.
'What are these stories I hear of you, young man? I have
been telling your father that when I was a schoolboy, a
lycéen—I, too, tried to meddle in politics. Take my advice, and keep clear of these things till you are older.
There are many things for the young: dancing, poetry,
and love. Politics to the old and the middle-aged. Of
course, I know your little escapade was nothing but a joke
. . . high spirits . . . natural mischief . . .'

The interview was galling and humiliating to Julian; he
disliked the Premier's bantering friendliness, through
which he was not sufficiently experienced to discern the
hidden mistrust, apprehension, and hostility. His father,
compelled to a secret and resentful pride in his son, was
conscious of these things. But Julian, his eyes fixed on the
middle button of the Premier's frock-coat, sullen and rebellious, tried to shut his ears to the prolonged murmur of

urbane derision. He wished to look down upon, to ignore Malteios, the unreal man, and this he could not do while he allowed those smooth and skilful words to flow unresisted in their suave cruelty over his soul. He shut his ears, and he felt only the hardening of his determination. He would go; he would leave Herakleion, only to return with increase of strength in the hour of fulfilment.

Dismissed, he set out for Kato's flat, hatless, in a mood of thunder. His violence was not entirely genuine, but he persuaded himself, for he had lately been with Eve, and the plausible influence of Herakleion was upon him. He strode down the street, aware that people turned to gaze at him as he went. On the quay, the immense Grbits rose suddenly up from the little green table where he sat drinking vermouth outside a café.

'My young friend,' he said, 'they tell me you are leaving Herakleion?

'They are wise,' he boomed. 'You would break their toys if you remained. But *I* remain; shall I watch for you? You will come back? I have hated the Greeks well. Shall we play a game with them? ha! ha!'

His huge laugh reverberated down the quay as Julian passed on, looking at the visiting card which the giant had just handed to him:—

SRGJAN GRBITS
Attaché à la Légation de S.M. le Roi des Serbes,
Croates, et Slovènes

'Grbits my spy!' he was thinking. 'Fantastic, fantastic.'

Kato's flat was at the top of a four-storied house on the quay. On the ground floor of the house was a cake-shop, and, like every other house along the sea-front, over every window hung a gay, striped sun blind that billowed slightly like a flag in the breeze from the sea. Inside the cake-shop a number of Levantines, dressed in their hot black, were eating sweet things off the marble counter. Julian could never get Eve past the cake-shop when they went to Kato's together; she would always wander in to eat *choux à la crême*, licking the whipped cream off her fingers with a guilty air until he lent her his handkerchief, her own being invariably lost.

Julian went into the house by a side-door, up the steep

narrow stairs, the walls painted in Pompeian red with a slate-coloured dado; past the first floor, where on two frosted glass doors ran the inscription: KONINKLJKE NEDERLANDSCHE STOOMBOOT-MAAISCHAPPIJ; past the second floor, where a brass plate said: Th. Mavrudis et fils, Cie. d'assurance; past the third floor, where old Grigoriu, the money-lender, was letting himself in by a latchkey; to the fourth floor, where a woman in the native dress of the Islands admitted him to Kato's flat.

The singer was seated on one of her low, carpet-covered divans, her throat and arms, as usual, bare, the latter covered with innumerable bangles; her knees wide apart and a hand placed resolutely upon each knee; before her stood Tsigaridis, the headman of Aphros, his powerful body encased in the blue English jersey Mrs Davenant had given him, and from the compression of which his pleated skirt sprang out so ridiculously. Beside Kato on the divan lay a basket of ripe figs which he had brought her. Their two massive figures disproportionately filled the already overcrowded little room.

They regarded Julian gravely.

'I am going away,' he said, standing still before their scrutiny, as a pupil before his preceptors.

Kato bowed her head. They knew. They had discussed whether they should let him go, and had decided that he might be absent from Herakleion until the next elections.

'But you will return, Kyrie?'

Tsigaridis spoke respectfully, but with urgent authority, much in the tone a regent might adopt towards a youthful king.

'Of course, I shall return,' Julian answered, and smiled and added, 'You mustn't lose faith, Tsantilas.'

The fisherman bowed with that dignity he inherited from unnamed but remotely ascending generations; he took his leave of Kato and the boy, shutting the door quietly behind him. Kato came up to Julian, who had turned away and was staring out of the window. From the height of this fourth story one looked down upon the peopled quay below, and saw distinctly the houses upon the distant Islands.

'You are sad,' she said.

She moved to the piano, which, like herself, was a great deal too big for the room, and which alone of all the pieces of furniture was not loaded with ornaments. Julian had often wondered, looking at the large expanse of lid, how Kato had so consistently resisted the temptation to put things upon it. The most he had ever seen there was a gilt basket of hydrangeas, tied with a blue ribbon, from which hung the card of the Premier.

He knew that within twenty-four hours he would be at sea, and that Herakleion as he would last have seen it—from the deck of the steamer, white, with many coloured sunblinds, and, behind it, Mount Mylassa, rising so suddenly, so threateningly, seemingly determined to crowd the man-built town off its narrow strip of coast into the water—Herakleion, so pictured, would be but a memory; within a week, he knew, he would be in England. He did not know when he would see Herakleion again. Therefore he abandoned himself, on this last evening, to Aphros, to the memory of Eve, and to romance, not naming, not linking the three that took possession of and coloured all the daylight of his youth, but quiescent, sitting on the floor, his knees clasped, and approaching again, this time in spirit, the island where the foam broke round the foot of the rocks and the fleet of little fishing-boats swayed like resting seagulls in the harbour. He scarcely noticed that, all this while, Kato was singing. She sang in a very low voice, as though she were singing a lullaby, and, though the words did not reach his consciousness, he knew that the walls of the room had melted into the warm and scented freedom of the terraces on Aphros when the vintage was at its height, and when the air, in the evening, was heavy with the smell of the grape. He felt Eve's fingers lightly upon his brows. He saw again her shadowy gray eyes, red mouth, and waving hair. He visualised the sparkle that crept into her eyes—strange eyes they were! deep-set, slanting upwards, so ironical sometimes, and sometimes so inexplicably sad—when she was about to launch one of her more caustic and just remarks. How illuminating her remarks could be! they always threw a new light; but she never insisted on their value; on the contrary, she passed carelessly on to something else. But whatever she touched, she lit. . . . One came to her with the expectation of being stimulated, perhaps a little bewildered, and one was not disappointed. He recalled her so vividly—yet recollection of her could never be really vivid; the construction of her personality was too subtle, too varied; as soon as one had left her one wanted to go back to her, thinking that this time, perhaps, one would succeed better in seizing and imprisoning the secret of her elusiveness. Julian caught himself smiling dreamily as he conjured her up. He heard the murmur of her seductive voice,—

'I love you, Julian.'

He accepted the words, which he had heard often from her lips, dreamily as part of his last, deliberate evening, so losing himself in his dreams that he almost failed to notice when the music died and the notes of Kato's voice slid from the recitative of her peasant songs into conversation with himself. She left the music-stool and came towards him where he sat on the floor.

'Julian,' she said, looking down at him, 'your cousin Eve, who is full of perception, says you are so primitive that the very furniture is irksome to you and that you dispense with it as far as you can. I know you prefer the ground to a sofa.'

He became shy, as he instantly did when the topic of his own personality was introduced. He felt dimly that Eve, who remorselessly dragged him from the woods into the glare of sunlight, alone had the privilege. At the same time he recognised her methods of appropriating a characteristic, insignificant in itself, and of building it up, touching it with her own peculiar grace and humour until it became a true and delicate attribute, growing into life thanks to her christening of it; a method truly feminine, exquisitely complimentary, carrying with it an insinuation faintly exciting, and creating a link quite separately personal, an understanding, almost an obligation to prove oneself true to her conception. . . .

'So you are leaving us?' said Kato, 'you are going to live among other standards, other influences, *"dont je ne connais point la puissance sur votre cœur."* How soon will it be before you forget? And how soon before you return? We want you here, Julian.'

'For the Islands?' he asked.

'For the Islands, and may I not say,' said Kato, spreading her hands with a musical clinking of all her bangles, 'for ourselves also? How soon will it be before you forget the Islands?' she forced herself to ask, and then, relapsing,

'Which will fade first in your memory, I wonder—the Islands? or Kato?'

'I can't separate you in my mind,' he said, faintly ill at ease.

'It is true that we have talked of them by the hour,' she answered, 'have we talked of them so much that they and I are entirely identified? Do you pay me the compliment of denying me the mean existence of an ordinary woman?'

He thought that by answering in the affirmative he would indeed be paying her the greatest compliment that lay within his power, for he would be raising her to the status of a man and a comrade. He said,—

'I never believed, before I met you, that a woman could devote herself whole-heartedly to her patriotism. We have the Islands in common between us; and, as you know, the Islands mean more than mere Islands to me: a great many things to which I could never give a name. And I am glad, yes, so glad, that our friendship has been, in a way, so impersonal—as though I were your disciple, and this flat my secret school, from which you should one day discharge me, saying "Go!"'

Never had he appeared to her so hopelessly inaccessible as now when he laid his admiration, his almost religious idealisation of her at her feet.

He went on,—

'You have been so infinitely good to me; I have come here so often, I have talked so much; I have often felt, when I went away, that you, who were accustomed to clever men, must naturally . . .'

'Why not say,' she interrupted, 'instead of "clever men," "men of my own age? my own generation"?'

He looked at her doubtfully, checked. She was standing over him, her hands on her hips, and he noticed the tight circles of fat round her bent wrists, and the dimples in every joint of her stumpy hands.

'But why apologise?" she added, taking pity on his embarrassment, with a smile, both forgiving and rueful for the ill she had brought upon herself. 'If you have enjoyed our talks, be assured I have enjoyed them too. For conversations to be as successful as ours have been, the enjoyment cannot possibly be one-sided. I shall miss them when you are gone. You go to England?'

After a moment she said,—

'Isn't it strange, when those we know so intimately in one place travel away to another place in which we have never seen them? What do I, Kato, know of the houses you will live in in England, or of your English friends? as some poet speaks, in a line I quoted to you just now, of all the influences *dont je ne connais pas la puissance sur votre cœur!* Perhaps you will even fall in love. Perhaps you will tell this imaginary woman with whom you are to fall in love, about our Islands?'

'No woman but you would understand,' he said.

'She would listen for your sake, and for your sake she would pretend interest. Does Eve listen when you talk about the Islands?'

'Eve doesn't care about such things. I sometimes think she cares only about herself,' he replied with some impatience.

'You ...' she began again, but, checking herself, she said instead, with a grave irony that was lost upon him, 'You have flattered me greatly to-day, Julian. I hope you may always find in me a wise preceptor. But I can only point the way. The accomplishment lies with you. We will work together?' She added, smiling, 'In the realms of the impersonal? A philosophic friendship? A Platonic alliance?'

When he left her, she was still, gallantly, smiling.

PART II
Eve

One

AFTER SPENDING nearly two years in exile, Julian was once more upon his way to Herakleion.

On deck, brooding upon a great coil of rope, his head bare to the winds, absorbed and concentrated, he disregarded all his surroundings in favour of the ever equi-distant horizon. He seemed to be entranced by its promise. He seemed, moreover, to form part of the ship on which he travelled; a part of it, crouching as he did always at the prow, as a figurehead forms part; part of the adventure, the winged gallantry, the eager onward spirit indissoluble from the voyage of a ship in the midst of waters from which no land is visible. The loneliness—for there is no loneliness to equal the loneliness of the sea—the strife of the wind, the generosity of the expanse, the pure cleanliness of the nights and days, met and matched his mood. At moments, feeling himself unconquerable, he tasted the full, rare, glory of youth and anticipation. He did not know which he preferred: the days full of sunlight on the wide blue sea, or the nights when the breeze was fresher against his face, and the road more mysterious, under a young moon that lit the ridges of the waves and travelled slowly past, overhead, across the long black lines of cordage and rigging. He knew only that he was happy as he had never been happy in his life.

His fellow-passengers had watched him when he joined the ship at Brindisi, and a murmur had run amongst them, 'Julian Davenant—son of those rich Davenants of Herakleion, you know—great wine-growers—they own a whole archipelago'; some one had disseminated the information even as Julian came up the gangway, in faded old gray flannels, hatless, in a rage with his porter, who appeared to be terrified out of all proportion. Then, suddenly, he had lost all interest in his luggage, tossed some money to the porter, and, walking for'ard, had thrown himself down on the heap of ropes and stared straight in front of him to sea, straining his eyes forward to where Greece might lie.

From here he had scarcely stirred. The people who watched him, benevolent and amused, thought him very young. They saw that he relieved the intensity of his vigil with absurd and childlike games that he played by himself, hiding and springing out at the sailors, and laughing immoderately when he had succeeded in startling them—he fraternised with the sailors, though with no one else—or when he saw somebody trip over a ring in the deck. His humour, like his body, seemed to be built on large and simple lines.... In the mornings he ran round and round the decks in rubber-soled shoes. Then again he flung himself down and continued with unseeing eyes to stare at the curve of the horizon.

Not wholly by design, he had remained absent from Herakleion for nearly two years. The standards and systems of life on that remote and beautiful seaboard had not faded for him, this time, with their usual astonishing rapidity; he had rather laid them aside carefully and deliberately, classified against the hour when he should take them from their wrappings; he postponed the consideration of the mission which had presented itself to him, and crushed down the recollection of what had been, perhaps, the most intoxicating of all moments—more intoxicating even, because more unexpected, than the insidious flattery of Eve—the moment when Paul had said to him beneath the fragmentary frescoes of the life of Saint Benedict, in a surprised voice, forced into admission,—

'You have the quality of leadership. You have it. You have the secret. The people will fawn to the hand that chastens.'

Paul, his tutor and preceptor, from whom he had first learnt, so imperceptibly that he scarcely recognised the teaching as a lesson, of the Islands and their problems both human and political, Paul had spoken these words to him, renouncing the authority of the master, stepping aside to admit the accession of the pupil. From the position of a regent, he had abased himself to that of a Prime Minister. Julian had accepted the acknowledgement with a momentary dizziness. In later moments of doubt, the words had flamed for him, bright with reassurance. And then he had banished them with the rest. That world of romance had been replaced by the world of healthy and prosaic things. The letters he periodically received from Eve irritated him because of their reminder of an existence he preferred to regard, for the moment, as in abeyance.

'And so you are gone: *veni, vidi, vici.* You were well started on your career of devastation! You hadn't done badly, all things considered. Herakleion has heaved an "Ouf!" of relief. You, unimpressionable? *Allons donc!* You, apathetic? You, placid, unemotional, unawakened? *Tu te payes ma tete!*

'Ah, the limitless ambition I have for you!

'I want you to rule, conquer, shatter, demolish.

'Haul down the simpering gods, the pampered gods, and put yourself in their place. It is in your power.

'Why not? You have *le feu sacré.* Stagnation is death, death. Burn their temples with fire, and trample their altars to dust.'

This letter, scrawled in pencil on a sheet of torn foolscap, followed him to England immediately after his departure. Then a silence of six months. Then he read, written on spacious yellow writing-paper, with the monogram E.D. embossed in a triangle of mother-of-pearl, vivid and extravagant as Eve herself—

'They are trying to catch me, Julian! I come quite near, quite near, and they hold very quiet their hand with the crumbs in it. I see the other hand stealing round to close upon me—then there's a flutter—*un battement d'ailes—l'oiseau s'est de nouveau dérobé!* They remain gazing after me, with their mouths wide open. They look so silly. And they haven't robbed me of one plume—not a single plume.

'Julian! Why this mania for capture? this wanting to take from me my most treasured possession—liberty? When I want to give, I'll give freely—largesse with both hands, showers of gold and flowers and precious stones—(don't say I'm not conceited!) but I'll never give my liberty, and I'll never allow it to be forced away from me. I should feel a traitor. I couldn't walk through a forest and hear the wind in the trees. I couldn't listen to music. (Ah, Julian! This afternoon

I steeped myself in music; Grieg, elf-like, mischievous, imaginative, romantic, so Latin sometimes in spite of his Northern blood. You would love Grieg, Julian. In the fairyland of music, Grieg plays gnome to Debussy's magician . . . Then "Khovantchina," of all music the most sublime, the most perverse, the most *bariolé*, the most abandoned, and the most desolate.) I could have no comradeship with a free and inspired company. I should have betrayed their secrets, bartered away their mysteries . . .'

He had wondered then whether she were happy. He had visualised her, turbulent, defiant; courting danger and then childishly frightened when danger overtook her; deliciously forthcoming, inventive, enthusiastic, but always at heart withdrawn; she expressed herself truly when she said that the bird fluttered away from the hand that would have closed over it. He knew that she lived constantly, from choice, in a storm of trouble and excitement. Yet he read between the lines of her letters a certain dissatisfaction, a straining after something as yet unattained. He knew that her heart was not in what she described as 'my little round of complacent amourettes.'

The phrase had awoken him with a smile of amusement to the fact that she was no longer a child. He felt some curiosity to see her again under the altered and advanced conditions of her life, yet, lazy and diffident, he shrank from the storm of adventure and responsibility which he knew would at once assail him. The indolence he felt sprang largely from the certainty that he could, at any moment of his choice, stretch out his hand to gether up again the threads that he had relinquished. He had surveyed Herakleion, that other world, from the distance and security of England. He had the conviction that it awaited him, and this conviction bore with it a strangely proprietary sense in which Eve was included. He had listened with amusement and tolerance to the accounts of her exploits, his sleepy eyes bent upon his informant with a quiet patience, as a man who listens to a familiar recital. He had dwelt very often upon the possibility of his return to Herakleion, but without a full or even a partial knowledge of his motives, postponed it. Yet all the while his life was a service, a dedication.

Then the letters which he received began to mention the forthcoming elections; a faint stir of excitement pervaded his correspondence; Eve, detesting politics, made no reference, but his father's rare notes betrayed an impatient and irritable anxiety; the indications grew, culminating in a darkly allusive letter which, although anonymous, he took to be from Grbits, and finally in a document which was a triumph of illiterate dignity, signed by Kato, Tsigaridis, Zapantiotis, and a double column of names that broke like a flight of exotic birds into the mellow enclosure of the Cathedral garden where it found him.

Conscious of his ripened and protracted strength, he took ship for Greece.

He had sent no word to announce his coming. A sardonic smile lifted one corner of his mouth as he foresaw the satisfaction of taking Eve by surprise. A standing joke between them (discovered and created, of course, by her, the inventive) was the invariable unexpectedness of his arrivals. He would find her altered, grown. An unreasoning fury possessed him, a jealous rage, not directed against any human being, but against Time itself, that it should lay hands upon Eve, his Eve, during his absence; taking, as it were, advantage while his back was turned. And though he had often professed to himself a lazy indifference to her devotion to him, Julian, he found intolerable the thought that that devotion might have been transferred elsewhere. He rose and strode thunderously down the deck, and one of his fellow-travellers, watching, whistled to himself and thought,—

'That boy has an ugly temper.'

Then the voyage became a dream to Julian; tiny islands, quite rosy in the sunlight, stained the sea here and there only a few miles distant, and along the green sea the ship drew a white, lacy wake, broad and straight, that ever closed behind her like an obliterated path, leaving the way of retreat trackless, and unavailable. One day he realised that the long, mountainous line which he had taken for a cloud-bank, was in point of fact the coast. That evening, a sailor told him, they were due to make Herakleion. He grew resentful of the apathy of passengers and crew. The coast-line became more and more distinct. Presently they were passing Aphros, and only eight miles lay between the

93

ship and the shore. The foam that gave it its name was breaking upon the rocks of the island. . . .

After that a gap occurred in his memory, and the scene slipped suddenly to the big frescoed drawing-room of his father's house in the *platia*, where the peace and anticipation of his voyage were replaced by the gaiety of voices, the blatancy of lights, and the strident energy of three violins and a piano. He had walked up from the pier after the innumerable delays of landing; it was then eleven o'clock at night, and as he crossed the *platia* and heard the music coming from the lighted and open windows of his father's house, he paused in the shadows, aware of the life that had gone on for over a year without him.

'And why is that surprising? I'm an astounding egotist,' he muttered.

He was still in his habitual gray flannels, but he would not go to his room to change. He was standing in the doorway of the drawing-room on the first floor, smiling gently at finding himself still unnoticed, and looking for Eve. She was sitting at the far end of the room between two men, and behind her the painted monkeys grimaced on the wall, swinging by hands and tails from the branches of the unconvincing trees. He saw her as seated in the midst of that ethereal and romantic landscape.

Skirting the walls, he made his way round to her, and in the angle he paused, and observed her. She was unconscious of his presence. Young Christopoulos bent towards her, and she was smiling into his eyes. . . . In eighteen months she had perfected her art.

Julian drew nearer, critically, possessively, and sarcastically observing her still, swift to grasp the essential difference. She, who had been a child when he had left her, was now a woman. The strangeness of her face had come to its own in the fullness of years, and the provocative mystery of her person, that withheld even more than it betrayed, now justified itself likewise. There seemed to be a reason for the red lips and ironical eyes that had been so incongruous, so almost offensive, in the face of the child. An immense fan of orange feathers drooped from her hand. Her hair waved turbulently round her brows, and seemed to cast a shadow over her eyes.

He stood suddenly before her.

For an instant she gazed up at him, her lips parted, her

breath arrested. He laughed easily, pleased to have bettered her at her own game of melodrama. He saw that she was really at a loss, clutching at her wits, at her recollection of him, trying desperately to fling a bridge across the gulf of those momentous months. She floundered helplessly in the abrupt renewal of their relations. Seeing this, he felt an arrogant exhilaration at the discomfiture which he had produced. She had awoken in him, without a word spoken, the tyrannical spirit of conquest which she induced in all men.

Then she was saved by the intervention of the room; first by Christopoulos shaking Julian's hand, then by dancers crowding round with exclamations of welcome and surprise. Mr Davenant himself was brought, and Julian stood confused and smiling, but almost silent, among the volubility of the guests. He was providing a sensation for lives greedy of sensation. He heard Madame Lafarge, smiling benevolently at him behind her lorgnon, say to Don Rodrigo Valdez,—

'C'est un original que ce garçon.'

They were all there, futile and vociferous. The few new-comers were left painfully out in the cold. They were all there: the fat Danish Excellency, her yellow hair fuzzing round her pink face; Condesa Valdez, painted like a cour-tesan; Armand, languid, with his magnolia-like complex-ion; Madame Delahaye, enterprising and equivocal; Julie Lafarge, thin and brown, timidly smiling; Panaïoannou in his sky-blue uniform; the four sisters Christopoulos, well to the front. These, and all the others. He felt that, at what-ever moment during the last eighteen months he had timed his return, he would have found them just the same, complete, none missing, the same words upon their lips. He accepted them now, since he had surrendered to Herakleion, but as for their reality as human beings, with the possible exception of Grbits the giant, crashing his way to Julian through people like an elephant pushing through a forest, and of the Persian Minister, hovering on the out-skirts of the group with the gentle smile still playing round his mouth, they might as well have been cut out of card-board. Eve had gone; he could see her nowhere. Alexan-der, presumably, had gone with her.

Captured at last by the Danish Excellency, Julian had a stream of gossip poured into his ears. He had been in exile for so long, he must be thirsty for news. A new English Minister had arrived, but he was said to be unsociable. He had been expected at the races on the previous Sunday, but had failed to put in an appearance. Armand had had an affair with Madame Delahaye. At a dinner-party last week, Rafaele, the Councillor of the Italian Legation, had not been given his proper place. The Russian Minister, who was the doyen of the *corps diplomatique*, had promised to look into the matter with the Chef du Protocole. Once etiquette was allowed to become lax ... The season had been very gay. Comparatively few political troubles. She disliked political troubles. She—confidentially—preferred personalities. But then she was only a woman, and foolish. She knew that she was foolish. But she had a good heart. She was not clever, like his cousin Eve.

Eve? A note of hostility and reserve crept into her expansiveness. Eve was, of course, very charming, though not beautiful. She could not be called beautiful, her mouth was too large and too red. It was almost improper to have so red a mouth; not quite *comme il faut* in so young a girl. Still, she was undeniably successful. Men liked to be amused, and Eve, when she was not sulky, could be very amusing. Her imitations were proverbial in Herakleion. Imitation was, however, an unkindly form of entertainment. It was perhaps a pity that Eve was so *moqueuse*. Nothing was sacred to her, not even things which were really beautiful and touching—patriotism, or moonlight, or art—even Greek art. It was not that she, Mabel Thyregod, disapproved of wit; she had even some small reputation for wit herself; no; but she held that there were certain subjects to which the application of wit was unsuitable. Love, for instance. Love was the most beautiful, the most sacred thing upon earth, yet Eve—a child, a chit—had no veneration either for love in the abstract or for its devotees in the flesh. She wasted the love that was offered her. She could have no heart, no temperament. She was perhaps fortunate. She, Mabel Thyregod, had always suffered from having too warm a temperament.

A struggle ensued between them, Fru Thyregod trying to force the personal note, and Julian opposing himself to its intrusion. He liked her too much to respond to her blatant advances. He wondered, with a brotherly interest, whether Eve were less crude in her methods.

The thought of Eve sent him instantly in her pursuit, leaving Fru Thyregod very much astonished and annoyed in the ball-room. He found Eve with a man he did not know sitting in her father's business-room. She was lying back in a chair, listless and absent-minded, while her companion argued with vehemence and exasperation. She exclaimed,—

'Julian again! another surprise appearance! Have you been wearing a cap of invisibility?'

Seeing that her companion remained silent in uncertainty, she murmured an introduction,—

'Do you know my cousin Julian? Prince Ardalion Miloradovitch.'

The Russian bowed with a bad grace, seeing that he must yield his place to Julian. When he had gone, unwillingly tactful and full of resentment, she twitted her cousin,—

'Implacable as always, when you want your own way! I notice you have neither outgrown your tyrannical selfishness nor left it behind in England.'

'I have never seen that man before; who is he?'

'A Russian. Not unattractive. I am engaged to him,' she replied negligently.

'You are going to marry him?'

She shrugged.

'Perhaps, ultimately. More probably not.'

'And what will he do if you throw him over?' Julian asked with a certain curiosity.

'Oh, he has a fine *je-m'en-fichisme*; he'll shrug his shoulders, kiss the tips of my fingers, and die gambling,' she answered.

When Eve said that, Julian thought that he saw the whole of Miloradovitch, whom he did not know, quite clearly; she had lit him up.

They talked then of a great many things, extraneous to themselves, but all the while they observed one another narrowly. She found nothing actually new in him, only an immense development along the old, careless, impersonal lines. In appearance he was as untidy as ever; large, slack-limbed, rough-headed. He, however, found much that was new in her; new that is, to his more experienced observation, but which, hitherto, in its latent form had slept undiscovered by his boyish eyes. His roaming glance took in the deliberate poise and provocative aloofness of her self-possession, the warm roundness of her throat and arms, the little *mouche* at the corner of her mouth, her little graceful hands, and white skin that here and there, in the shadows, gleamed faintly gold, as though a veneer of amber had been brushed over the white; the pervading sensuousness that glowed from her like the actual warmth of a slumbering fire. He found himself banishing the thought of Milora-dovitch. . . .

'Have you changed?' he said abruptly. 'Look at me.'

She raised her eyes, with the assurance of one well-ac-customed to personal remarks; a slow smile crept over her lips.

'Well, your verdict?'

'You are older, and your hair is brushed back.'

'Is that all?'

'Do you expect me to say that you are pretty?'

'Oh, no,' she said, snapping her fingers, 'I never expect compliments from you, Julian. On the other hand, let me pay you one. Your arrival, this evening, has been a triumph. Most artistic. Let me congratulate you. You know of old that I dislike being taken by surprise.'

'That's why I do it.'

'I know,' she said, with sudden humility, the marvellous organ of her voice sinking surprisingly into the rich luxuri-ance of its most sombre contralto.

He noted with a fresh enjoyment the deep tones that broke like a honeyed caress upon his unaccustomed ear. His imagination bore him away upon a flight of images that left him startled by their emphasis no less than by their fantasy. A cloak of black velvet, he thought to him-self, as he continued to gaze unseeingly at her; a dusky voice, a gipsy among voices! the purple ripeness of a plum; the curve of a Southern cheek; the heart of red wine. All things seductive and insinuating. It matched her soft indolence, her exquisite subtlety, her slow, ironical smile.

'Your delicious vanity,' he said unexpectedly, and, put-ting out his hand he touched the hanging fold of silver net which was bound by a silver ribbon round one of her slen-der wrists.

Two

HERAKLEION. The white town. The sun. The precipitate coast, and Mount Mylassa soaring into the sky. The distant slope of Greece. The low islands lying out in the jewelled sea. The diplomatic round, the calculations of gain, the continuous and plaintive music of the Islands, the dream of rescue, the ardent championship of the feebler cause, the strife against wealth and authority. The whole fabric of youth ... These were the things abruptly rediscovered and renewed.

The elections were to take place within four days of Julian's arrival. Father Paul, no doubt, could add to the store of information Kato had already given him. But Father Paul was not to be found in the little tavern he kept in the untidy village close to the gates of the Davenants' country house. Julian reined up before it, reading the familiar name, Xenodochion Olympos, above the door, and calling out to the men who were playing bowls along the little gravelled bowling alley to know where he might find the priest. They could not tell him, nor could the old islander Tsigaridis, who sat near the door, smoking a cigar, and dribbling between his fingers the beads of a bright green rosary.

'The *papá* is often absent from us,' added Tsigaridis, and Julian caught the grave inflection of criticism in his tone.

The somnolent heat of the September afternoon lay over the squalid dusty village; in the whole length of its street no life stirred; the dogs slept; the pale pink and blue houses were closely shuttered, with an effect of flatness and desertion. Against the pink front of the tavern splashed the shadows of a great fig-tree, and upon its threshold, but on one side the tree had been cut back to prevent any shadows from falling across the bowling-alley.

Julian rode on, enervated by the too intense heat and the glare, and, giving up his horse at his uncle's stables, wandered in the shade under the pergola of gourds at the bottom of the garden.

He saw Father Paul coming towards him across the grass between the lemon-trees; the priest walked slowly, his head bent, his hands clasped behind his back, a spare black figure among the golden fruit. So lean, so lank he appeared, his natural height accentuated by his square black cap; so sallow his bony face in contrast to his stringy red hair. Julian likened him to a long note of exclamation. He advanced unaware of Julian's presence, walking as though every shuffling step of his flat, broadtoed shoes were an accompaniment to some laborious and completed thought.

'Perhaps,' Julian reflected, watching him, 'by the time he reaches me he'll have arrived at his decision.'

He speculated amusedly as to the priest's difficulties: an insurgent member of the flock? a necessary repair to the church? Nothing, nothing outside Herakleion. A tiny life! A priest, a man who had forsworn man's birthright. The visible in exchange for the invisible world. A life concentrated and intense; tight-handed, a round little ball of a life. No range, no freedom. Village life under a microscope; familiar faces and familiar souls. Julian seemed to focus suddenly the rays of the whole world into a spot of light which was the village, and over which the priest's thin face was bent poring with a close, a strained expression of absorption, so that his benevolent purpose became almost a force of evil, prying and inquisitive, and from which the souls under his charge strove to writhe away in vain. To break the image, he called out aloud,—

'You were very deeply immersed in your thoughts, father?'

'Yes, yes,' Paul muttered. He took out his handkerchief to pass it over his face, which Julian now saw with surprise was touched into high lights by a thin perspiration.

'Is anything wrong?' he asked.

'Nothing wrong. Your father is very generous,' the priest added irrelevantly.

Julian, still under the spell, inquired as to his father's generosity.

'He has promised me a new iconostase,' said Paul, but

he spoke from an immense distance, vagueness in his eyes, and with a trained, obedient tongue. 'The old iconostase is in a disgraceful state of dilapidation,' he continued, with a new, uncanny energy; 'when we cleaned out the panels we found them hung with bats at the back, and not only bats, but, do you know, Julian, the mice had nested there; the mice are a terrible plague in the church. I am obliged to keep the consecrated bread in a biscuit tin, and I do not like doing that; I like to keep it covered over with a linen cloth; but no, I cannot, all on account of the mice. I have set traps, and I had got a cat, but since she caught her foot in one of the traps she has gone away. I am having great trouble, great trouble with the mice.'

'I know,' said Julian, 'I used to have mice in my rooms at Oxford.'

'A plague!' cried Paul, still fiercely energetic, but utterly remote. 'One would wonder, if one were permitted to wonder, why He saw fit to create mice. I never caught any in my traps; only the cat's foot. And the boy who cleans the church ate the cheese. I have been very unfortunate—very unfortunate with the mice,' he added.

Would they never succeed in getting away from the topic? The garden was populated with mice, quick little gray objects darting across the path. And Paul, who continued to talk vehemently, with strange, abrupt gestures, was not really there at all.

'Nearly two years since you have been away,' he was saying. 'I expect you have seen a great deal; forgotten all about Paul? How do you find your father? Many people have died in the village; that was to be expected. I have been kept busy, funerals and christenings. I like a full life. And then I have the constant preoccupation of the church; the church, yes. I have been terribly concerned about the iconostase. I have blamed myself bitterly for my negligence. That, of course, was all due to the mice. A man was drowned off these rocks last week; a stranger. They say he had been losing in the casino. I have been into Herakleion once or twice, since you have been away. But it is too noisy. The trams, and the glare ... It would not seem noisy to you. You no doubt welcome the music of the world. You are young, and life for you contains no problems. But I am very happy; I should not like you to think I was not perfectly happy. Your father and your uncle are peculiarly considerate and generous men. Your uncle has promised to pay for the installation of the new iconostase and the removal of the old one. I forgot to tell you that. Completely perished, some of the panels ... And your aunt, a wonderful woman.'

Julian listened in amazement. The priest talked like a wound-up and crazy machine, and all the while Julian was convinced that he did not know a word he was saying. He had once been grave, earnest, scholarly, even wise ... He kept taking off and putting on his cap, to the wild disordering of his long hair.

'He's gone mad,' Julian thought in dismay.

Julian despaired of struggling out of the quicksands that sucked at their feet. He thought desperately that if the priest would come back, would recall his spirit to take control of his wits, all might be well. The tongue was babbling in an empty body while the spirit journeyed in unknown fields, finding there what excruciating torment? Who could tell! For the man was suffering, that was clear; he had been suffering as he walked across the grass, but he had suffered then in controlled silence, spirit and mind close-locked and allied in the taut effort of endurance; now, their alliance shattered by the sound of a human voice, the spirit had fled, sweeping with it the furies of agony, and leaving the mind bereaved, chattering emptily, noisily, in the attempt at concealment. He, Julian, was responsible for this revelation of the existence of an unguessed secret. He must repair the damage he had done.

'Father!' he said, interrupting, and he took the priest strongly by the wrist.

Their eyes met.

'Father!' Julian said again. He held the wrist with the tensest effort of his fingers, and the eyes with the tensest effort of his will. He saw the accentuated cavities of the priest's thin face, and the pinched lines of suffering at the corners of the mouth. Paul had been strong, energetic, masculine. Now his speech was random, and he quavered as a palsied old man. Even his personal cleanliness had, in a measure, deserted him; his soutane was stained, his hair lank and greasy. He confronted Julian with a sacred and piteous cowardice, compelled, yet seeking escape, then as he slowly steadied himself under Julian's grip the succeeding emotions were reflected in his eyes: first shame; then a horrified grasping after his self-respect; finally, most touching of all, confidence and gratitude; and Julian, seeing the cycle completed and knowing that Paul was again master of himself, released the wrist and asked, in the most casual voice at his command, 'All right?" He had the sensation of having saved some one from falling.

Paul nodded without speaking. Then he began to ask Julian as to how he had employed the last eighteen months, and they talked for some time without reference to the unaccountable scene that had passed between them. Paul talked with his wonted gentleness and interest, the strangeness of his manner entirely vanished; Julian could have believed it a hallucination, but for the single trace left in the priest's disordered hair. Red strands hung abjectly down his back. Julian found his eyes drawn towards them in a horrible fascination, but, because he knew the scene must be buried unless Paul himself chose to revive it, he kept his glance turned away with conscious deliberation.

He was relieved when the priest left him.

'Gone to do his hair'—the phrase came to his mind as he saw the priest walk briskly away, tripping with the old familiar stumble over his soutane, and saw the long wisps faintly red on the black garment. 'Like a woman—exactly!' he uttered in revolt, clenching his hand at man's degradation. 'Like a woman, long hair, long skirt; ready to listen to order people's troubles. Unnatural existence; unnatural? it's unnatural to the point of viciousness. No wonder the man's mind is unhinged.'

He was really troubled about his friend, the more so that loyalty would keep him silent and allow him to ask no questions. He thought, however, that if Eve volunteered any remarks about Paul it would not be disloyal to listen. The afternoon was hot and still; Eve would be indoors. The traditions of his English life still clung to him sufficiently to make him chafe vaguely against the idleness of the days; he resented the concession to the climate. A demoralising place. A place where priests let their hair grow long, and went temporarily mad . . .

He walked in the patchy shade of the lemon-trees towards the house in a distressed and irascible frame of mind. He longed for action; his mind was never content to dwell long unoccupied. He longed for the strife the elections would bring. The house glared very white, and all the green shutters were closed; behind them, he knew, the windows would be closed too. Another contradiction. In England, when one wanted to keep a house cool, one opened the windows wide.

He crossed the veranda; the drawing-room was dim and empty. How absurd to paint sham flames on the ceiling in a climate where the last thing one wanted to remember was fire. He called,—

'Eve!'

Silence answered him. A book lying on the floor by the writing-table showed him that she had been in the room; no one else in the house would read Albert Samain. He picked it up and read disgustedly,—

> '. . . Des roses! des roses encore!
> Je les adore à la souffrance.
> Elles ont la sombre attirance
> Des choses qui donnent la mort.'

'Nauseating!' he cried, flinging the book from him.

Certainly the book was Eve's. Certainly she had been in the room, for no one else would or could have drawn that mask of a faun on the blotting paper. He looked at it carelessly, then with admiration; what malicious humour she had put into those squinting eyes, that slanting mouth! He turned the blotting paper idly—how like Eve to draw on the blotting paper!—and came on other drawings: a demon, a fantastic castle, a half-obliterated sketch of himself. Once he found his name, in elaborate architectural lettering, repeated all over the page. Then he found a letter of which the three first words: 'Eternal, exasperating Eve!' and the last sentence, '. . . votre réveil qui doit être charmant dans le désordre fantaisiste de votre chambre,' made him shut the blotter in a scurry of discretion.

Here were all the vivid traces of her passage, but where was she? Loneliness and the lack of occupation oppressed him. He lounged away from the writing-table, out into the wide passage which ran all round the central court. He paused there, his hands in his pockets, and called again,—

'Eve!'

'Eve!' the echoing passage answered startlingly.

Presently another more tangible voice came to him as

he stood staring disconsolately through the windows into the court.

'Were you calling Mith Eve, Mathter Julian? The'th rethting. Thall I tell her?'

He was pleased to see Nana, fat, stayless, shipshod, slovenly, benevolent. He kissed her, and told her she was fatter than ever.

'Glad I've come back, Nannie?'

'Why, yeth, thurely, Mathter Julian.'

Nana's demonstrations were always restrained, respectful. She habitually boasted that although life in the easy South might have induced her to relax her severity towards her figure, she had never allowed it to impair her manners.

'Can I go up to Eve's room, Nannie?'

'I thuppoth tho, my dear.'

'Nannie, you know, you ought to be an old Negress.'

'Why, dear Lord! me black?'

'Yes; you'd be ever so much more suitable.'

He ran off to Eve's room upstairs, laughing, boyish again after his boredom and irritability. He had been in Eve's room many times before, but with his fingers on the door handle he paused. Again that strange vexation at her years had seized him.

He knocked.

Inside, the room was very dim; the furniture bulked large in the shadows. Scent, dusk, luxury lapped round him like warm water. He had an impression of soft, scattered garments, deep mirrors, chosen books, and many little bottles. Suddenly he was appalled by the insolence of his own intrusion—an unbeliever bursting into a shrine. He stood silent by the door. He heard a drowsy voice singing in a murmur an absurd childish rhyme,—

> 'Il était noir comme un corbeau,
> Ali, Ali, Ali, Alo,
> Macachebono,
> La Roustah, la Mougah, la Roustah,
> la Mougah,
> Allah!
> 'Il était de bonne famille,
> Sa mère élevait des chameaux,
> Macachebono . . .'

He discerned the bed, the filmy veils of the muslin mosquito curtains, falling apart from a baldaquin. The lazy voice, after a moment of silence, queried,—

'Nana?'

It was with an effort that he brought himself to utter,—

'No; Julian.'

With an upheaval of sheets he heard her sit upright in bed, and her exclamation,—

'Who said you might come in here?'

At that he laughed, quite naturally.

'Why not? I was bored. May I come and talk to you?'

He came round the corner of the screen and saw her sitting up, her hair tumbled and dark, her face indistinct, her shoulders emerging white from a foam of lace.

He sat down on the edge of her bed, the details of the room emerging slowly from the darkness; and she herself becoming more distinct as she watched him, her shadowy eyes half sarcastic, half resentful.

'Sybarite!' he said.

She only smiled in answer, and put out one hand towards him. It fell listlessly on to the sheets as though she had no energy to hold it up.

'You child,' he said, 'you make me feel coarse and vulgar beside you. Here am I, burning for battle, and there you lie, wasting time, wasting youth, half-asleep, luxurious, and quite unrepentant.'

'Surely even you must find it too hot for battle?'

'I don't find it too hot to wish that it weren't too hot. You, on the other hand, abandon yourself contentedly; you are pleased that it is too hot for you to do anything but glide voluptuously into a siesta in the middle of the day.'

'You haven't been here long, remember, Julian; you're still brisk from England. Only wait; Herakleion will overcome you.'

'Don't!' he cried out startlingly. Don't say it! It's prophetic. I shall struggle against it; I shall be the stronger.'

She only laughed murmurously into her pillows, but he was really stirred; he stood up and walked about the room, launching spasmodic phrases.

'You and Herakleion, you are all of a piece.—You shan't drag me down.—Not if I am to live here.—I know one loses one's sense of values here. I learnt that when I last went away to England. I've come back on my guard.—I'm determined to remain level-headed.—I refuse to be impressed by fantastic happenings . . .'

'Why do you stop so abruptly?' Did her voice mock him?

He had stopped, remembering Paul. Already he had blundered against something he did not understand. An impulse came to him to confide in Eve; Eve lying there, quietly smiling with unexpressed but unmistakable irony; Eve so certain that, sooner or later, Herakleion would conquer him. He could confide in her. And then, as he hesitated, he knew suddenly that Eve was not trustworthy.

He began again walking about the room, betraying by no word that a moment of revelation, important and dramatic, had come and passed on the tick of a clock. Yet he knew he had crossed a line over which he could now never retrace his steps. He would never again regard Eve in quite the same light. He absorbed the alteration with remarkable rapidity into his conception of her. He supposed that the knowledge of her untrustworthiness had always lain dormant in him waiting for the test which should some day call it out; that was why he was so little impressed by what he had mistaken for new knowledge.

'Julian, sit down; how restless you are. And you look so enormous in this room, you frighten me.'

He sat down, closer to her than he had sat before, and began playing with her fingers.

'How soft your hand is. It is quite boneless,' he said, crushing it together; 'it's like a little pigeon. So you think Herakleion will beat me? I dare say you are right. Shall I tell you something? When I was on my way here, from England, I determined that I would allow myself to be beaten. I don't know why I had that moment of revolt just now. Because I am quite determined to let myself drift with the current, whether it carry me towards adventures or towards lotus-land.'

'Perhaps towards both.'

'Isn't that too much to hope?'

'Why? They are compatible. C'est le sort de la jeunesse.'

'Prophesy adventures for me!'

'My dear Julian! I'm far too lazy.'

'Lotus-land, then?'

'This room isn't a bad substitute,' she proffered.

He wondered then at the exact extent of her meaning. He was accustomed to the amazing emotional scenes she had periodically created between them in childhood—scenes which he never afterwards could rehearse to himself; scenes whose fabric he never could dissect, because it was more fantastic, more unreal, than gossamer; scenes in which storm, anger, and heroics had figured; scenes from which he had emerged worried, shattered, usually with the ardent impress of her lips on his, and brimming with self-reproach. A calm existence was not for her; she would neither understand nor tolerate it.

The door opened, and old Nana came shuffling in.

'Mith Eve, pleath, there'th a gentleman downstairth to thee you. Here'th hith card.'

Julian took it.

'Eve, it's Malteios.'

That drowsy voice, indifferent and melodious,—

'Tell him to go away, Nana; tell him I am resting.'

'But, dearie, what'll your mother thay?'

'Tell him to go away, Nana.'

'He'th the Prime Minithter,' Nana began doubtfully.

'Eve!' Julian said in indignation.

'But, Mith Eve, you know he came latht week and you forgot he wath coming and you wath out.'

'Is that so, Eve? Is he here by appointment with you to-day?'

'No.'

'I shall go down to him and find out whether you are speaking the truth.'

He went downstairs, ignoring Eve's voice that called him back. The Premier was in the drawing-room, examining the insignificant ornaments on the table. Their last meeting had been a memorable one, in the painted room overlooking the *platia*.

When their greetings were over, Julian said,—

'I believe you were asking for my cousin, sir?'

'That is so. She promised me,' said the Premier, a sly look coming over his face, 'that she would give me tea to-day. Shall I have the pleasure of seeing her?'

'What,' thought Julian, 'does this old scapegrace politician, who must have his mind and his days full of the coming elections, want with Eve? and want so badly that

he can perform the feat of coming out here from Herakleion in the heat of the afternoon?'

Aloud he said, grimly because of the lie she had told
him,—

'She will be with you in a few moments, sir.'

In Eve's dark room, where Nana still stood fatly and
hopelessly expostulating, and Eve pretended to sleep, he
spoke roughly,—

'You lied to me as usual. He is here by appointment. He
is waiting. I told him you would not keep him waiting
long. You must get up.'

'I shall do nothing of the sort. What right have you to
dictate to me?'

'You're making Mathter Julian croth—and he tho
thweet-tempered alwayth,' said Nana's warning voice.

'Does she usually behave like this, Nana?'

'Oh, Mathter Julian, it'th dreadful—and me alwayth
thaving her from her mother, too. And loothing all her
thingth, too, all the time. I can't keep anything in it'th
plathe. Only three dayth ago the lotht a diamond ring, but
the never cared. The Thpanith gentleman thent it to her,
and the never thanked him, and then lotht the ring. And
the never notithed or cared. And the getth dretheth and
dretheth, and won't put them on twith. And flowerth and
chocolatheth thent her—they all thpoil her tho—and the
biteth all the chocolatheth in two to thee what'th inthide,
and throwth them away and thayth the dothn't like them.
That exathperating, the ith.'

'Leave her to me, Nannie.'

'Mith Naughtineth,' said Nana, as she left the room.

They were alone.

'Eve, I am really angry. That old man!'

She turned luxuriously on to her back, her arms flung
wide, and lay looking at him.

'You are very anxious that I should go to him. You are
not very jealous of me, are you, Julian?'

'Why does he come?' he asked curiously. 'You never
told me . . .'

'There are a great many things I never tell you, my
dear.'

'It is not my business and I am not interested,' he answered, 'but he has come a long way in the heat to see

109

you, and I dislike your callousness. I insist upon you getting up.'

She smiled provokingly. He dropped on his knees near her.

'Darling, to please me?'

She gave a laugh of sudden disdain.

'Fool! I might have obeyed you; now you have thrown away your advantage.'

'Have I?' he said, and, slipping his arm beneath her, he lifted her up bodily. 'Where shall I put you down?' he asked, standing in the middle of the room and holding her. 'At your dressing-table?'

'Why don't you steal me, Julian?' she murmured, settling herself more comfortably in his grasp.

'Steal you? what on earth do you mean? explain!' he said.

'Oh, I don't know; if you don't understand, it doesn't matter,' she replied with some impatience, but beneath her impatience he saw that she was shaken, and, flinging one arm round his neck, she pulled herself up and kissed him on the mouth. He struggled away, displeased, brotherly, and feeling the indecency of that kiss in that darkened room, given by one whose thinly-clad, supple body he had been holding as he might a child's.

'You have a genius for making me angry, Eve.'

He stopped: she had relaxed suddenly, limp and white in his arms; with a long sigh she let her head fall back, her eyes closed. The warmth of her limbs reached him through the diaphanous garment she wore. He thought he had never before seen such abandonment of expression and attitude; his displeasure deepened, and an uncomplimentary word rose to his lips.

'I don't wonder . . .' flashed through his mind.

He was shocked, as a brother might be at the betrayal of his sister's sexuality.

'Eve!' he said sharply.

She opened her eyes, met his, and came to herself.

'Put me down!' she cried, and as he set her on her feet, she snatched at her Spanish shawl and wrapped it round her. 'Oh!' she said, an altered being, shamed and outraged, burying her face, 'go now, Julian—go, go, go.'

He went, shaking his head in perplexity: there were too many things in Harakleion he failed to understand. Paul,

Eve, Malteios. This afternoon with Eve, which should have been natural, had been difficult. Moments of illumination were also moments of a profounder obscurity. And why should Malteios return to-day, when in the preceding week, according to Nana, he had been so casually forgotten? Why so patient, so long-suffering, with Eve? Was it possible that he should be attracted by Eve? It seemed to Julian, accustomed still to regard her as a child, very improbable. Malteios! The Premier! And the elections beginning within four days—that he should spare the time! Rumour said that the elections would go badly for him; that the Stavridists would be returned. A bad look-out for the Islands if they were. Rumour said that Stavridis was neglecting no means, no means whatsoever, by which he might strengthen his cause. He was more unscrupulous, younger, more vigorous, than Malteios. The years of dispossession had added to his determination and energy. Malteios had seriously prejudiced his popularity by his liaison with Kato, a woman, as the people of Herakleion never forgot, of the Islands, and an avowed champion of their cause. Was it possible that Eve was mixed up in Malteios' political schemes? Julian laughed aloud at the idea of Eve interesting herself in politics. But perhaps Kato herself, for whom Eve entertained one of her strongest and most enduring enthusiasms, had taken advantage of their friendship to interest Eve in Malteios' affairs? Anything was possible in that preposterous state. Eve, he knew, would mischievously and ignorantly espouse any form of intrigue. If Malteios came with any other motive he was an old satyr—nothing more.

Julian's mind strayed again to the elections. The return of the Stavridis party would mean certain disturbances in the Islands. Disturbances would mean an instant appeal for leadership. He would be reminded of the day he had spent, the only day of his life, he thought, on which he had truly lived, on Aphros. Tsigaridis would come, grave, insistent, to hold him to his undertakings, a figure of comedy in his absurdly picturesque clothes, but also a figure full of dignity with his unanswerable claim. He would bring forward a species of moral blackmail, to which Julian, ripe for adventure and sensitive to his obligations, would surely surrender. After that there would be no drawing back ...

'I have little hope of victory,' said Malteios, to whom Julian, in search of information, had recourse; and hinted with infinite suavity and euphemism, that the question of election in Herakleion depended largely, if not entirely, on the condition and judicious distribution of the party funds. Stavridis, it appeared, had controlled larger subscriptions, more trustworthy guarantees. The Christopoulos, the largest bankers, were unreliable. Alexander had political ambitions. An under-secretaryship . . . Christopoulos *père* had subscribed, it was true, to the Malteios party, but while his right hand produced the miserable sum from his right pocket, who could tell with what generosity his left hand ladled out the drachmæ into the gaping Stavridis coffers? Safe in either eventuality. Malteios knew his game.

The Premier enlarged blandly upon the situation, regretful, but without indignation. As a man of the world, he accepted its ways as Herakleion knew them. Julian noted his gentle shrugs, his unfinished sentences and innuendoes. It occurred to him that the Premier's frankness and readiness to enlarge upon political technique were not without motive. Buttoned into his high frock-coat, which the climate of Herakleion was unable to abolish, he walked softly up and down the parquet floor between the lapis columns, his fingers loosely interlaced behind his back, talking to Julian. In another four days he might no longer be Premier, might be merely a private individual, unostentatiously working a dozen strands of intrigue. The boy was not to be neglected as a tool. He tried him on what he conceived to be his tenderest point.

'I have not been unfavourable to your islanders during my administration,'—then, thinking the method perhaps a trifle crude, he added, 'I have even exposed myself to the attack of my opponents on that score; they have made capital out of my clemency. Had I been a less disinterested man, I should have had greater foresight. I should have sacrificed my sense of justice to the demands of my future.'

He gave a deprecatory and melancholy smile.

'Do I regret the course I chose? Not for an instant. The responsibility of a statesman is not solely towards himself or his adherents. He must set it sternly aside in favour of the poor, ignorant destinies committed to his care. I lay down my office with an unburdened conscience.'

He stopped in his walk and stood before Julian, who, with his hands thrust in his pockets, had listened to the discourse from the depths of his habitual arm-chair.

'But you, young man, are not in my position. The door I seek is marked Exit; the door you seek, Entrance. I think I may, without presumption, as an old and finished man, offer you a word of prophecy.' He unlaced his fingers and pointed one of them at Julian. 'You may live to be the saviour of an oppressed people, a not unworthy mission. Remember that my present opponents, should they come to power, will not sympathise with your efforts, as I myself—who knows?—might have sympathised.'

Julian, acknowledging the warning, thought he recognised the style of the Senate Chamber, but failed to recognise the sentiments he had heard expressed by the Premier on a former occasion, on this same subject of his interference in the affairs of the Islands. He ventured to suggest as much. The Premier's smile broadened, his deprecatory manner deepened.

'Ah, you were younger then; hot-headed; I did not know how far I could trust you. Your intentions, excellent; but your judgment perhaps a little precipitate? Since then, you have seen the world; you are a man. You have returned, no doubt, ready to pick up your weapon you tentatively fingered as a boy. You will no longer be blinded by sentiment, you will weigh your actions nicely in the balance. And you will remember the goodwill of Platon Malteios?'

He resumed his soft walk up and down the room.

'Within a few weeks you may find yourself in the heart of strife. I see you as a young athlete on the threshold, doubtless as generous as most young men, as ambitious, as eager. Discard the divne foolishness of allowing ideas, not facts, to govern your heart. We live in Herakleion, not in Utopia. We have all shed, little by little, our illusions. . . .'

After a sigh, the depth of whose genuineness neither he nor Julian could accurately diagnose, he continued, brightening as he returned to the practical,—

'Stavridis—a harsher man than I. He and your islanders would come to grips within a month. I should scarcely deplore it. A question based on the struggle of nationality—for, it cannot be denied, the Italian blood of your islanders severs them irremediably from the true Greek of Herakleion—such questions cry for decisive settlement even at the cost of a little blood-letting. Submission or liberty, once and for all. That is preferable to the present irritable shilly-shally.'

'I know the alternative I should choose,' said Julian.

'Liberty?—the lure of the young,' said Malteios, not unkindly. 'I said that I should scarcely deplore such an attempt, for it would fail; Herakleion could never tolerate for long the independence of the Islands. Yes, it would surely fail. But from it good might emerge. A friendlier settlement, a better understanding, a more cheerful submission. Believe me,' he added, seeing the cloud of obstinate disagreement upon Julian's face, 'never break your heart over the failure. Your Islands would have learnt the lesson of the inevitable; and the great inevitable is perhaps the least intolerable of all human sorrows. There is, after all, a certain kindliness in the fate which lays the obligation of sheer necessity upon our courage.'

For a moment his usual manner had left him; he recalled it with a short laugh.

'Perhaps the thought that my long years of office may be nearly at an end betrays me into this undue melancholy,' he said flippantly; 'pay no attention, young man. Indeed, whatever I may say, I know that you will cling to your ideas of revolt. Am I not right?'

Once more the keen, sly look was in his eyes, and Julian knew that only the Malteios who desired the rupture of the Islands with his own political adversary, remained. He felt, in a way, comforted to be again upon the familiar ground; his conception of the man had been momentarily disarranged.

'Your Excellency is very shrewd,' he replied, politely and evasively.

Malteios shrugged and smiled the smile that had such real charm; and as he shrugged and smiled the discussion away into the region of such things dismissed, his glance travelled beyond Julian to the door, his mouth curved into a more goatish smile amidst his beard, and his eyes narrowed into two slits till his whole face resembled the mask of the old faun that Eve had drawn on the blotting paper.

'Mademoiselle!' he murmured, advancing towards Eve, who, dressed in white, appeared between the lapis-lazuli columns.

Three

MADAME LAFARGE gave a picnic which preceded the day of the elections, and to Julian Davenant it seemed that he was entering a cool, dark cavern roofed over with mysterious greenery after riding in the heat across a glaring plain. The transition from the white Herakleion to the deep valley, shut in by steep, terraced hills covered with olives, ilexes, and myrtles—a valley profound, haunted, silent, hallowed by pools of black-green shadow—consciousness of the transition stole over him soothingly, as his pony picked its way down the stony path of the hill-side. He had refused to accompany the others. Early in the morning he had ridden over the hills, so early that he had watched the sunrise, and had counted, from a summit, the houses on Aphros in the glassy limpidity of the Grecian dawn. The morning had been pure as the treble notes of a violin, the sea below bright as a pavement of diamonds. The Islands lay, clear and low, delicately yellow, rose, and lilac, in the serene immensity of the dazzling waters. They seemed to him to contain every element of enchantment; cleanly of line as cameos, yet intangible as a mirage, rising lovely and gracious as Aphrodite from the white flashes of their foam, fairy islands of beauty and illusion in a sea of radiant and eternal youth.

A stream ran through the valley, and near the banks of the stream, in front of a clump of ilexes, gleamed the marble columns of a tiny ruined temple. Julian turned his pony loose to graze, throwing himself down at full length beside the stream and idly pulling at the orchids and magenta cyclamen which grew in profusion. Towards midday his solitude was interrupted. A profession of victorias accompanied by men on horseback began to wind down the steep road into the valley; from afar he watched them coming, conscious of distaste and boredom, then remembering that Eve was of the party, and smiling to himself a little in relief. She would come, at first silent, unobtrusive, almost sulky; then little by little the spell of their intimacy would steal over him, and by a word or a glance they would be linked, the whole system of their relationship developing itself anew, a system elaborated by her, as he well knew; built up of personal, whimsical jokes; stimulating, inventive, she had to a supreme extent the gift of creating such a web, subtly, by meaning more than she said and saying less than she meant; giving infinite promise, but, ever postponing fulfilment.

'A flirt?' he wondered to himself, lazily watching the string of carriages in one of which she was.

But she was more elemental, more dangerous, than a mere flirt. On that account, and because of her wide and penetrative intelligence, he could not relegate her to the common category. Yet he thought he might safely make the assertion that no man in Herakleion had altogether escaped her attraction. He thought he might apply this generalisation from M. Lafarge, or Malteios, or Don Rodrigo Valdez, down to the chasseur who picked up her handkerchief. (Her handkerchief! ah, yes! she could always be traced, as in a paper-chase, by her scattered possessions—a handkerchief, a glove, a cigarette-case, a gardenia, a purse full of money, a powder-puff—frivolities doubly delightful and doubly irritating in a being so terrifyingly elemental, so unassailably and sarcastically intelligent.) Eve, the child he had known unaccountable, passionate, embarrassing, who had written him the precocious letters on every topic in a variety of tongues, exceedingly imaginative, copiously illustrated, bursting occasionally into erratic and illegible verse; Eve with her desperate and excessive passions; Eve, grown to womanhood, grown into a firebrand! He had been entertained, but at the same time slightly offended, to find her grown; his conception of her was disarranged; he had felt almost a sense of outrage in seeing her heavy hair piled upon her head; he had looked curiously at the uncovered nape of her neck, the hair brushed upwards and slightly curling, where once it had hung thick and plaited; he had noted with an irritable shame the softness of her throat in the evening dress she had worn when first he had seen her. He banished violently the recollection of her in that brief moment when in his anger he had lifted her out of her bed and had carried her across the room in his arms. He banished it with a shudder and a revulsion, as he might have banished a suggestion of incest.

Springing to his feet, he went forward to meet the carriages; the shadowed valley was flicked by the bright uniforms of the chasseurs on the boxes and the summer dresses of the women in the victorias; the laughter of the Danish Excellency already reached his ears above the hum of talk and the sliding hoofs of the horses as they advanced cautiously down the hill, straining back against their harness, and bringing with them at every step a little shower of stones from the rough surface of the road. The younger men, Greeks, and secretaries of legations, rode by the side of the carriages. The Danish Excellency was the first to alight, fat and babbling in a pink muslin dress with innumerable flounces; Julian turned aside to hide his smile. Madame Lafarge descended with her customary weightiness, beaming without benevolence but with a tyrannical proprietorship over all her guests. She graciously accorded her hand to Julian. The chasseurs were already busy with wicker baskets.

'The return to Nature,' Alexander Christopoulos whispered to Eve.

Julian observed that Eve looked bored and sulky; she detested large assemblies, unless she could hold their entire attention, preferring the more intimate scope of the *tête-à-tête*. Amongst the largest gatherings she usually contrived to isolate herself and one other, with whom she conversed in whispers. Presently, he knew, she would be made to recite, or to tell anecdotes, involving imitation, and this she would perform, at first languidly, but warming with applause, and would end by dancing—he knew her programme! He rarely spoke to her, or she to him, in public. She would appear to ignore him, devoting herself to Don Rodrigo, or to Alexander, or, most probably, to the avowed admirer of some other woman. He had frequently brought his direct and masculine arguments to bear against this practice. She listened without replying, as though she did not understand.

Fru Thyregod was more than usually sprightly.

'Now, Armand, you lazy fellow, bring me my camera; this day has to be immortalised; I must have pictures of all you beautiful young men for my friends in Denmark.

117

Fauns in a Grecian grave! Let me peep whether any of you have cloven feet.'

Madame Lafarge put up her lorgnon, and said to the Italian Minister in a not very low voice,—

'I am so fond of dear Fru Thyregod, but she is terribly vulgar at times.'

There was a great deal of laughter over Fru Thyregod's sally, and some of the young men pretended to hide their feet beneath napkins.

'Eve and Julie, you must be the nymphs,' the Danish Excellency went on.

Eve took no notice; Julie looked shy, and the sisters Christopoulos angry at not being included.

'Now we must all help to unpack; that is half the fun of the picnic,' said Madame Lafarge, in a business-like tone.

Under the glare of her lorgnon Armand and Madame Delahaye attacked one basket; they nudged and whispered to one another, and their fingers became entangled under the cover of the paper wrappings. Eve strolled away, Valdez followed her. The Persian Minister who had come unobtrusively, after the manner of a humble dog, stood gently smiling in the background. Julie Lafarge never took her adoring eyes off Eve. The immense Grbits had drawn Julian on one side, and was talking to him, shooting out his jaw and hitting Julian on the chest for emphasis. Fru Thyregod, with many whispers, collected a little group to whom she pointed them out, and photographed them.

'Really,' said the Danish Minister peevishly, to Condesa Valdez, 'my wife is the most foolish woman I know.'

During the picnic every one was very gay, with the exception of Julian, who regretted having come, and of Miloradovitch, of whom Eve was taking no notice at all. Madame Lafarge was especially pleased with the success of her expedition. She enjoyed the intimacy that existed amongst all her guests, and said as much in an aside to the Roumanian Minister.

'You know, *chère Excellence,* I have known most of these dear friends so long; we have spent happy years together in different capitals; that is the best of diplomacy: *ce qu'il y a de beau dans la carrière c'est qu' on se retrouve toujours.*'

'It is not unlike a large family, one may say,' replied the Roumanian.

'How well you phrase it!' exclaimed Madame Lafarge. 'Listen, everybody: His Excellency has made a real *mot d' esprit*, he says diplomacy is like a large family.'

Eve and Julian looked up, and their eyes met.

'You are not eating anything, Ardalion Semeonovitch,' said Armand (he had once spent two months in Russia) to Miloradovitch, holding out a plate of sandwiches.

'No, nor do I want anything,' said Miloradovitch rudely, and he got up, and walked away by himself.

'Dear me! *ces Russes!* what manners!' said Madame Lafarge, pretending to be amused; and everybody looked facetiously at Eve.

'I remember once, when I was in Russia, at the time that Stolypin was Prime Minister,' Don Rodrigo began, 'there was a serious scandal about one of the Empress's ladies-in-waiting and a son of old Princess Golucheff—you remember old Princess Golucheff, Excellency? she was a Bariatinsky, a very handsome woman, and Serge Radziwill killed himself on her account—he was a Pole, one of the Kieff Radziwills, whose mother was commonly supposed to be *au mieux* with Stolypin (though Stolypin was not at all that kind of man; he was *très province*), and most people thought that was the reason why Serge occupied such a series of the highest Court appointments, in spite of being a Pole—the Poles were particularly unpopular just then; I even remember that Stanislas Aveniev, in spite of having a Russian mother—she was an Orloff, and her jewels were proverbial even in Petersburg—they had all been given her by the Grand Duke Boris—Stanislas Aveniev was obliged to resign his commission in the Czar's guard. However, Casimir Golucheff . . .' but everybody had forgotten the beginning of his story and only Madame Lafarge was left politely listening.

Julian overheard Eve reproducing, in an undertone to Armand, the style and manner of Don Rodrigo's conversation. He also became aware that, between her sallies, Fru Thyregod was bent upon retaining his attention for herself.

He was disgusted with all this paraphernalia of social construction, and longed ardently for liberty on Aphros. He wondered whether Eve were truly satisfied, or whether she played the part merely with the humorous gusto of an artist, caught up in his own game; he wondered to what extent her mystery was due to her life's pretence?

Later, he found himself drifting apart with the Danish Excellency; he drifted, that is, beside her, tall, slack of limb, absent of mind, while she tripped with apparent heedlessness, but with actual determination of purpose. As she tripped she chattered. Fair and silly, she demanded gallantry of men, and gallantry of a kind—perfunctory, faintly pitying, apologetic—she was accorded. She had enticed Julian away, with a certain degree of skill, and was glad. Eve had scowled blackly, in the one swift glance she had thrown them.

'Your cousin enchants Don Rodrigo, it is clear,' Fru Thyregod said with malice as they strolled.

Julian turned to look back. He saw Eve sitting with the Spanish Minister on the steps of the little temple. In front of the temple, the ruins of the picnic stained the valley with bright frivolity; bits of white paper fluttered, table-cloths remained spread on the ground, and laughter echoed from the groups that still lingered hilariously; the light dresses of the women were gay, and their parasols floated above them like coloured bubbles against the darkness of the ilexes.

'What desecration of the Dryads' grove,' said Fru Thyregod, 'let us put it out of sight,' and she gave a little run forward, and then glanced over her shoulder to see if Julian were following her.

He came, unsmiling and leisurely. As soon as they were hidden from sight among the olives, she began to talk to him about himself, walking slowly, looking up at him now and then, and prodding meditatively with the tip of her parasol at the stones upon the ground. He was, she said, so free. He had his life before him. And she talked about herself, of the shackles of her sex, the practical difficulties of her life, her poverty, her effort to hide beneath a gay exterior a heart that was not gay.

'Carl,' she said, alluding to her husband, 'has indeed charge of the affairs of Norway and Sweden also in Herakleion, but Herakleion is so tiny, he is paid as though he were a Consul.'

Julian listened, dissecting the true from the untrue; although he knew her gaiety was no effort, but merely the child of her innate foolishness, he also knew that her poverty was a source of real difficulties to her, and he felt towards her a warm, though a bored and slightly contemptuous, friendliness. He listened to her babble, thinking more of the stream by which they walked, and of the little magenta cyclamen that grew in the shady, marshy places on its banks.

Fru Thyregod was speaking of Eve, a topic round which she perpetually hovered in an uncertainty of fascination and resentment.

'Do you approve of her very intimate friendship with that singer, Madame Kato?'

'I am very fond of Madame Kato myself, Fru Thyregod.'

'Ah, you are a man. But for Eve ... a girl ... After all, what is Madame Kato but a common woman, a woman of the people, and the mistress of Malteios into the bargain?'

Fru Thyregod was unwontedly serious. Julian had not yet realised to what extent Alexander Christopoulos had transferred his attention to Eve.

'You know I am an unconventional woman; every one who knows me even a little can see that I am unconventional. But when I see a child, a nice child, like your cousin Eve, associated with a person like Kato, I think to myself, "Mabel, that is unbecoming." '

She repeated,—

'And yet I have been told that I was too unconventional. Yes, Carl has often reproached me, and my friends too. They say, "Mabel, you are too soft-hearted, and you are too unconventional." What do you think?'

Julian ignored the personal. He said,—

'I should not describe Eve as a "nice child." '

'No? Well, perhaps not. She is too ... too ...' said Fru Thyregod, who, not having very many ideas of her own, liked to induce other people into supplying the missing adjective.

'She is too important,' Julian said gravely.

The adjective in this case was unexpected. The Danish Excellency could only say,—

'I think I know what you mean.'

Julian, perfectly well aware that she did not, and caring nothing whether she did or no, but carelessly willing to illuminate himself further on the subject, pursued,—

'Her frivolity is a mask. Her instincts alone are deep; *how* deep, it frightens me to think. She is an artist, although, she may never produce art. She lives in a world of her own, with its own code of morals and values. The Eve that we all know is a sham, the produce of her own pride and humour. She is laughing at us all. The Eve we know is entertaining, cynical, selfish, unscrupulous. The real Eve is ...' he paused, and brought out his words with a satisfied finality, 'a revel and an idealist.'

Then, glancing at his bewildered companion, he laughed and said,—

'Don't believe a word I say, Fru Thyregod: Eve is nineteen, bent only upon enjoying her life to the full.'

He knew, nevertheless, that he had swept together the loose wash of his thought into a concrete channel; and rejoiced.

Fru Thyregod passed to a safer topic. She liked Julian, and understood only one form of excitement.

'You bring with you such a breath of freshness and originality,' she said, sighing, 'into our stale little world.'

His newly-found good humour coaxed him into responsiveness.

'No world can surely ever be stale to you, Fru Thyregod; I always think of you as endowed with perpetual youth and gaiety.'

'Ah, Julian, you have perfect manners, to pay so charming a compliment to an old woman like me.'

She neither thought her world stale or little, nor herself old, but pathos had often proved itself of value.

'Everybody knows, Fru Thyregod, that you are the life and soul of Herakleion.'

They had wandered into a little wood, and sat down on a fallen tree beside the stream. She began again prodding at the ground with her parasol, keeping her eyes cast down. She was glad to have captured Julian, partly for her own sake, and partly because she knew that Eve would be annoyed.

'How delightful to escape from all our noisy friends,' she said; 'we shall create quite a scandal; but I am too unconventional to trouble about that. I cannot sympathise with those limited, conventional folk who always consider appearances. I have always said, "One should be natural. Life is too short for the conventions." Although, I think one should refrain from giving pain. When I was a girl, I was a terrible tomboy.'

He listened to her babble of coy platitudes, contrasting her with Eve.

'I never lost my spirits,' she went on, in the meditative tone she thought suitable to *tête-à-tête* conversations—it provoked intimacy, and afforded agreeable relief to her more social manner; a woman, to be charming, must be several-sided; gay in public, but a little wistful philosophy was interesting in private; it indicated sympathy, and betrayed a thinking mind,—'I never lost my spirits, although life has not always been very easy for me; still, with good spirits and perhaps a little courage one can continue to laugh, isn't that the way to take life? and on the whole I have enjoyed mine and my little adventures too, my little harmless adventures; Carl always laughs and says, "You will always have adventures, Mabel, so I must make the best of it,"—he says that, though he has been very jealous at times. Poor Carl,' she said reminiscently, 'perhaps I have made him suffer; who knows?'

Julian looked at her; he supposed that her existence was made up of such experiments, and know that the arrival of every new young man in Herakleion was to her a source of flurry and endless potentialities which, alas, never fulfilled their promise, but which left her undaunted and optimistic for the next affray.

'Why do I always talk about myself to you?' she said, with her little laugh; 'you must blame yourself for being too sympathetic.'

He scarcely knew how their conversation progressed; he wondered idly whether Eve conducted hers upon the same lines with Don Rodrigo Valdez, or whether she had been claimed by Miloradovitch, to whom she said she was engaged. Did she care for Miloradovitch? he was immensely rich, the owner of jewels and oil-mines, remarkably good-looking; dashing, and a gambler. At diplomatic gatherings he wore a beautiful uniform. Julian had seen Eve dancing with him; he had seen the Russian closely following her out of a room, bending forward to speak to her, and her ironical eyes raised for an instant over the slow movement of her fan. He had seen them disappear together, and the provocative poise of her white shoulders, and the richness of the beautiful uniform, had remained imprinted on his memory.

He awoke with dismay to the fact that Fru Thyregod had taken off her hat.

She had a great quantity of soft, yellow hair into which she ran her fingers, lifting its weight as though oppressed. He supposed that the gesture was not so irrelevant to their foregoing conversation, of which he had not noticed a word, as it appeared to be. He was startled to find himself saying in a tone of commiseration,—

'Yes, it must be very heavy.'

'I wish that I could cut it all off,' Fru Thyregod cried petulantly. 'Why, to amuse you, only look . . .' and to his horror she withdrew a number of pins and allowed her hair to fall in a really beautiful cascade over her shoulders. She smiled at him, parting the strands before her eyes.

At that moment Eve and Miloradovitch came into view, wandering side by side down the path.

Of the four, Miloradovitch alone was amused. Julian was full of a shamefaced anger towards Fru Thyregod, and between the two women an instant enmity sprang into being like a living and visible thing. The Russian drew near to Fru Thyregod with some laughing compliment; she attached herself desperately to him as a refuge from Julian. Julian and Eve remained face to face with one another.

'Walk with me a little,' she said, making no attempt to disguise her fury.

'My dear Eve,' he said, when they were out of earshot, 'I should scarcely recognise you when you put on that expression.'

He spoke frigidly. She was indeed transformed, her features coarsened and unpleasing, her soft delicacy vanished. He could not believe that he had ever thought her rare, exquisite, charming.

'I don't blame you for preferring Fru Thyregod,' she returned.

'I believe your vanity to be so great that you resent any man speaking to any other woman but yourself,' he said, half persuading himself that he was voicing a genuine conviction.

'Very well, if you choose to believe that,' she replied.

They walked a little way in angry silence.

'I detest all women,' he added presently.

'Including me?'

'Beginning with you.'

He was reminded of their childhood with its endless disputes, and made an attempt to restore their friendship.

'Come, Eve, why are we quarrelling? I do not make you jealous scenes about Miloradovitch.'

'Far from it,' she said harshly.

'Why should he want to marry you?' he began, his anger rising again. 'What qualities have you? Clever, seductive, and entertaining! But, on the other hand, selfish, jealous, unkind, pernicious, indolent, vain. A bad bargain. If he knew you as well as I . . . Jealousy! It amounts to madness.'

'I am perhaps not jealous where Miloradovitch is concerned,' she said.

'Then spare me the compliment of being jealous of me. You wreck affection; you will wreck your life through your jealousy and exorbitance.'

'No doubt,' she replied in a tone of so much sadness that he became remorseful. He contrasted, moreover, her violence, troublesome, inconvenient, as it often was, with the standardised and distasteful little inanities of Fru Thyregod and her like, and found Eve preferable.

'Darling, you never defend yourself; it is very disarming.'

But she would not accept the olive-branch he offered.

'Sentimentality becomes you very badly, Julian; keep it for Fru Thyregod.'

'We have had enough of Fru Thyregod,' he said, flushing.

'It suits you to say so; I do not forget so easily. Really, Julian, sometimes I think you very commonplace. From the moment you arrived until to-day, you have never been out of Fry Thyregod's pocket. Like Alexander, once. Like any stray young man.'

'Eve!' he said, in astonishment at the outrageous accusation.

'My little Julian, have you washed the lap-dog to-day? Carl always says, "Mabel, you are fonder of your dogs than of your children—you are really dreadful," but I don't think that's quite fair,' said Eve, in so exact an imitation of Fru Thyregod's voice and manner that Julian was forced to smile.

She went on,—

'I expect too much of you. My imagination makes of you something which you are not. I so despise the common herd that I persuaded myself that you are above it. I can persuade myself of anything,' she said scathingly, wounding him in the recesses of his most treasured vanity—her good opinion of him; 'I persuade myself that you are a Titan amongst men, almost a god, but in reality, if I could see you without prejudice, what are you fit for? to be Fru Thyregod's lover!'

'You are mad,' he said, for there was no other reply.

'When I am jealous, I am mad,' she flung at him.

'But if you are jealous of me ...' he said, appalled. 'Supposing you were ever in love, your jealousy would know no bounds. It is a disease. It is the ruin of our friendship.'

'Entirely.'

'You are inordinately perverse.'

'Inordinately.'

'Supposing I were to marry, I should not dare—what an absurd thought—to introduce you to my wife.'

A truly terrible expression came into her eyes; they narrowed to little slits, and turned slightly inwards; as though herself aware of it, she bent to pick the little cyclamen.

'Are you trying to tell me, Julian ...'

'You told me you were engaged to Miloradovitch.'

She stood up, regardless, and he saw the tragic pallor of her face. She tore the cyclamen to pieces beneath her white fingers.

'It is true, then?' she said, her voice dead.

He began to laugh.

'You do indeed persuade yourself very easily.'

'Julian, you must tell me. You must. Is it true?'

'If it were?'

'I should have to kill you—or myself,' she replied with the utmost gravity.

'You are mad,' he said again, in the resigned tone of one who states a perfectly established fact.

'If I am mad, you are unutterably cruel,' she said, twisting her fingers together; 'will you answer me, yes or no? I believe it is true,' she rushed on, immolating herself, 'you have fallen in love with some women in England, and she, naturally, with you. Who is she? You have promised to marry her. You, whom I thought so free and splendid, to load yourself with the inevitable fetters!'

'I should lose caste in your eyes?' he asked, thinking to himself that Eve was, when roused, scarcely a civilised being. 'But if you marry Miloradovitch you will be submitting to the same fetters you think so degrading.'

'Miloradovitch,' she said impatiently, 'Miloradovitch will no more ensnare me than have the score of people I have been engaged to since I last saw you. You are still evading your answer.'

'You will never marry?' he dwelt on his discovery.

'Nobody that I loved,' she replied without hesitation, 'but, Julian, Julian, you don't answer my question?'

'Would you marry me if I wanted you to?' he asked carelessly.

'Not for the world, but why keep me in suspense? only answer me, are you trying to tell me that you have fallen in love? If so, admit it, please, at once, and let me go; don't you see, I am leaving Fru Thyregod on one side, I ask you in all humility now, Julian.'

'For perhaps the fiftieth time since you were thirteen,' he said, smiling.

'Have you tormented me long enough?'

'Very well: I am in love with the Islands, and with nothing and nobody else.'

'Then why had Frau Thyregod her hair down her back? You're lying to me, and I despise you doubly for it,' she reverted, humble no longer, but aggressive.

'Fru Thyregod again?' he said, bewildered.

'How little I trust you,' she broke out; 'I believe that you deceive me at every turn. Kato, too; you spend hours in Kato's flat. What do you do there? You write letters to people of whom I have never heard. You dined with the Thyregods twice last week. Kato sends you notes by hand from Herakleion when you are in the country. You see the Islands as dust to throw in my eyes, but I am not blinded.'

'I have had enough of this!' he cried.

'You are like everybody else,' she insisted; 'you enjoy mean entanglements, and you cherish the idea of marriage. You want a home, like everybody else. A faithful wife. Children. I loathe children,' she said violently. 'You are very different from me. You are tame. I have deluded myself into thinking we were alike. You are tame, respectable. A good citizen. You have all the virtues. I will live to show you how different we are. Ten years hence, you will say to your wife, "No, my dear, I really cannot allow you to know that poor Eve." And your wife, well trained, submissive, will agree.'

He shrugged his shoulders, accustomed to such storms, and knowing that she only sought to goad him into a rage.

'In the meantime, go back to Fru Thyregod; why trouble to lie to me? And to Kato, go back to Kato. Write to the woman in England, too. I will go to Miloradovitch, or to any of the others.'

He was betraying into saying,—

'The accusation of mean entanglements comes badly from your lips.'

In her heart she guessed pretty shrewdly at his real relation towards women: a self-imposed austerity, with violent relapses that had no lasting significance, save to leave him with his contemptuous distaste augmented. His mind was too full of other matters. For Kato alone he had a profound esteem.

Eve answered his last remark,—

'I will prove to you the little weight of my entanglements, by dismissing Miloradovitch to-day; you have only to say the word.'

'You would do that—without remorse?'

'Miloradovitch is nothing to me.'

'You are something to him—perhaps everything.'

'*Cela ne me regarde pas,*' she replied. 'Would you do as much for me? Fru Thyregod, for instance? or Kato?'

Interested and curious, he said,—

'To please you, I should give up Kato?'

'You would not?'

'Most certainly I should not. Why suggest it? Kato is your friend as much as mine. Are all women's friendships so unstable?'

'Be careful, Julian: you are on the quicksands.'

'I have had enough of these topics,' he said, 'will you leave them?'

'No; I choose my own topics; you shan't dictate to me.'

'You would sacrifice Miloradovitch without a thought,

128

to please me—why should it please me?—but you would not forgo the indulgence of your jealousy! I am not grateful. Our senseless quarrels,' he said, 'over which we squander so much anger and emotion.' But he did not stop to question what lay behind their important futility. He passed his hand wearily over his hair, 'I am deluded sometimes into believing in their reality and sanity. You are too difficult. You ... you distort and bewitch, until one expects to wake up from a dream. Sometimes I think of you as a woman quite apart from other women, but at other times I think you live merely by and upon fictitious emotion and excitement. Must your outlook be always so narrowly personal? Kato, thank Heaven, is very different. I shall take care to choose my friends amongst men, or amongst women like Kato,' he continued, his exasperation rising.

'Julian, don't be so angry: it isn't my fault that I hate politics.'

He grew still angrier at her illogical short-cut to the reproach which lay, indeed, unexpressed at the back of his mind.

'I never mentioned politics. I know better. No man in his senses would expect politics from any woman so demoralisingly feminine as yourself. Besides, that isn't your rôle. Your rôle is to be soft, idle; a toy; a siren; the negation of enterprise. Work and woman—the terms contradict one another. The woman who works, or who tolerates work, is only half a woman. The most you can hope for,' he said with scorn, 'is to inspire—and even that you do unconsciously, and very often quite against your will. You sap our energy; you sap and you destroy.'

She had not often heard him speak with so much bitterness, but she did not know that his opinions in this more crystallised form dated from that slight moment in which he had divined her own untrustworthiness.

'You are very wise. I forget whether you are twenty-two or twenty-three?'

'Oh, you may be sarcastic. I only know that I will never have my life wrecked by women. To-morrow the elections take place, and, after that, whatever their result, I belong to the Islands.'

'I think I see you with a certain clearness,' she said

more gently, 'full of illusions, independence, and young generosities—*nous passons tous par l'à.*'

'Talk English, Eve, and be less cynical; if I am twenty-two, as you reminded me, you are nineteen.'

'If you could find a woman who was a help and not a hindrance?' she suggested.

'Ah!' he said, 'the Blue Bird! I am not likely to be taken in; I am too well on my guard.—Look!' he added, 'Fru Thyregod and your Russian friend; I leave you to them,' and before Eve could voice her indignation he had disappeared into the surrounding woods.

Four

ON THE NEXT DAY, the day of the elections, which was also the anniversary of the Declaration of Independence, Herakleion blossomed suddenly, and from the earliest hour, into a striped and fluttering gaudiness. The sun shone down upon a white town beflagged into an astonishing gaiety. Everywhere was whiteness, whiteness, and brilliantly coloured flags. White, green, and orange, dazzling in the sun, vivid in the breeze. And, keyed up to match the intensity of the colour, the band blared brassily, unremittingly, throughout the day from the centre of the *platia*.

A parrot-town, glaring and screeching; a monkey-town, gibbering, excited, inconsequent. All the shops, save the sweet-shops, were shut, and the inhabitants flooded into the streets. Not only had they decked their houses with flags, they had also decked themselves with ribbons, their women with white dresses, their children with bright bows, their carriages with paper streamers, their horses with sun-bonnets. Bands of young men, straw-hatted, swept arm-in-arm down the pavements, adding to the din with mouth organs, mirlitons, and tin trumpets. The trams flaunted posters in the colours of the contending parties. Immense char-à-bancs, roofed over with brown holland and drawn by teams of mules, their harness hung with bells and red tassels, conveyed the voters to the polling-booths amid the cheers and imprecations of the crowd.

Herakleion abandoned itself deliriously to political carnival.

In the immense, darkened rooms of the houses on the *platia*, the richer Greeks idled, concealing their anxiety. It was tacitly considered beneath their dignity to show themselves in public during that day. They could but await the fruition or the failure of their activities during the preceding weeks. Heads of households were for the most part

131

morose, absorbed in calculations and regrets. Old Christopoulos, looking more bleached than usual, wished he had been more generous. That secretaryship for Alexander ... In the great sala of his house he paced restlessly up and down, biting his finger nails, and playing on his fingers the tune of the many thousand drachmæ he might profitably have expended. The next election would not take place for five years. At the next election he would be a great deal more lavish.

He had made the same resolution at every election during the past thirty years.

In the background, respectful of his silence, themselves dwarfed and diminutive in the immense height of the room, little knots of his relatives and friends whispered together, stirring cups of tisane. Heads were very close together, glances at old Christopoulos very frequent. Visitors, isolated or in couples, strolled in unannounced and informally, stayed for a little, strolled away again. A perpetual movement of such circulation rippled through the houses in the *platia* throughout the day, rumour assiduous in its wake. Fru Thyregod alone, with her fat, silly laugh, did her best wherever she went to lighten the funereal oppression of the atmosphere. The Greeks she visited were not grateful. Unlike the populace in the streets, they preferred taking their elections mournfully.

By midday the business of voting was over, and in the houses of the *platia* the Greeks sat round their luncheon-tables with the knowledge that the vital question was now decided, though the answer remained as yet unknown, and that in the polling-booths an army of clerks sat feverishly counting, while the crowd outside, neglectful of its meal, swarmed noisily in the hope of news. In the houses of the *platia*, on this one day of the year, the Greeks kept open table. Each vast dining-room, carefully darkened and indistinguishable in its family likeness from its neighbour in the house on either side, offered its hospitality under the inevitable chandelier. In each, the host greeted the new-comer with the same perfunctory smile. In each, the busy servants came and went, carrying dishes and jugs of orangeade—for Levantine hospitality, already heavily strained, boggled at wine—among the bulky and old-fashioned sideboards. All joyousness was absent from these gatherings, and the closed shutters served to exclude, not only the heat, but also the strains of the indefatigable band playing on the *platia*.

Out in the streets the popular excitement hourly increased, for if the morning had been devoted to politics, the afternoon and evening were to be devoted to the annual feast and holiday of the Declaration of Independence. The national colours, green and orange, seemed trebled in the town. They hung from every balcony and were reproduced in miniature in every buttonhole. Only here and there an islander in his fustanelle walked quickly with sulky and averted eyes, rebelliously innocent of the brilliant cocarde, and far out to sea the rainbow islands shimmered with never a flag to stain the distant whiteness of the houses upon Aphros.

The houses of the *platia* excelled all others in the lavishness of their patriotic decorations. The balconies of the club were draped in green and orange, with the arms of Herakleion arranged in the centre in electric lights for the evening illumination. The Italian Consulate drooped its complimentary flag. The house of Platon Malteios—Premier or ex-Premier? no one knew—was almost too ostentatiously patriotic. The cathedral, on the opposite side, had its steps carpeted with red and the spaciousness of its porch festooned with the colours. From the central window of the Davenant house, opposite the sea, a single listless banner hung in motionless folds.

It had, earlier in the day, occasioned a controversy.

Julian had stood in the centre of the frescoed drawing-room, flushed and constrained.

'Father, that flag on our house insults the Islands. It can be seen even from Aphros!'

'My dear boy, better that it should be seen from Aphros than that we should offend Herakleion.'

'What will the islanders think?'

'They are accustomed to seeing it there every year.'

'If I had been at home . . .'

'When this house is yours, Julian, you will no doubt do as you please; so long as it is mine, I beg you not to interfere.'

Mr Davenant had spoken in his curtest tones. He had added,—

'I shall go to the cathedral this afternoon.'

The service in the cathedral annually celebrated the independence of Herakleion. Julian slipped out of the house, meaning to mix with the ill-regulated crowd that began to collect on the *platia* to watch for the arrival of the notables, but outside the door of the club he was discovered by Alexander Christopoulos who obliged him to follow him upstairs to the Christopoulos drawing-room.

'My father is really too gloomy for me to confront alone,' Alexander said, taking Julian's arm and urging him along; 'also I have spent the morning in the club, which exasperates him. He likes me to sit at home while he stands looking at me and mournfully shaking his head.'

They came into the sala together, where old Christopoulos paced up and down in front of the shuttered windows, and a score of other people sat whispering over their cups of tisane. White dresses, dim mirrors, and the dull gilt of furniture gleamed here and there in the shadows of the vast room.

'Any news? any news?' the banker asked of the two young men.

'You know quite well, father, that no results are to be declared until seven o'clock this evening.'

Alexander opened a section of a Venetian blind, and as a shaft of sunlight fell startlingly across the floor a blare of music burst equally startlingly upon the silence.

'The *platia* is crowded already,' said Alexander, looking out.

The hum of the crowd became audible, mingled with the music; explosions of laughter, and some unexplained applause. The shrill cry of a seller of iced water rang immediately beneath the window. The band in the centre continued to shriek remorselessly an antiquated air of the Paris boulevards.

'At what time is the procession due?' asked Fru Thyregod over Julian's shoulder.

'At five o'clock; it should arrive at any moment,' Julian said, making room for the Danish Excellency.

'I adore processions,' cried Fru Thyregod, clapping her hands, and looking brightly from Julian to Alexander.

Alexander whispered to Julie Lafarge, who had come up,—

'I am sure Fru Thyregod has gone from house to house and from Legation to Legation, and has had a meal at each to-day.'

Somebody suggested,—

'Let us open the shutters and watch the procession from the balconies.'

'Oh, what a good idea!' cried Fru Thyregod, clapping her hands again and executing a pirouette.

Down in the *platia* an indefinite movement was taking place; the band stopped playing for the first time that day, and began shuffling with all its instruments to one side. Voices were then heard raised in tones of authority. A cleavage appeared in the crowd, which grew in length and width as though a wedge were being gradually driven into that reluctant confusion of humanity.

'A path for the procession,' said old Christopoulos, who, although not pleased at that frivolous flux of his family and guests on to the balconies of his house, had joined them, overcome by his natural curiosity.

The path cut in the crowd now ran obliquely across the *platia* from the end of the rue Royale to the steps of the cathedral opposite, and upon it the confetti with which the whole *platia* was no doubt strewn became visible. The police with truncheons in their hands, were pressing the people back to widen the route still further. They wore their gala hats, three-cornered, with upright plumes of green and orange nodding as they walked.

'Look at Sterghiou,' said Alexander.

The Chief of Police rode vaingloriously down the route looking from left to right, and saluting with his free hand. The front of his uniform was crossed with broad gold hinges, and plaits of yellow braid disappeared mysteriously into various pockets. One deduced whistles; pencils; perhaps a knife. Although he did not wear feathers in his hat, one knew that only the utmost self-restraint had preserved him from them.

Here the band started again with a march, and Sterghiou's horse shied violently and nearly unseated him.

'The troops!' said old Christopoulos with emotion.

Debouching from the rue Royale, the army came marching four abreast. As it was composed of only four hundred men, and as it never appeared on any other day of the year, its general Panaïoannou always mobilised it in its entirely on the national festival. This entailed the temporary closing of all casino in order to release the croupiers, who were nearly all in the ranks, and led to a yearly dispute between the General and the board of administration.

'There was once a croupier,' said Alexander, 'who was admitted to the favour of a certain grand-duchess until the day when, indiscreetly coming into the dressing-room where the lady was arranging and improving her appearance, he said, through sheer force of habit, "Madame, les yeux sont faits?" and was dismissed for ever by her reply, "Rien ne va plus."'

The general himself rode in the midst of his troops, in his sky-blue uniform, to which the fantasy of his Buda-Pesth costumier had added for the occasion a slung Hussar jacket of white cloth. His gray moustache was twisted fiercely upwards, and curved like a scimitar across his face. He rode with his hand on his hip, slowly scanning the windows and balconies of the *platia*, which by now were crowded with people, gravely saluting his friends as he passed. Around him marched his bodyguard of six, a captain and five men; the captain carried in one hand a sword, and in the other—nobody knew why—a long frond of palm.

The entire army tramped by, hot, stout, beaming, and friendly. At one moment some one threw down a handful of coins from a window, and the ranks were broken in a scramble for the coppers. Julian, who was leaning apart in a corner of his balcony, heard a laugh like a growl behind him as the enormous hand of Grbits descended on his shoulder.

'Remember the lesson, young man: if you are called upon to deal with the soldiers of Herakleion, a fistful of silver amongst them will scatter them.'

Julian thought apprehensively that they must be overheard, but Grbits continued in supreme unconsciousness,—

'Look at their army, composed of shop-assistants and croupiers. Look at their general—a general in his spare moments, but in the serious business of his life a banker and an intriguer like the rest of them. I doubt whether he has ever seen anything more dead in his life than a dead dog in a gutter. I could pick him up and squash in his head like an egg.'

Grbits extended his arm and slowly unfolded the fingers of his enormous hand. At the same time he gave his great laugh that was like the laugh of a good-humoured ogre.

'At your service, young man,' he said, displaying the full breadth of his palm to Julian, 'whenever you stand in need of it. The Stavridists will be returned to-day; lose no time; show them your intentions.'

He impelled Julian forward to the edge of the balcony and pointed across to the Davenant house.

'That flag, young man: see to it that it disappears within the hour after the results of the elections are announced.'

The army was forming itself into two phalanxes on either side of the cathedral steps. Panaïoannou caracoled up and down shouting his orders, which were taken up and repeated by the busy officers on foot. Meanwhile the notables in black coats were arriving in a constant stream that flowed into the cathedral; old Christopoulos had already left the house to attend the religious ceremony; the foreign Ministers and Consuls attended out of compliment to Herakleion; Madame Lafarge had rolled down the route in her barouche with her bearded husband; Malteios had crossed the *platia* from his own house, and Stavridis came, accompanied by his wife and daughters. Still the band played on, the crowd laughed, cheered, or murmured in derision, and the strident cries of the water-sellers rose from all parts of the *platia*.

Suddenly the band ceased to play, and in the hush only the hum of the crowd continued audible.

The religious procession came walking very slowly from the rue Royale, headed by a banner and by a file of young girls, walking two by two, in white dresses, with wreaths of roses on their heads. As they walked they scattered sham roses out of baskets, the gesture reminiscent of the big picture in the Senate-room. It was customary for the Premier of the Republic to walk alone, following these young girls, black and grave in his frock-coat after their virginal white, but on this occasion, as no one knew who the actual Premier was, a blank space was left to represent the problematical absentee. Following the space came the Premier's habitual escort, a posse of police; it should have been a platoon of soldiers, but Panaïoannou always refused to consent to such a diminution of his army.

'They say,' Grbits remarked to Julian in this connection,

'that the general withdraws even the sentries from the frontier to swell his ranks.'

'Herakleion is open to invasion,' said Julian, smiling.

Grbits replied sententiously, with the air of one creating a new proverb,—

'Herakleion is open to invasion, but who wants to invade Herakleion?'

The crowd watched the passage of the procession with the utmost solemnity. Not a sound was now heard but the monotonous step of feet. Religious awe had hushed political hilarity. Archbishop and bishops; archimandrites and *papás* of the country districts, passed in a mingling of scarlet, purple and black. All the pomp of Herakleion had been pressed into service—all the clamorous, pretentious pomp, shouting for recognition, beating on a hollow drum; designed to impress the crowd; and perhaps, also, to impress, beyond the crowd, the silent Islands that possessed no army, no clergy, no worldly trappings, but that suffered and struggled uselessly, pitiably, against the tinsel tyrant in vain but indestructible rebellion.

As five o'clock drew near, the entire population seemed to be collected in the *platia*. The white streak that had marked the route of the procession had long ago disappeared, and the square was now, seen from above, only a dense and shifting mass of people. In the Christopoulos drawing-room, where Julian still lingered, talking to Grbits and listening to the alternate foolishness, fanaticism, and ferocious good-humour of the giant, the Greeks rallied in numbers with only one topic on their lips. Old Christopoulos was frankly biting his nails and glancing at the clock; Alexander but thinly concealed his anxiety under a dribble of his usual banter. The band had ceased playing, and the subtle ear could detect an inflection in the very murmur of the crowd.

'Let us go on to the balcony again,' Grbits said to Julian; 'the results will be announced from the steps of Malteios' house.'

They went out; some of the Greeks followed them, and all pressed behind, near the window openings.

'It is a more than usually decisive day for Herakleion,' said old Christopoulos, and Julian knew that the words were spoken at, although not to, him.

He felt that the Greeks looked upon him as an intruder, wishing him away so that they might express their opinions freely, but in a spirit of contrariness he remained obstinately.

A shout went up suddenly from the crowd: a little man dressed in black, with a top-hat, and a great many white papers in his hand, had appeared in the frame of Malteios' front-door. He stood on the steps, coughed nervously, and dropped his papers.

'Inefficient little rat of a secretary!' cried Alexander in a burst of fury.

'Listen!' said Grbits.

A long pause of silence from the whole *platia*, in which one thin voice quavered, reaching only the front row of the crowd.

'Stavridis has it,' Grbits said quietly, who had been craning over the edge of the balcony. His eyes twinkled maliciously; delightedly, at Julian across the group of mortified Greeks. 'An immense majority,' he invented, enjoying himself.

Julian was already gone. Slipping behind old Christopoulos, whose saffron face had turned a dirty plum colour, he made his way downstairs and out into the street. A species of riot, in which the police, having failed successfully to intervene, were enthusiastically joining, had broken out in the *platia*. Some shouted for Stavridis, some for Malteios; some railed derisively against the Islands. People threw their hats into the air, waved their arms, and kicked up their legs. Some of them were vague as to the trend of their own opinions, others extremely determined, but all were agreed about making as much noise as possible. Julian passed unchallenged to his father's house.

Inside the door he found Aristotle talking with three islanders. They laid hold of him, urgent though respectful, searching his face with eager eyes.

'It means revolt at last; you will not desert us, Kyrie?'

He replied,—

'Come with me, and you will see.'

They followed him up the stairs, pressing closely after him. On the landing he met Eve and Kato, coming out of the drawing-room. The singer was flushed, two gold wheat-ears trembled in her hair and she had thrown open the front of her dress. Eve hung on her arm.

'Julian!' Kato exclaimed, 'you have heard, Platon has gone?'

In her excitement she inadvertently used Malteios' Christian name.

'It means,' he replied, 'that Stavridis, now in power, will lose no time in bringing against the Islands all the iniquitous reforms we know he contemplates. It means that the first step must be taken by us.'

His use of the pronoun ranged himself, Kato, Aristotle, the three islanders, and the invisible Islands into an instant confederacy. Kato responded to it,—

'Thank God, for this.'

They waited in complete confidence for his next words. He had shed his aloofness, and all his efficiency of active leadership was to the fore.

'Where is my father?'

'He went to the Cathedral; he has not come home yet, Kyrie.'

Julian passed into the drawing-room, followed by Eve and Kato and the four men. Outside the open window, fastened to the balcony, flashed the green and orange flag of Herakleion. Julian took a knife from his pocket, and, cutting the cord that held it withdrew flag and flag-staff into the room and flung it on the ground.

'Take it away,' he said to the islanders, 'or my father will order it to be replaced. And if he orders another to be hung out in its place,' he added, looking at them with severity, 'remember there is no other flag in the house, and none to be bought in Herakleion.'

At that moment a servant from the country-house came hurriedly into the room, drew Julian unceremoniously aside, and broke into an agitated recital in a low voice. Eve heard Julian saying,—

'Nicolas sends for me? But he should have given a reason. I cannot come now, I cannot leave Herakleion.'

And the servant,—

'Kyrie, the major-domo impressed upon me that I must on no account return without you. Something has occurred, something serious. What it is I do not know. The carriage is waiting at the back entrance; we could not drive across the *platia* on account of the crowds.'

'I shall have to go, I suppose,' Julian said to Eve and Kato. 'I will go at once, and will return, if possible, this evening. Nicolas would not send without an excellent reason, though he need not have made this mystery. Possibly a message from Aphros . . . In any case, I must go.'

'I will come with you,' Eve said unexpectedly.

Five

IN ALMOST UNBROKEN SILENCE they drove out to the country-house, in a hired victoria, to the quick, soft trot of the two little lean horses, away from the heart of the noisy town; past the race-course with its empty stands; under the ilex-avenue in a tunnel of cool darkness; along the road, redolent with magnolias in the warmth of the evening; through the village, between the two white lodges; and round the bend of the drive between the bushes of eucalyptus. Eve had spoken, but he had said abruptly,—

'Don't talk; I want to think,' and she, after a little gasp of astonished indignation, had relapsed languorous into her corner, her head propped on her hand, and her profile alone visible to her cousin. He saw, in the brief glance that he vouchsafed her, that her red mouth looked more than usually sulky, in fact not unlike the mouth of a child on the point of tears, a very invitation to inquiry, but, more from indifference than deliberate wisdom, he was not disposed to take up the challenge. He too sat silent, his thoughts flying over the day, weighing the consequences of his own action, trying to forecast the future. He was far away from Eve, and she knew it. At times he enraged and exasperated her almost beyond control. His indifference was an outrage on her femininity. She knew him to be utterly beyond her influence: taciturn when he chose, ill-tempered when he chose, exuberant when he chose, rampageous, wild; insulting to her at moments; domineering whatever his mood, and regardless of her wishes; yet at the same time unconscious of all these things. Alone with her now, he had completely forgotten her presence by his side.

Her voice broke upon his reflections,—

'Thinking of the Islands, Julian?' and her words joining

like a cogwheel smoothly on to the current of his mind, he answered naturally,—

'Yes.'

'I thought as much. I have something to tell you. You may not be interested. I am no longer engaged to Miloradovitch.'

'Since when?'

'Since yesterday evening. Since you left me, and ran away into the woods. I was angry, and vented my anger on him.'

'Was that fair?'

'He has you to thank. It has happened before—with others.'

Roused for a second from his absorption, he impatiently shrugged his shoulders, and turned his back, and looked out over the sea. Eve was again silent, brooding and resentful in her corner. Presently he turned towards her, and said angrily, reverting to the Islands,—

'You are the vainest and most exorbitant woman I know. You resent one's interest in anything but yourself.'

As she did not answer, he added,—

'How sulky you look; it's very unbecoming.'

Was no sense of proportion or of responsibility ever to weigh upon her beautiful shoulders? He was irritated, yet he knew that his irritation was half-assumed, and that in his heart he was no more annoyed by her fantasy than by the fantasy of Herakleion. They matched each other; their intangibility, their instability, were enough to make a man shake his fists to Heaven, yet he was beginning to believe that their colour and romance—for he never dissociated Eve and Herakleion in his mind—were the dearest treasures of his youth. He turned violently and amazingly upon her.

'Eve, I sometimes hate you, damn you; but you are the rainbow of my days.'

She smiled, and, enlightened, he perceived with interest, curiosity, and amused resignation, the clearer grouping of the affairs of his youthful years. Fantasy to youth! Sobriety to middle-age! Carried away, he said to her,—

'Eve! I want adventure, Eve!'

Her eyes lit up in instant response, but he could not read her inward thought, that the major part of his adventure should be, not Aphros, but herself. He noted, however, her lighted eyes, and leaned over to her.

'You are a born adventurer, Eve, also.'

She remained silent, but her eyes continued to dwell on him, and to herself she was thinking, always sardonic although the matter was of such perennial, such all-eclipsing importance to her,—

'A la bonne heure, he realises my existence.'

'What a pity you are not a boy; we could have seen the adventure of the Islands through together.'

('The Islands always!' she thought reufully.)

'I should like to cross to Aphros to-night,' he murmured, with absent eyes . . .

('Gone again,' she thought. 'I held him for a moment.')

When they reached the house no servants were visible, but in reply to the bell a young servant appeared, scared, white-faced, and, as rapidly disappearing, was replaced by the old major-domo. He burst open the door into the passage, a crowd of words pressing on each other's heels in his mouth; he had expected Julian alone; when he saw Eve, who was idly turning over the letters that awaited her, he clapped his hand tightly over his lips, and stood, struggling with his speech, balancing himself in his arrested impetus on his toes.

'Well, Nicolas?' said Julian.

The major-domo exploded, removing his hand from his mouth,—

'Kyrie! a word alone . . .' and as abruptly replaced the constraining fingers.

Julian followed him through the swing door into the servants' quarters, where the torrent broke loose.

'Kyrie, a disaster! I have sent men with a stretcher. I remained in the house myself looking for your return. Father Paul—yes, yes, it is he—drowned—yes, drowned—at the bottom of the garden. Come, Kyrie, for the love of God. Give directions. I am too old a man. God be praised, you have come. Only hasten. The men are there already with lanterns.'

He was clinging helplessly to Julian's wrist, and kept moving his fingers up and down Julian's arm, twitching fingers that sought reassurance from firmer muscles, in a

144

distracted way, while his eyes beseechingly explored Julian's face.

Julian, shocked, jarred, incredulous, shook off the feeble fingers in irritation. The thing was an outrage on the excitement of the day. The transition to tragedy was so violent that he wished, in revolt, to disbelieve it.

'You must be mistaken, Nicolas!'

'Kyrie, I am not mistaken. The body is lying on the shore. You can see it there. I have sent lanterns and a stretcher. I beg of you to come.'

He spoke, tugging at Julian's sleeve, and as Julian remained unaccountably immovable he sank to his knees, clasping his hands and raising imploring eyes. His fustanelle spread its pleats in a circle on the stone floor. His story had suddenly become vivid to Julian with the words, 'The body is lying on the shore'; 'drowned,' he had said before, but that had summoned no picture. The body was lying on the shore. The body! Paul, brisk, alive, familiar, now a body, merely. The body! had a wave, washing forward, deposited it gently, and retreated without its burden? or had it floated, pale-faced under the stars, till some man, looking by chance down at the sea from the terrace at the foot of the garden, caught that pale, almost phosphorescent gleam rocking on the swell of the water?

The old major-domo followed Julian's stride between the lemon-trees, obsequious and conciliatory. The windows of the house shone behind them, the house of tragedy, where Eve remained as yet uninformed, uninvaded by the solemnity, the reality, of the present. Later, she would have to be told that a man's figure had been wrenched from their intimate and daily circle. The situation appeared grotesquely out of keeping with the foregoing day, and with the wide and gentle night.

From the paved walk under the pergola of gourds rough steps led down to the sea. Julian, pausing, perceived around the yellow squares of the lanterns the indistinct figures of men, and heard their low, disconnected talk breaking intermittently on the continuous wash of the waves. The sea that he loved filled him with a sudden revulsion for the indifference of its unceasing movement after its murder of a man. It should, in decency, have remained quiet, silent; impenetrable, unrepentant, perhaps;

145

inscrutable, but at least silent; its murmur echoed almost as the murmur of a triumph. . . .

He descended the steps. As he came into view, the men's fragmentary talk died away; their dim group fell apart; he passed between them, and stood beside the body of Paul.

Death. He had never seen it. As he saw it now, he thought that he had never beheld anything so incontestably real as its irrevocable stillness. Here was finality; here was defeat beyond repair. In the face of this judgment no revolt was possible. Only acceptance was possible. The last word in life's argument had been spoken by an adversary for long remote, forgotten; an adversary who had remained ironically dumb before the babble, knowing that in his own time, with one word, he could produce the irrefutable answer. There was something positively satisfying in the faultlessness of the conclusion. He had not thought that death would be like this. Not cruel, not ugly, not beautiful, not terrifying—merely unanswerable. He wondered now at the multitude of sensations that had chased successively across his mind or across his vision: the elections, Fru Thyregod, the jealousy of Eve, his incredulity and resentment at the news, his disinclination for action, his indignation against the indifference of the sea; these things were vain when here, at his feet, lay the ultimate solution.

Paul lay on his back, his arms straight down his sides, and his long, wiry body closely sheathed in the wet soutane. The square toes of his boots stuck up, close together, like the feet of a swathed mummy. His upturned face gleamed white with a tinge of green in the light of the lanterns, and appeared more luminous than they. So neat, so orderly he lay; but his hair, alone disordered, fell in wet red wisps across his neck and along the ground behind his head.

At that moment from the direction of Herakleion there came a long hiss and a rush of bright gold up into the sky; there was a crackle of small explosions, and fountains of gold showered against the night as the first fireworks went up from the quays. Rockets soared, bursting into coloured stars among the real stars, and plumes of golden light spread themselves dazzlingly above the sea. Faint sounds of cheering were borne upon the breeze.

The men around the body of the priest waited, ignorant and bewildered, relieved that some one had come to take command. Their eyes were bent upon Julian as he stood looking down; they thought he was praying for the dead. Presently he became aware of their expectation, and pronounced with a start,—

'Bind up his hair!'

Fingers hastened clumsily to deal with the stringy red locks; the limp head was supported, and the hair knotted somehow into a semblance of its accustomed roll. The old major-domo quavered in a guilty voice, as though taking the blame for carelessness,—

'The hat is lost, Kyrie.'

Julian let his eyes travel over the little group of men, islanders all, with an expression of searching inquiry.

'Which of you made this discovery?'

It appeared that one of them, going to the edge of the sea in expectation of the fireworks, had noticed, not the darkness of the body, but the pallor of the face, in the water not far out from the rocks. He had waded in and drawn the body ashore. Dead Paul lay there deaf and indifferent to this account of his own finding.

'No one can explain. . . .'

Ah, no! and he, who could have explained, was beyond the reach of their curiosity. Julian looked at the useless lips, unruffled even by a smile of sarcasm. He had known Paul all his life, had learnt from him, travelled with him, eaten with him, chaffed him lightly, but never, save in that one moment when he had gripped the priest by the wrist and had looked with steadying intention into his eyes, had their intimate personalities brushed in passing. Julian had no genius for friendship ... He began to see that this death had ended an existence which had run parallel with, but utterly walled off from, his own.

In shame the words tore themselves from him,—

'Had he any trouble?'

The men slowly, gravely, mournfully shook their heads. They could not tell. The priest had moved amongst them, charitable, even saintly; yes, saintly, and one did not expect confidences of a priest. A priest was a man who received the confidences of other men. Julian heard, and, possessed by a strong desire, a necessity, for self-accusation, he said to them in a tone of urgent and impersonal justice, as one

147

who makes a declaration, expecting neither protest nor acquiescence,—

'I should have inquired into his loneliness.'

They were slightly startled, but, in their ignorance, not over-surprised, only wondering why he delayed in giving the order to move the body on to the stretcher and carry it up to the church. Farther up the coast, the rockets continued to soar, throwing out bubbles of green and red and orange, fantastically tawdry. Julian remained staring at the unresponsive corpse, repeating sorrowfully,—

'I should have inquired—yes, I should have inquired— into his loneliness.'

He spoke with infinite regret, learning a lesson, shedding a particle of his youth. He had taken for granted that other men's lives were as promising, as full of dissimulated eagerness, as his own. He had walked for many hours up and down Paul's study, lost in an audible monologue, expounding his theories, tossing his rough head, emphasising, enlarging, making discoveries, intent on his egotism, hewing out his convictions, while the priest sat by the table, leaning his head on his hand, scarcely contributing a word, always listening. During those hours, surely, his private troubles had been forgotten? Or had they been present, gnawing, beneath the mask of sympathy? A priest was a man who received the confidences of other men!

'Carry him up,' Julian said, 'carry him up to the church.'

He walked away alone as the dark cortège set itself in movement, his mind strangely accustomed to the fact that Paul would no longer frequent their house and that the long black figure would no longer stroll, tall and lean, between the lemon-trees in the garden. The fact was more simple and more easily acceptable than he could have anticipated. It seemed already quite an old-established fact. He remembered with a shock of surprise, and a raising of his eyebrows, that he yet had to communicate it to Eve. He knew it so well himself that he thought every one else must know it too. He was immeasurably more distressed by the tardy realisation of his own egotism in regard to Paul, than by the fact of Paul's death.

He walked very slowly, delaying the moment when he must speak to Eve. He sickened at the prospect of the numerous inevitable inquiries that would be made to him by both his father and his uncle. He would never hint to them that the priest had had a private trouble. He rejoiced to remember his former loyalty, and to know that Eve remained ignorant of that extraordinary, unexplained conversation when Paul had talked about the mice. Mice in the church! He, Julian, must see to the decent covering of the body. And of the face, especially of the face.

An immense golden wheel flared out of the darkness; whirled, and died away above the sea.

In the dim church the men had set down the stretcher before the iconostase. Julian felt his way cautiously amongst the rush-bottomed chairs. The men were standing about the stretcher, their fishing caps in their hands, awed into a whispering mysticism which Julian's voice harshly interrupted,—

'Go for a cloth, one of you—the largest cloth you can find.'

He had spoken loudly in defiance of the melancholy peace of the church, that received so complacently within its ready precincts the visible remains from which the spirit, troubled and uncompanioned in life, had fled. He had always thought the church complacent, irritatingly remote from pulsating human existence, but never more so than now when it accepted the dead body as by right, firstly within its walls, and lastly within its ground, to decompose and rot, the body of its priest, among the bodies of other once vital and much-enduring men.

'Kyrie, we can find only two large cloths, one a dust-sheet, and one a linen cloth to spread over the altar. Which are we to use?'

'Which is the larger?'

'Kyrie, the dust-sheet, but the altar-cloth is of linen edged with lace.'

'Use the dust-sheet; dust to dust,' said Julian bitterly.

Shocked and uncomprehending, they obeyed. The black figure now became a white expanse, under which the limbs and features defined themselves as the folds sank into place.

'He is completely covered over?'

'Completely, Kyrie.'

'The mice cannot run over his face?'

'Kyrie, no!'

'Then no more can be done until one of you ride into Herakleion for the doctor.'

He left them, re-entering the garden by the side-gate which Paul had himself constructed with his capable, carpenter's hands. There was now no further excuse for delay; he must exchange the darkness for the unwelcome light, and must share out his private knowledge to Eve. Those men, fisherfolk, simple folk, had not counted as human spectators, but rather as part of the brotherhood of night, nature, and the stars.

He waited for Eve in the drawing-room, having assured himself that she had been told nothing, and there, presently, he saw her come in, her heavy hair dressed high, a fan and a flower drooping from her hand, and a fringed Spanish shawl hanging its straight silk folds from her escaping shoulders. Before her indolence, and her slumbrous delicacy, he hesitated. He wildly thought that he would allow the news to wait. Tragedy, reality, were at that moment so far removed from her. . . . She said in delight, coming up to him, and forgetful that they were in the house in obedience to a mysterious and urgent message,—

'Julian, have you seen the fireworks? Come out into the garden. We'll watch.'

He put his arm through her bare arm,—

'Eve, I must tell you something.'

'Fru Thyregod?' she cried, and the difficulty of his task became all but insurmountable.

'Something serious. Something about Father Paul.'

Her strange eyes gave him a glance of undefinable suspicion.

'What about him?'

'He has been found, in the water, at the bottom of the garden.'

'In the water?'

'In the sea. Drowned.'

He told her all the circumstances, doggedly, conscientiously, under the mockery of the tinsel flames that streamed out from the top of the columns, and of the distant lights flashing through the windows, speaking as a man who proclaims in a foreign country a great truth bought by the harsh experience of his soul, to an audience unconversant with his alien tongue. This truth that he had won, in the presence of quiet stars, quieter death, and simple men, was desecrated by its recital to a vain woman in a room where the very architecture was based on falsity. Still he persevered, believing that his own intensity of feeling must end in piercing its way to the foundations of her heart. He laid bare even his harassing conviction of his neglected responsibility,—

'I should have suspected . . . I should have suspected. . . .'

He looked at Eve; she had broken down and was sobbing, Paul's name mingled incoherently with her sobs. He did not doubt that she was profoundly shocked, but with a new-found cynicism he ascribed her tears to shock rather than to sorrow. He himself would have been incapable of shedding a single tear. He waited quietly for her to recover herself.

'Oh, Julian! Poor Paul! How terrible to die like that, alone, in the sea, at night. . . .' For a moment her eyes were expressive of real horror, and she clasped Julian's hand, gazing at him while all the visions of her imagination were alive in her eyes. She seemed to be on the point of adding something further, but continued to cry for a few moments, and then said, greatly sobered, 'You appear to take for granted that he has killed himself?'

He considered this. Up to the present no doubt whatever had existed in his mind. The possibility of an accident had not occurred to him. The very quality of repose and peace that he had witnessed had offered itself to him as the manifest evidence that the man had sought the only solution for a life grown unendurable. He had acknowledged the man's wisdom, bowing before his recognition of the conclusive infallibility of death as a means of escape. Cowardly? so men often said, but circumstances were conceivable—circumstances in the present case unknown, withheld, and therefore not to be violated by so much as a hazarded guess—circumstances were conceivable in which no other course was to be contemplated. He replied with gravity,—

'I do believe he put an end to his life.'

The secret reason would probably never be disclosed; even if it came within sight, Julian must now turn his eyes the other way. The secret which he might have, nay, should have, wrenched from his friend's reserve while he still lived, must remain sacred and unprofaned now that he was dead. Not only must he guard it from his own

151

knowledge, but from the knowledge of others. With this resolution he perceived that he had already blundered.

'Eve, I have been wrong; this thing must be presented as an accident. I have no grounds for believing that he took his life. I must rely on you to support me. In fairness on poor Paul ... He told me nothing. A man has a right to his own reticence.'

He paused, startled at the truth of his discovery, and cried out, taking his head between his hands,—

'Oh God! the appalling loneliness of us all!'

He shook his head despairingly for a long moment with his hands pressed over his temples. Dropping his hands with a gesture of discouragement and lassitude, he regarded Eve.

'I've found things out to-night, I think I've aged by five years. I know that Paul suffered enough to put an end to himself. We can't tell what he suffered from. I never intended to let you think he had suffered. We must never let any one else suspect it. But imagine the stages and degrees of suffering which led him to that state of mind; imagine his hours, his days, and specially his nights. I looked on him as a village priest, limited to his village; I thought his long hair funny; God forgive me, I slightly despised him. You, Eve, you thought him ornamental, a picturesque appendage to the house. And all that while, he was moving slowly towards the determination that he must kill himself ... Perhaps, probably, he took his decision yesterday, when you and I were at the picnic. When Fru Thyregod ... For months, perhaps, or for years, he had been living with the secret that was to kill him. He knew, but no one else knew. He shared his knowledge with no one. I think I shall never look at a man again without awe, and reverence, and terror.'

He was trembling strongly, discovering his fellows, discovering himself, his glowing eyes never left Eve's face. He went on talking rapidly, as though eager to translate all there was to translate into words before the aroused energy deserted him.

'You vain, you delicate, unreal thing, do you understand at all? Have you ever seen a dead man? You don't know the meaning of pain. You inflict pain for your amusement. You thing of leisure, you toy! Your deepest emotion is your jealousy. You can be jealous even where you cannot

152

love. You make a plaything of men's pain—you woman! You can change your personality twenty times a day. You can't understand a man's slow, coherent progression; he, always the same person, scarred with the wounds of the past. To wound you would be like wounding a wraith.'

Under the fury of his unexpected outburst, she protested,—

'Julian, why attack me? I've done, I've said, nothing.'

'You listened uncomprehendingly to me, thinking if you thought at all, that by to-morrow I should have forgotten my mood of to-night. You are wrong. I've gone a step forward to-day. I've learnt ... Learnt, I mean, to respect men who suffer. Learnt the continuity and the coherence of life. Days linked to days. For you, an episode is an isolated episode.'

He softened.

'No wonder you look bewildered. If you want the truth, I am angry with myself for my blindness towards Paul. Poor little Eve! I only meant half I said.'

'You meant every word; one never speaks the truth so fully as when one speaks it unintentionally.'

He smiled, but tolerantly and without malice.

'Eve betrays herself by the glibness of the axiom. You know nothing of truth. But I've seen truth to-night. All Paul's past life is mystery, shadow, enigma to me, but at the same time there is a central light—blinding, incandescent light—which is the fact that he suffered. Suffered so much that, a priest, he preferred the supreme sin to such suffering. Suffered so much that, a man, he preferred death to such suffering! All his natural desire for life was conquered. That irresistible instinct, that primal law, that persists even to the moment when darkness and unconsciousness overwhelm us—the fight for life, the battle to retain our birthright—all this was conquered. The instinct to escape from life became stronger than the instinct to preserve it! Isn't that profoundly illuminating?'

He paused.

'That fact sweeps, for me, like a great searchlight over an abyss of pain. The pain the man must have endured before he arrived at such a reversal of his religion and of his most primitive instinct! His world was, at the end, turned upside down. A terrifying nightmare. He took the only course. You cannot think how final death is—so final, so simple. So simple. There is no more to be said. I had no idea . . .'

He spoke himself with the simplicity he was trying to express. He said again, candidly, evenly, in a voice from which all the emotion had passed,—

'So simple.'

They were silent for a long time. He had forgotten her, and she was wondering whether she dared now recall him to the personal. She had listened, gratified when he attacked her, resentful when he forgot her, bored with his detachment, but wise enough to conceal both her resentment and her boredom. She had worshipped him in his anger, and had admired his good looks in the midst of his fire. She had been infinitely more interested in him than in Paul. Shocked for a moment by Paul's death, aware of the stirrings of pity, she had quickly neglected both for the sake of the living Julian.

She reviewed a procession of phrases with which she might recall his attention.

'You despise me, Julian.'

'No, I only dissociate you. You represent a different sphere. You belong to Herakleion. I love you—in your place.'

'You are hurting me.'

He put his hands on her shoulders and turned her towards the light. She let him have his way, with the disconcerting humility he had sometimes found in her. She bore his inspection mutely, her hands dropping loosely by her sides, fragile before his strength. He found that his thoughts had swept back, away from death, away from Paul, to her sweetness and her worthlessness.

'Many people care for you—more fools they,' he said. 'You and I, Eve, must be allies now. You say I despise you. I shall do so less if I can enlist your loyalty in Paul's cause. He has died as the result of an accident. Are you to be trusted?'

He felt her soft shoulders move in the slightest shrug under the pressure of his hands.

'Do you think,' she asked, 'that you will be believed?'

'I shall insist upon being believed. There is no evidence—is there?—to prove me wrong.'

As she did not answer, he repeated his question, then released her in suspicion.

'What do you know? tell me!'

After a very long pause, he said quietly,—

'I understand. There are many ways of conveying information. I am very blind about some things. Heavens! if I had suspected that truth, either you would not have remained here, or Paul would not have remained here. A priest! Unheard of ... A priest to add to your collection. First Miloradovitch, now Paul. Moths pinned upon a board. He loved you? Oh,' he cried in a passion, 'I see it all: he struggled, you persisted—till you secured him. A joke to you. Not a joke now—surely not a joke, even to you—but a triumph. Am I right? A triumph! A man, dead for you. A priest. You allowed me to talk, knowing all the while.'

'I am very sorry for Paul,' she said absently.

He laughed at the pitiably inadequate word.

'Have the courage to admit that you are flattered. More flattered than grieved. Sorry for Paul—yes, toss him that conventional tribute before turning to the luxury of your gratified vanity. That such things can be! Surely men and women live in different worlds?'

'But, Julian, what could I do?'

'He told you he loved you?'

She acquiesced, and he stood frowning at her, his hands buried in his pockets and his head thrust forward, picturing the scenes, which had probably been numerous, between her and the priest, letting his imagination play over the anguish of his friend and Eve's indifference. That she had not wholly discouraged him, he was sure. She would not so easily have let him go. Julian was certain, as though he had observed their interviews from a hidden corner, that she had amusedly provoked him, watched him with half-closed, ironical eyes, dropped him a judicious word in her honeyed voice, driven him to despair by her disregard, raised him to joy by her capricious friendliness. They had had every opportunity for meeting. Eve was strangely secretive. All had been carried on unsuspected. At this point he spoke aloud, almost with admiration,—

'That you, who are so shallow, should be so deep!'

A glimpse of her life had been revealed to him, but what secrets remained yet hidden? The veils were lifting from his simplicity; he contemplated, as it were, a new world—Eve's world, ephemerally and clandestinely populated. He contemplated it in fascination, acknowledging that here was an additional, a separate art, insistent for recognition, dominating, imperative, forcing itself impudently upon mankind, exasperating to the straight-minded because it imposed itself, would not be denied, was subtle, pretended so unswervingly to dignity that dignity was accorded it by a credulous humanity—the art which Eve practised, so vain, so cruel, so unproductive, the most fantastically prosperous of impostors!

She saw the marvel in his eyes, and smiled slightly.

'Well, Julian?'

'I am wondering,' he cried, 'wondering! trying to pierce to your mind, your peopled memory, your present occupation, your science. What do you know? what have you heard? What have you seen? You, so young ... Who are not young. How many secrets like the secret of Paul are buried away in your heart? That you will never betray? Do you ever look forward to the procession of your life? You, so young. I think you have some extraordinary, instinctive, inherited wisdom, some ready-made heritage, bequeathed to you by generations, that compensates for the deficiencies of your own experience. Because you are so young. And so old, that I am afraid.'

'Poor Julian,' she murmured. A gulf of years lay between them, and she spoke to him as a woman to a boy. He was profoundly shaken, while she remained quiet, gently sarcastic, pitying towards him, who, so vastly stronger than she, became a bewildered child upon her own ground. He had seen death, but she had seen, toyed with, dissected the living heart. She added, 'Don't try to understand. Forget me and be yourself. You are annoying me.'

She had spoken the last words with such impatience, that, torn from his speculations, he asked,—

'Annoying you? Why?'

After a short hesitation she gave him the truth,—

'I dislike seeing you at fault.'

He passed to a further bewilderment.

'I want you infallible.'

Rousing herself from the chair where she had been indolently lying, she said in the deepest tones of her contralto voice,—

'Julian, you think me worthless and vain; you condemn me as that without the charity of any further thought.

You are right to think me heartless towards those I don't love. You believe that I spend my life in vanity. Julian, I only ask to be taken away from my life; I have beliefs, and I have creeds, both of my own making, but I'm like a ship without a rudder. I'm wasting my life in vanity. I'm capable of other things. I'm capable of the deepest good, I know, as well as of the most shallow evil. Nobody knows, except perhaps Kato a little, how my real life is made up of dreams and illusions that I cherish. People are far more unreal to me than my own imaginings. One of my beliefs is about you. You mustn't ever destroy it. I believe you could do anything.'

'No, no,' he said, astonished.

But she insisted, lit by the flame of her conviction.

'Yes, anything. I have the profoundest contempt for the herd—to which you don't belong. I have believed in you since I was a child; believed in you, I mean, as something Olympian of which I was frightened. I have always known that you would justify my faith.'

'But I am ordinary, normal!' he said, defending himself. He mistrusted her profoundly; wondered what attack she was engineering. Experience of her had taught him to be sceptical.

'Ah, don't you see, Julian, when I am sincere?' she said, her voice breaking. 'I am telling you now one of the secrets of my heart, if you only knew it. The gentle, the amiable, the pleasant—yes, they're my toys. I'm cruel, I suppose. I'm always told so. I don't care; they're worth nothing. It does their little souls good to pass through the mill. But you, my intractable Julian. . . .'

'Kyrie,' said Nicolas, appearing, 'Tsantilas Tsigaridis, from Aphros, asks urgently whether you will receive him?'

'Bring him in,' said Julian, conscious of relief, for Eve's words had begun to trouble him.

Outside, the fireworks continued to flash like summer lightning.

Six

TSIGARIDIS came forward into the room, his fishing cap between his fingers, and his white hair standing out in bunches of wiry curls round his face. Determination was written in the set gravity of his features, even in the respectful bow with which he came to a halt before Julian. Interrupted in their conversation, Eve had fallen back, half lying, in her arm-chair, and Julian, who had been pacing up and down, stood still with folded arms, a frown cleaving a deep valley between his brows. He spoke to Tsigaridis,—

'You asked for me, Tsantilas?'

'I am a messenger, Kyrie.'

He looked from the young man to the girl, his age haughty towards their youth, his devotion submissive towards the advantage of their birth. He said to Julian, using almost the same words as he had used once before,—

'The people of Aphros are the people of your people,' and he bowed again.

Julian had recovered his self-possession; he no longer felt dazed and bewildered as he had felt before Eve. In speaking to Tsigaridis he was speaking of things he understood. He knew very well the summons Tsigaridis was bringing him, the rude and fine old man, single-sighted as a prophet, direct and unswerving in the cause he had at heart. He imagined, with almost physical vividness, the hand of the fisherman on his shoulder, impelling him forward.

'Kyrie,' Tsigaridis continued, 'to-day the flag of Herakleion flew from the house of your honoured father until you with your own hand threw it down. I was in Herakleion, where the news was brought to me, and there is no doubt that by now it is known also on Aphros. Your action can be interpreted only in one way. I know that to-day'—he crossed himself devoutly—'Father Paul, who was our friend and yours, has met his death; I break in upon your sorrow; I dared not wait; even death must not delay me. Kyrie, I come up to bring you back to Aphros.'

'I will go to-night,' said Julian without hesitation. 'My father and my uncle are in Herakleion, and I will start from here before they can stop me. Have you a boat?'

'I can produce one,' said Tsigaridis, very erect, and looking at Julian with shining eyes.

'Then I will meet you at the private jetty in two hours' time. We shall be unnoted in the darkness, and the illuminations will be over by then.'

'Assuredly,' said the fisherman.

'We go in all secrecy,' Julian added. 'Tsantilas, listen: can you distribute two orders for me by nightfall? I understand that you have organised a system of communications?'

The old man's face relaxed slowly from its stern dignity; it softened into a mixture of slyness and pride and tenderness—the tenderness of a father for his favourite child. Almost a smile struggled with his lips. A strange contortion troubled his brows. Slowly and portentously, he winked.

'Then send word to Aphros,' said Julian, 'that no boat be allowed to leave the Islands, and send word round the mainland recalling every available islander. Is it possible? I know that every islander in Herakleion to-night is sitting with boon companions in buried haunts, talking, talking, talking. Call them together, Tsantilas.'

'It will be done, Kyrie.'

'And Madame Kato—she must be informed.'

'Kyrie, she sends you a message that she leaves Herakleion by to-night's train for Athens. When her work is done in Athens, she also will return to Aphros.'

Tsigaridis took a step forward and lifted Julian's hands to his lips as was his wont. He bowed, and with his patriarchal gravity left the room.

Julian in a storm of excitement flung himself upon his knees beside Eve's chair.

'Eve!' he cried. 'Oh, the wild adventure! Do you understand? It has come at last. Paul—I had almost forgotten the Islands for him, and now I must forget him for the Is-

159

lands. Too much has happened to-day. To-morrow all Herakleion will know that the Islands have broken away, and that I and every islander are upon Aphros. They will come at first with threats; they will send representatives. I shall refuse to retract our declaration. Then they will begin to carry out their threats. Panaïoannou—think of it!—will organise an attack with boats.' He became sunk in practical thought, from which emerging he said more slowly and carefully. 'They will not dare to bombard the island because they know that Italy and Greece are watching every move, and with a single man-of-war could blow the whole town of Herakleion higher than Mount Mylassa. Kato will watch over us from Athens ... They will dare to use no more than reasonable violence. And they will never gain a footing.'

Eve was leaning forward; she put both hands on his shoulders as he knelt.

'Go on talking to me,' she said, 'my darling.'

In a low, intense voice, with unseeing eyes, he released all the flood of secret thought that he had, in his life, expressed only to Paul and to Kato.

'I went once to Aphros, more than a year ago; you remember. They asked me then, through Tsigaridis, whether I could champion them if they needed championship. I said I would. Father was very angry. He is incomprehensibly cynical about the Islands, so cynical that I have been tempted to think him merely mercenary, anxious to live at peace with Herakleion for the sake of his profits. He is as cynical as Malteios, or any stay-in-power politician here. He read me a lecture and called the people a lot of rebellious good-for-nothings. Eve, what do I care? One thing is true, one thing is real: those people suffer. Everything on earth is empty, except pain. Paul suffered, so much that he preferred to die. But a whole people doesn't die. I went away to England, and I put Herakleion aside, but at the bottom of my heart I never thought of anything else; I knew I was bound to those people, and I lived, I swear to you, with the sole idea that I should come back, and that this adventure of rescue would happen some day exactly as it is happening now. I thought of Kato and of Tsigaridis as symbolical, almost mythological beings; my tutelary deities; Kato vigorous, and Tsigaridis stern. Eve, I would rather die than read disappointment in that man's eyes. I never made him many promises, but he must find me better than my word.'

He got up and walked once or twice up and down the room, beating his fist against his palm and saying,—

'Whatever good I do in my life, will be done in the Islands.'

He came back and stood by Eve.

'Eve, yesterday morning when I rode over the hills I saw the Islands lying out in the sea ... I thought of father, cynical and indifferent, and of Stavridis, a self-seeker. I wondered whether I should grow into that. I thought that in illusion lay the only loveliness.'

'Ah, how I agree!' she said fervently.

He dropped on his knees again beside her, and she put her fingers lightly on his hair.

'When Tsigaridis came, you were telling me that you believed in me—Heaven knows why. For my part, I only believe that one can accomplish when one has faith in a cause, and is blind to one's own fate. And I believe that the only cause worthy of such faith, is the redemption of souls from pain. I set aside all doubt. I will listen to no argument, and I will walk straight towards the object I have chosen. If my faith is an illusion, I will make that illusion into a reality by the sheer force of my faith.'

He looked up at Eve, whose eyes were strangely intent on him.

'You see,' he said, fingering the fringe of her Spanish shawl, 'Herakleion is my battleground, and if I am to tilt against windmills it must be in Herakleion. I have staked out Herakleion for my own, as one stakes out a claim in a gold-mining country. The Islands are the whole adventure of youth for me.'

'And what am I?' she murmured to him.

He looked at her without appearing to see her; he propped his elbow on her knee, leant his chin in his palm, and went on talking about the Islands.

'I know that I am making the thing into a religion, but then I could never live, simply drifting along. Aimless ... I don't understand existence on those terms. I am quite prepared to give everything for my idea; father can disinherit me, and I know I am very likely to be killed. I don't care. I may be mistaken; I may be making a blunder, an error of judgment. I don't care. Those people are mine. Those Islands are my faith. I am blind.'

'And you enjoy the adventure,' she said.

'Of course, I enjoy the adventure. But there is more in it than that,' he said, shaking his head; 'there is conviction, burnt into me. Fanatical. Whoever is ready to pay the ultimate price for his belief, has a right to that belief. Heaven preserve me,' he cried, showing his fist, 'from growing like father, or Malteios, or Stavridis. Eve, you understand.'

She murmured again,—

'And what am I? What part have I got in this world of yours?'

Again he did not appear to hear her, but making an effort to get up, he said,—

'I promised to meet Tsantilas, and I must go,' but she pressed her hands on his shoulders and held him down.

'Stay a little longer. I want to talk to you.'

Kneeling there, he saw at last that her mouth was very resolute and her eyes full of a desperate decision. She sat forward in her chair, so close to him that he felt the warmth of her body, and saw that at the base of her throat a little pulse was beating quickly.

'What is it, Eve?'

'This,' she said, 'that if I let you go I may never see you again. How much time have you?'

He glanced at the heavy clock between the lapis columns.

'An hour and a half.'

'Give me half an hour.'

'Do you want to stop me from going?'

'Could I stop you if I tried?'

'I should never listen to you.'

'Julian,' she said, 'I rarely boast, as you know, but I am wondering now how many people in Herakleion would abandon their dearest ideals for me? If you think my boast is empty—remember Paul.'

He paused for a moment, genuinely surprised by the point of view she presented to him.

'But I am different,' he said then, quite simply and with an air of finality.

She laughed a low, delighted laugh.

'You have said it: you are different. Of course you are different. So different, that you never notice me. People

162

cringe to me—oh, I may say this to you—but you, Julian, either you are angry with me or else you forget me.'

She looked at the clock, and for the first time a slight loss of self-assurance came over her, surprising and attractive in her, who seemed always to hold every situation in such contemptuous control.

'Only half an hour,' she said, 'and I have to say to you all that which I have been at such pains to conceal— hoping all the while that you would force the gates of my concealment, trample on my hypocrisy!'

Her eyes lost their irony and became troubled; she gazed at him with the distress of a child. He was uneasily conscious of his own embarrassment; he felt the shame of taking unawares the self-reliant in a moment of weakness, the mingled delight and perplexity of the hunter who comes suddenly upon the nymph, bare and gleaming, at the edge of a pool. All instinct of chivalry urged him to retreat until she should have recovered her self-possession. He desired to help her, tender and protective; and again, relentlessly, he would have outraged her reticence, forced her to the uttermost lengths of self-revelation, spared her no abasement, enjoyed her humiliation. Simultaneously, he wanted the triumph over her pride, the battle joined with a worthy foe; and the luxury of comforting her new and sudden pathos, as he alone, he knew, could comfort it. She summoned in him, uncivilised and wholly primitive, a passion of tyranny and a passion of possessive protection.

He yielded to the former, and continued to look at her in expectation, without speaking.

'Help me a little, Julian,' she murmured piteously, keeping her eyes bent on her hands, which were lying in her lap. 'Look back a little, and remember me. I can remember you so well: coming and going and disregarding me, or furiously angry with me; very often unkind to me; tolerant of me sometimes; negligently, insultingly, certain of me always!'

'We used to say that although we parted for months, we always came together again.'

She raised her eyes, grateful to him, as he still knelt on the floor in front of her, but he was not looking at her; he was staring at nothing, straight in front of him.

'Julian,' she said, and spoke of their childhood, knowing

163

that her best hope lay in keeping his thoughts distant from the present evening.

Her distress, which had been genuine, had passed. She had a vital game to play, and was playing it with the full resources of her ability. She swept the chords lightly, swift to strike again that chord which had whispered in response. She bent a little closer to him.

'I have always had this belief in you, of which I told you. You and I both have in us the making of fanatics. We never have led, and never should lead, the tame life of the herd.'

She touched him with that, and regained command over his eyes, which this time she held unswervingly. But, having forced him to look at her, she saw a frown gathering on his brows; he sprang to his feet, and made a gesture as if to push her from him.

'You are playing with me; if you saw me lying dead on that rug you would turn from me as indifferently as from Paul.'

At this moment of her greatest danger, as he stood towering over her, she dropped her face into her hands, and he looked down only upon the nape of her neck and her waving hair. Before he could speak she looked up again, her eyes very sorrowful under plaintive brows.

'Do I deserve that you should say that to me? I never pretended to be anything but indifferent to those I didn't love. I should have been more hypocritical. You despise me now, so I pay the penalty of my own candour. I have not the pleasant graces of a Fru Thyregod, Julian; not towards you, that is. I wouldn't offer you the insult of an easy philandering. I might make your life a burden; I might even kill you. I know I have often been impossible towards you in the past. I should probably be still more impossible in the future. If I loved you less, I should, no doubt, love you better. You see that I am candid.'

He was struck, and reflected: she spoke truly, there was indeed a vein of candour which contradicted and redeemed the petty deceits and untruthfulnesses which so exasperated and offended him. But he would not admit his hesitation.

'I have told you a hundred times that you are cruel and vain and irredeemably worthless.'

She answered after a pause, in the deep and wonderful voice which she knew so well how to use,—

'You are more cruel than I; you hurt me more than I can say.'

He resisted his impulse to renounce his words, to pretend that he had chosen them in deliberate malice. As he said nothing, she added,—

'Besides, have I ever shown myself any of those things to you? I haven't been cruel to you; I haven't even been selfish; you have no right to find fault with me.'

She had blundered; he flew into a rage.

'Your damned feminine reasoning! Your damned personal point of view! I can see well enough the fashion in which you treat other men. I don't judge you only by your attitude towards myself.'

Off her guard, she was really incapable of grasping his argument; she tried to insist, to justify herself, but before his storm of anger she cowered away.

'Julian, how you frighten me.'

'You only pretend to be frightened.'

'You are brutal; you mangle every word I say,' she said hopelessly.

He had reduced her to silence; he stood over her threateningly, much as a tamer of wild beasts who waits for the next spring of the panther. Desperate, her spirit flamed up again, and she cried,—

'You treat me monstrously; I am a fool to waste my time over you; I am accustomed to quite different treatment.'

'You are spoilt; you are accustomed to flattery—flattery which means less than nothing,' he sneered, stamping upon her attempt at arrogance.

'Ah, Julian!' she said, suddenly and marvellously melting, and leaning forward she stretched out both hands towards him, so that he was obliged to take them, and she drew him down to his knees once more beside her, and smiled into his eyes, having taken command and being resolved that no crisis of anger should again arise to estrange them, 'I shall never have flattery from you, shall I? my turbulent, impossible Julian, whose most meagre compliment I have treasured ever since I can remember! but it is over now, my time of waiting for you'—she still held his hands, and the smile with which she looked at him transfigured all her face.

He was convinced; he trembled. He strove against her faintly,—

'You choose your moment badly; you know that I must leave for Aphros.'

'You cannot!' she cried in indignation.

As his eyes hardened, she checked herself; she knew that for her own safety she must submit to his will without a struggle. Spoilt, irrational as she was, she had never before so dominated her caprice. Her wits were all at work, quick slaves to her passion.

'Of course you must go,' she said.

She played with his fingers, her head bent low, and he was startled by the softness of her touch.

'What idle hands,' he said, looking at them; 'you were vain of them, as a child.'

But she did not wish him to dwell upon her vanity.

'Julian, have I not been consistent, all my life? Are you taking me seriously? Do you know that I am betraying all the truth? One hasn't often the luxury of betraying all the truth. I could betray even greater depths of truth, for your sake. Are you treating what I tell you with the gravity it deserves? You must not make a toy of my secret. I have no strength of character, Julian. I suppose, in its stead, I have been given strength of love. Do you want what I offer you? Will you take the responsibility of refusing it?'

'Is that a threat?' he asked, impressed and moved.

She shrugged slightly and raised her eyebrows; he thought he had never so appreciated the wonderful nobility of her face.

'I am nothing without the person I love. You have judged me yourself: worthless—what else?—cruel, vain. All that is true. Hitherto I have tried only to make the years pass by. Do you want me to return to such an existence?'

His natural vigour rebelled against her frailty.

'You are too richly gifted, Eve, to abandon yourself to such slackness of life.'

'I told you I had no strength of character,' she said with bitterness, 'what are my gifts, such as they are, to me? You are the thing I want.'

'You could turn your gifts to any account.'

'With you, yes.'

'No, independently of me or any other human being. One stands alone in work. Work is impersonal.'

'Nothing is impersonal to me, she replied morosely, 'that's my tragedy.'

She flung out her hands.

'Julian, I cherish such endless dreams! I loathe my life of petty adventures; I undertake them only in order to forget the ideal which until now has been denied me. I have crushed down the vision of life with you, but always it has remained at the back of my mind, so wide, so open, a life so free and so full of music and beauty, Julian! I would work—for you. I would create—for you. I don't want to marry you, Julian. I value my freedom above all things. Bondage is not for you or me. But I'll come with you anywhere—to Aphros if you like.'

'To Aphros?' he repeated.

'Why not?'

She put in, with extraordinary skill,—

'I belong to the Islands no less than you.'

Privately she thought,—

'If you knew how little I cared about the Islands!'

He stared at her, turning her words over in his mind. He was as reckless as she, but conscientiously he suggested,—

'There may be danger.'

'I am not really a coward, only in the unimportant things. And you said yourself that they could never invade the island,' she added with complete confidence in his statement.

He dreamt aloud,—

'I have only just found her. This is Herakleion! She might, who knows? be of use to Aphros.'

She wondered which consideration weighed most heavily with him.

'You were like my sister,' he said suddenly.

She gave a rueful smile, but said nothing.

'No, no!' he cried, springing up. 'This can never be; have you bewitched me? Let me go, Eve; you have been playing a game with me.'

She shook her head very slowly and tears gathered in her eyes.

'Then the game is my whole life, Julian; put me to any test you choose to prove my sincerity.'

She convinced him against his will, and he resented it.

'You have deceived me too often.'

'I have been obliged to deceive you, because I could not tell you the truth.'

'Very plausible,' he muttered.

She waited, very well acquainted with the vehemence of his moods and reactions. She was rewarded; he said next, with laughter lurking in his eyes,—

'Ever since I can remember, I have quarrelled with you several times a day.'

'But this evening we have no time to waste in quarrelling,' she replied, relieved, and stretching out her hands to him again. As he took them, she added in a low voice, 'You attract me fatally, my refractory Julian.'

'We will go to Aphros,' he said, 'as friends and colleagues.'

'On any terms you choose to dictate,' she replied with ironical gravity.

A flash of clear-sightedness pierced his attempt at self-deception; he saw the danger into which they were deliberately running, he and she, alone amidst fantastic happenings, living in fairyland, both headstrong and impatient creatures, unaccustomed to forgo their whims, much less their passions. . . . He was obliged to recognise the character of the temple which stood at the end of the path they were treading, and of the deity to whom it was dedicated; he saw the temple with the eyes of his imagination as vividly as his mortal eyes would have seen it: white and lovely amongst cypresses, shadowy within; they would surely enter. Eve he certainly could not trust; could he trust himself? His honesty answered no. She observed the outward signs of what was passing in his mind, he started, he glanced at her, a look of horror and vigorous repudiation crossed his face, his eyes dwelt on her, then she saw—for she was quick to read him—by the slight toss of his head that he had banished sagacity.

'Come on to the veranda,' she said, tugging at his hand.

They stood on the veranda, watching the lights in the distance; the sky dripped with gold; balls of fire exploded into sheaves of golden feathers, into golden fountains and golden rain; golden slashes like the blades of scimitars cut across the curtain of night. Eve cried out with delight.

168

Fiery snakes rushed across the sky, dying in a shower of sparks. At one moment the whole of the coast-line was lit up by a violent light, which most marvellously gleamed upon the sea.

'Fairyland!' cried Eve, clapping her hands.

She had forgotten Aphros. She had forgotten Paul.

The fireworks were over. Tsigaridis pulled strongly and without haste at his oars across a wide sea that glittered now like black diamonds under the risen moon. The water rose and fell beneath the little boat as gently and as regularly as the breathing of a sleeper. On a milky sky, spangled with stars, the immense moon hung flat and motionless, casting a broad path of rough silver up the blackness of the waters, and illuminating a long stretch of little broken clouds that lay above the horizon like the vertebræ of some gigantic crocodile. The light at the tip of the pier showed green, for they saw it still from the side of the land, but as they drew farther out to sea and came on a parallel line with the light, they saw it briefly half green, half ruby; then, as they passed it, looking back they saw only the ruby glow. Tsigaridis rowed steadily, silently but for the occasional drip of the water with the lifting of an oar, driving his craft away from the lights of the mainland—the stretch of Herakleion along the coast—towards the beckoning lights in the heart of the sea.

For ahead of them clustered the little yellow lights of the sheerly-rising village on Aphros; isolated lights, three or four only, low down at the level of the harbour, then, after a dark gap representing the face of the cliff, the lights in the houses, irregular, tier above tier. But it was not to these yellow lights that the glance was drawn. High above them all, upon the highest summit of the island, flared a blood-red beacon, a fierce and solitary stain of scarlet, a flame like a flag, like an emblem, full of hope as it leapt towards the sky, full of rebellion as it tore its angry gash across the night. In the moonlight the tiny islands of the group lay darkly outlined in the sea, but the moonlight, placid and benign, was for them without significance: only the beacon, insolently red beneath the pallor of the moon, burned for them with a message that promised to all men strife, to others death, and to the survivors liberty.

The form of Aphros was no more than a silhouette under the moon, a silhouette that rose, humped and shadowy, bearing upon its crest that flower of flame; dawn might break upon an island of the purest loveliness, colour blown upon it as upon the feathers of a bird, fragile as porcelain, flushed as an orchard in blossom; to-night it lay mysterious, unrevealed, with that single flame as a token of the purpose that burned within its heart. Tenderness, loveliness, were absent from the dark shape crowned by so living, so leaping an expression of its soul! Here were resolution, anticipation, hope, the perpetual hope of betterment, the undying chimera, the sublime illusion, the lure of adventure to the rebel and the idealist alike. The flame rang out like a bugle call in the night, its glare in the darkness becoming strident indeed as the note of a bugle in the midst of silence.

A light breeze brushed the little boat as it drew away from the coast, and Tsigaridis with a word of satisfaction shipped his oars and rose, the fragile craft rocking as he moved; Eve and Julian, watching from the prow, saw a shadow creep along the mast and the triangular shape of a sail tauten itself darkly against the path of the moon. Tsigaridis sank back into an indistinguishable block of intenser darkness in the darkness at the bottom of the boat. A few murmured words had passed,—

'I will take the tiller, Tsigaridis.'

'Malista, Kyrie,' and the silence had fallen again, the boat sailing strongly before the breeze, the beacon high ahead, and the moon brilliant in the sky. Eve, not daring to speak, glanced at Julian's profile as she sat beside him. He was scowling. Had she but known, he was intensely conscious of her nearness, assailed again with that now familiar ghost, the ghost of her as he had once held her angrily in his arms, soft, heavy, defenceless; and his fingers as they closed over the tiller closed as delicately as upon the remembered curves of her body; she had taken off her hat, and the scent of her hair reached him, warm, personal; she was close to him, soft, fragrant, silent indeed, but mysteriously alive; the desire to touch her grew, like the desire of thirst; life seemed to envelop him with a strange completeness. Still a horror held him back: was it Eve, the child to whom he had been brotherly? or Eve, the woman? but in spite of his revulsion—for it was not his habit to control his desires—he changed the tiller to the other hand, and his free arm fell round her shoulders; he felt her instant yielding, her movement nearer towards him, her shortened breath, the falling back of her head; he knew that her eyes were shut; his fingers moulded themselves lingeringly round her throat; she slipped still lower within the circle of his arm, and his hand, almost involuntarily, trembled over the softness of her breast.

PART III
Aphros

One

IN THE large class-room of the school-house the dejected group of Greek officials sat among the hideous yellow desks and benches of the school-children of Aphros. Passion and indignation had spent themselves fruitlessly during the preceding evening and night. To do the islanders justice, the Greeks had not been treated with incivility. But all demands for an interview with the highest authority were met not only with a polite reply that the highest authority had not yet arrived upon the island, but also a refusal to disclose his name. The Greek officials, having been brought from their respective lodgings to the central meeting-point of the school, had been given the run of two class-rooms, one for the men, of whom there were, in all, twenty, and one for the women, of whom there were only six. They were told that they might communicate, but that armed guards would be placed in both rooms. They found most comfort in gathering, the six-and-twenty of them, in the larger class-room, while the guards, in their kilted dresses, sat on chairs, two at each entrance, with suspiciously modern and efficient-looking rifles laid across their knees.

A large proportion of the officials were, naturally, those connected with the school. They observed morosely that all notices in the pure Greek of Herakleion had already been removed, also the large lithographs of Malteios and other former Presidents, so that the walls of pitch pine—the school buildings were modern, and of wood—were now ornamented only with maps, anatomical diagrams, and some large coloured plates published by some English manufacturing firm for advertisement; there were three children riding a gray donkey, and another child trying on a sun-bonnet before a mirror; but any indication of the relationship of Aphros to Herakleion there was none.

'It is revolution,' the postmaster said gloomily.

The guards would not speak. Their natural loquacity was in abeyance before the first fire of their revolutionary ardour. From vine-cultivators they had become soldiers, and the unfamiliarity of the trade filled them with self-awe and importance. Outside, the village was surprisingly quiet; there was no shouting, no excitement; footsteps passed rapidly to and fro, but they seemed to be the footsteps of men bent on ordered business; the Greeks could not but be impressed and disquieted by the sense of organisation.

'Shall we be allowed to go free?' they asked the guards.

'You will know when he comes,' was all the guards would reply.

'Who is he?'

'You will know presently.'

'Has he still not arrived?'

'He has arrived.'

'We heard nothing; he must have arrived during the night.'

To this they received no answer, nor any to their next remark,—

'Why so much mystery? It is, of course, the scatter-brained young Englishman.'

The guards silently shrugged their shoulders, as much as to say, that any one, even a prisoner, had a right to his own opinion.

The school clock pointed to nine when the first noise of agitation began in the street. It soon became clear that a large concourse of people was assembling in the neighbourhood of the school; a slight excitement betrayed itself by some shouting and laughter, but a voice cried 'Silence!' and silence was immediately produced. Those within the school heard only the whisperings and rustlings of a crowd. They were not extravagantly surprised, knowing the islanders to be an orderly, restrained, and frugal race, their emotions trained into the sole channel of patriotism, which here was making its supreme demand upon their self-devotion. The Greeks threw wondering glances at the rifles of the guards. Ostensibly school-teachers, post and telegraph clerks, and custom-house officers, they were, of course, in reality the spies of the government of Herakleion, and as such should have had knowledge of the presence of such weapons on the island. They reflected that, undesirable as was a prolonged imprisonment in the school-house, at the mercy of a newly-liberated and probably rancorous population, a return to Herakleion might prove a no less undesirable fate at the present juncture.

Outside, some sharp words of command were followed by the click of weapons on the cobblestones; the post-master looked at the chief customs-house clerk, raised his eyebrows, jerked his head, and made a little noise: 'Tcha!' against his teeth, as much as to say, 'The deceitful villains! under our noses!' but at the back of his mind was, 'No further employment, no pension, for any of us.' A burst of cheering followed in the street. The voice cried 'Silence!' again, but this time was disregarded. The cheering continued for some minutes, the women's note joining in with the men's deep voices, and isolated words were shouted, all with the maximum of emotion. The Greeks tried to look out of the windows, but were prevented by the guards. Some one in the street began to speak, when the cheering had died away, but through the closed windows it was impossible to distinguish the words. A moment's hush followed this speaking, and then another voice began, reading impressively—it was obvious, from the unhesitating and measured scansion, that he was reading. Sections of his address, or proclamation, whichever it was, were received with deep growls of satisfaction from the crowd. At one moment he was wholly interrupted by repeated shouts of 'Viva! viva! viva!' and when he had made an end thunderous shouts of approval shook the wooden building. The Greeks were by now very pale; they could not tell whether this proclamation did not contain some reference, some decision, concerning themselves.

After the proclamation, another voice spoke, interrupted at every moment by various cries of joy and delight, especially from the women; the crowd seemed alternately rocked with enthusiasm, confidence, fire, and laughter. The laughter was not the laughter of amusement so much as the grim laughter of resolution and fraternity; an extraordinarily fraternal and unanimous spirit seemed to prevail. Then silence again, broken by voices in brief confabulation, and then the shifting of the crowd which, to judge from the noise, was pressing back against the school buildings in order to allow somebody a passage down the street.

The door opened, and Zapantiotis, appearing, announced,—

'Prisoners, the President.'

The words created a sensation among the little herd of hostages, who, for comfort and protection, had instinctively crowded together. They believed themselves miraculously rescued, at least from the spite and vengeance of the islanders, and expected to see either Malteios or Stavridis, frock-coated and top-hatted, in the doorway. Instead, they saw Julian Davenant, flushed, untidy, bareheaded, and accompanied by two immense islanders carrying rifles.

He paused and surveyed the little speechless group, and a faint smile ran over his lips at the sight of the confused faces of his prisoners. They stared at him, readjusting their ideas: in the first instance they had certainly expected Julian, then for one flashing moment they had expected the President of Herakleion, then they were confronted with Julian. A question left the lips of the postmaster,—

'President of what?'

Perhaps he was tempted madly to think that neither Malteios, nor Stavridis, but Julian, had been on the foregoing day elected President of Herakleion.

Zapantiotis answered gravely,—

'Of the Archipelago of San Zacharie.'

'Are we all crazy?' cried the postmaster.

'You see, gentlemen,' said Julian, speaking for the first time, 'that the folly of my grandfather's day has been revived.'

He came forward and seated himself at the schoolmaster's desk, his bodyguard standing a little behind him, one to each side.

'I have come here,' he said, 'to choose amongst you one representative who can carry to Herakleion the terms of the proclamation which has just been read in the marketplace outside. These terms must be communicated to the present government. Zapantiotis, hand the proclamation to these gentlemen.'

The outraged Greeks came closer together to read the proclamation over each other's shoulder; it set forth that the islands constituting the Archipelago of San Zacharie, and including the important island of Aphros, by the present proclamation, and after long years of oppression, declared themselves a free and independent republic under the presidency of Julian Henry Davenant, pending the formation of a provisional government; that if unmolested they were prepared to live in all peace and neighbourly good-fellowship with the republic of Herakleion, but that if molested in any way they were equally prepared to defend their shores and their liberty to the last drop of blood in the last man upon the Islands.

There was a certain nobleness in the resolute gravity of the wording.

Julian wore a cryptic smile as he watched the Greeks working their way through this document, which was in the Italianate Greek of the Islands. Their fingers pointed certain paragraphs out to one another, and little repressed snorts came from them, snorts of scorn and of indignation, and glances were flung at Julian lounging indifferently in the schoolmaster's chair. The doors had been closed to exclude the crowd, and of the islanders, only Zapantiotis and the guards remained in the room. Although it was early, the heat was beginning to make itself felt, and the flies were buzzing over the window-panes.

'If you have finished reading, gentlemen,' said Julian presently, 'I shall be glad if you will decide upon a representative, as I have much to attend to; a boat is waiting to take him and these ladies to the shore.'

Immense relief was manifested by the ladies.

'This thing,' said the head of the school, hitting the proclamation with his closed fingers, 'is madness; I beg you, young man—I know you quite well—to withdraw before it is too late.'

'I can have no argument; I give you five minutes to decide,' Julian replied, laying his watch on the desk.

His followers had no longer cause to fret against his indecision.

Seeing him determined, the Greeks excitedly conferred; amongst them the idea of self-preservation, rather than of self-immolation, was obviously dominant. Herakleion, for all the displeasure of the authorities, was, when it came to the point, preferable to Aphros in the hands of the islanders and their eccentric, if not actually bloodthirsty, young leader. The postmaster presented himself as senior member of the group; the schoolmaster as the most erudite, therefore the most fitted to represent his colleagues before

179

the Senate; the head clerk of the customs-house urged his claim as having the longest term of official service. The conference degenerated into a wrangle.

'I see, gentlemen, that I must take the decision out of your hands,' Julian said at length, breaking in upon them, and appointed the customs-house clerk.

But in the market-place, whither the Greek representative and the women of the party were instantly hurried, the silent throng of population waited in packed and coloured ranks. The men stood apart, arms folded, handkerchiefs bound about their heads under their wide straw hats—they waited, patient, confident, unassuming. None of them was armed with rifles, although many carried a pistol or a long knife slung at his belt; the customs-house clerk, through all his confusion of mingled terror and relief, noted the fact; if he delivered it at a propitious moment, it might placate an irate Senate. No rifles, or, at most, eight in the hands of the guards! Order would very shortly be restored in Aphros.

Nevertheless, that sense of organisation, of discipline, of which the Greeks had been conscious while listening to the assembling of the crowd through the boards of the school-house, was even more apparent here upon the market-place. These islanders knew their business. A small file of men detached itself as an escort for the representative and the women. Julian came from the school at the same moment with his two guards, grim and attentive, behind him. A movement of respect produced itself in the crowd. The customs-house clerk and his companions were not allowed to linger, but were marched away to the steps which led down to the jetty. They carried away with them as their final impression of Aphros the memory of the coloured throng and of Julian, a few paces in advance, watching their departure.

The proclamation, the scene in the school-house, remained as the prelude to the many pictures which populated Julian's memory, interchangeably, of that day. He saw himself, speaking rarely, but, as he knew, to much purpose, seated at the head of a table in the village assembly-room, and, down each side of the table, the principal men of the Islands, Tsigaridis and Zapantiotis on his either hand, grave counsellors; he heard their speech, unreproducibly magnificent, because a bodyguard of facts supported every phrase; because, in the background, thronged the years of endurance and the patient, steadfast hope. He heard the terms of the new constitution, and the oath of resolution to which every man subscribed. With a swimming brain, and his eyes fixed upon the hastily-restored portrait of his grandfather, he heard the references to himself as head of the state—a state in which the citizens numbered perhaps five thousand. He heard his own voice, issuing orders whose wisdom was never questioned: no boat to leave the Islands, no boats to be admitted to the port, without his express permission, a system of sentries to be instantly instituted and maintained, day and night. As he delivered these orders, men rose in their places, assuming the responsibility, and left the room to execute them without delay.

He saw himself later, still accompanied by Tsigaridis and Zapantiotis, but having rid himself of his two guards, in the interior of the island, on the slopes where the little rough stone walls retained the terraces, and where between the trunks of the olive-trees the sea moved, blue and glittering, below. Here the island was dry and stony; mule-paths, rising in wide, low steps, wandered up the slopes and lost themselves over the crest of the hill. A few goats moved restlessly among cactus and bramble-bushes, cropping at the prickly stuff, and now and then raising their heads to bleat for the kids that, more light-hearted because not under the obligation of searching for food amongst the vegetation, leapt after one another, up and down, in a happy chain on their little stiff certain legs from terrace to terrace. An occasional cypress rose in a dark spire against the sky. Across the sea, the town of Herakleion lay, white, curved, and narrow, with its coloured sunblinds no bigger than butterflies, along the strip of coast that Mount Mylassa so grudgingly allowed it.

The stepped paths being impassable for carts, Tsigaridis had collected ten mules with panniers, that followed in a string. Julian rode ahead upon another mule; Zapantiotis walked, his tall staff in his hand, and his dog at his heels. Julian remembered idly admiring the health which enabled this man of sixty-five to climb a constantly-ascending path under a burning sun without showing any signs of exhaustion. As they went, the boy in charge of the mules droned out a mournful native song which Julian recognised as having heard upon the lips of Kato. The crickets chirped unceasingly, and overhead the seagulls circled uttering their peculiar cry.

They had climbed higher, finally leaving behind them the olive-terraces and coming to a stretch of vines, the autumn vine-leaves ranging through every shade of yellow, red, and orange; here, away from the shade of the olives, the sun burned down almost unbearably, and the stones of the rough walls were too hot for the naked hand to touch. Here it was that the grapes were spread out, drying into currants—a whole terrace heaped with grapes, over which a party of young men, who sat playing at dice beneath a rough shelter made out of reeds and matting, were mounting guard.

Julian, knowing nothing of this business, and present only out of interested curiosity, left the command to Zapantiotis. A few stone-pines grew at the edge of the terrace; he moved his mule into their shade while he watched. They had reached the summit of the island—no doubt, if he searched far enough, he would come across the ruins of last night's beacon, but he preferred to remember it as a living thing rather than to stumble with his foot against ashes, gray and dead; he shivered a little, in spite of the heat, at the thought of that flame already extinguished—and from the summit he could look down upon both slopes, seeing the island actually as an island, with the sea below upon every side, and he could see the other islands of the group, speckled around, some of them too tiny to be inhabited, but all deserted now, when in the common cause every soul had been summoned by the beacon, the preconcerted signal, to Aphros. He imagined the little isolated boats travelling across the moonlit waters during the night, as he himself had travelled; little boats, each under its triangular sail, bearing the owner, his women, his children, and such poor belongings as he could carry, making for the port or the creeks of Aphros, relying for shelter upon the fraternal hospitality of the inhabitants. No doubt they, like himself, had travelled with their eyes upon the beacon. . . .

The young men, grinning broadly and displaying a zest they would not have contributed towards the mere routine of their lives, had left their skeleton shelter and had fallen to work upon the heaps of drying grapes with their large, purple-stained, wooden shovels. Zapantiotis leant upon his staff beside Julian's mule.

"See, Kyrie!' he had said. 'It was a crafty thought, was it not? Ah, women! only a woman could have thought of such a thing.'

'A woman?'

'Anastasia Kato,' the overseer had replied, reverent towards the brain that had contrived thus craftily for the cause, but familiar towards the great singer—of whom distinguished European audiences spoke with distant respect—as towards a woman of his own people. He probably, Julian had reflected, did not know of her as a singer at all.

Beneath the grapes rifles were concealed, preserved from the fruit by careful sheets of coarse linen; rifles, gleaming, modern rifles, laid out in rows; a hundred, two hundred, three hundred; Julian had no means of estimating.

He had dismounted and walked over to them; the young men were still shovelling back the fruit, reckless of its plenty, bringing more weapons and still more to light. He had bent down to examine more closely.

'Italian,' he had said then, briefly, and had met Tsigaridis' eye, had seen the slow, contented smile which spread on the old man's face, and which he had discreetly turned aside to conceal.

Then Julian, with a glimpse of all those months of preparation, had ridden down from the hills, the string of mules following his mule in single file, the shining barrels bristling out of the panniers, and in the market-place he had assisted, from the height of his saddle, at the distribution of the arms. Two hundred and fifty, and five hundred rounds of ammunition to each. ... He thought of the nights of smuggling represented there, of the catch of fish—the 'quick, shining harvest of the sea'—beneath which lay the deadlier catch that evaded the eyes of the customs-house clerks. He remembered the robbery at the casino, and was illuminated. Money had not been lacking.

These were not the only pictures he retained of that day; the affairs to which he was expected to attend seemed to be innumerable; he had sat for hours in the village assembly-room, while the islanders came and went, surprisingly capable, but at the same time utterly reliant upon him. Throughout the day no sign came from Herakleion. Julian grew weary, and could barely restrain his thoughts from wandering to Eve. He would have gone to her room before leaving the house in the morning, but she had refused to see him. Consequently the thought of her had haunted him all day. One of the messages which reached him as he sat in the assembly-room had been from her: Would he send a boat to Herakleion for Nana?

He had smiled, and had complied, very much doubting whether the boat would ever be allowed to return. The message had brought him, as it were, a touch from her, a breath of her personality which clung about the room long after. She was near at hand, waiting for him, so familiar, yet so unfamiliar, so undiscovered. He felt that after a year with her much would still remain to be discovered; that there was, in fact, no end to her interest and her mystery. She was of no ordinary calibre, she who could be, turn by turn, a delicious or plaintive child, a woman of ripe seduction, and—in fits and starts—a poet in whose turbulent and undeveloped talent he divined startling possibilities! When she wrote poetry she smothered herself in ink, as he knew; so mingled in her were the fallible and the infallible. He refused to analyse his present relation to her; a sense, not of hypocrisy, but of decency, held him back; he remembered all too vividly the day he had carried her in his arms; his brotherliness had been shocked, offended, but since then the remembrance had persisted and had grown, and now he found himself, with all that brotherliness of years still ingrained in him, full of thoughts and on the brink of an adventure far from brotherly. He tried not to think these thoughts. He honestly considered them degrading, incestuous. But his mood was ripe for adventure; the air was full of adventure; the circumstances were unparalleled; his excitement glowed—he left the assembly-room, walked rapidly up the street, and entered the Davenant house, shutting the door behind him.

The sounds of the street were shut out, and the water plashed coolly in the open courtyard; two pigeons walked prinking round the flat edge of the marble basin, the male cooing and bowing absurdly, throwing out his white chest, ruffling his tail, and putting down his spindly feet with fussy precision. When Julian appeared, they fluttered away to the other side of the court to resume their convention of lovemaking. Evening was falling, warm and suave, and overhead in the still blue sky floated tiny rosy clouds. In the cloisters round the court the frescoes of the life of Saint Benedict looked palely at Julian, they so faded, so washed-out, he so young and so full of strength. Their pallor taught him that he had never before felt so young, so reckless, or so vigorous.

He was astonished to find Eve with the son of Zapantiotis, learning from him to play the flute in the long, low room which once had been the refectory and which ran the full length of the cloisters. Deeply recessed windows, with heavy iron gratings, looked down over the roofs of the village to the sea. In one of these windows Eve leaned against the wall holding the flute to her lips, and young Zapantiotis, eager, handsome, showed her how to place her fingers upon the holes. She looked defiantly at Julian.

'Nico has rescued me,' she said; 'but for him I should have been alone all day. I have taught him to dance.' She pointed to a gramophone upon a table.

'Where did that come from?' Julian said, determined not to show his anger before the islander.

'From the café,' she replied.

'Then Nico had better take it back; they will need it,' Julian said, threats in his voice, 'and he had better see whether his father cannot find him employment; we have not too many men.'

'You left me the whole day,' she said when Nico had gone; 'I am sorry I came with you, Julian; I would rather go back to Herakleion; even Nana has not come. I did not think you would desert me.'

He looked at her, his anger vanished, and she was surprised when he answered her gently, even amusedly,—

'You are always delightfully unexpected and yet characteristic of yourself: I come back, thinking I shall find you alone, perhaps glad to see me, having spend an unoccupied day, but no, I find you with the best-looking scamp of the village, having learnt from him to play the flute, taught him to dance, and borrowed a gramophone from the local café!'

He put his hands heavily upon her shoulders with a gesture she knew of old.

'I suppose I love you,' he said roughly, and then seemed

indisposed to talk of her any more, but told her his plans and arrangements, to which she did not listen.

They remained standing in the narrow window-recess, leaning, opposite to one another, against the thick stone walls of the old Genoese building. Through the grating they could see the sea, and, in the distance, Herakleion.

'It is sufficiently extraordinary,' he remarked, gazing across the bay, 'that Herakleion has made no sign. I can only suppose that they will try force as soon as Panaïoannou can collect his army, which, as it was fully mobilised no later than yesterday, ought not to take very long.'

'Will there be fighting?' she asked, with a first show of interest.

'I hope so,' he replied.

'I should like you to fight,' she said.

Swaying as he invariably did between his contradictory opinions of her, he found himself inwardly approving her standpoint, that man, in order to be worthy of woman, must fight, or be prepared to fight, and to enjoy the fighting. From one so self-indulgent, so pleasure-loving, so reluctant to face any unpleasantness of life, he might pardonably have expected the less heroic attitude. If she resented his absence all day on the business of preparations for strife, might she not equally have resented the strife that called him from her side? He respected her appreciation of physical courage, and remodelled his estimate to her advantage.

To his surprise, the boat he had sent for Nana returned from Herakleion. It came, indeed, without Nana, but bearing in her place a letter from his father:—

'Dear Julian,—By the courtesy of M. Stavridis—by whose orders this house is closely guarded, and for which I have to thank your folly—I am enabled to send you this letter, conditional on M. Stavridis's personal censorship. Your messenger has come with your astonishing request that your cousin's nurse may be allowed to return with the boat to Aphros. I should have returned with it myself in the place of the nurse, but for M. Stavridis's very natural objection to my rejoining you or leaving Herakleion.

'I am at present too outraged to make any comment upon your behaviour. I try to convince myself that you must be completely insane. M. Stavridis, however, will shortly take drastic steps to restore you to sanity. I trust only that no harm will befall you—for I remember still that you are my son—in the process. In the meantime, I demand of you most urgently, in my own name and that of your uncle and aunt, that you will send back your cousin without delay to Herakleion. M. Stavridis has had the great kindness to give his consent to this. A little consideration will surely prove to you that in taking her with you to Aphros you have been guilty of a crowning piece of folly from every point of view. I know you to be headstrong and unreflecting. Try to redeem yourself in this one respect before it is too late.

'I fear that I should merely be wasting my time by attempting to dissuade you from the course you have chosen with regards to the Islands. My poor misguided boy, do you not realise that your effort is *bound* to end in disaster, and will serve but to injure those you most desire to help?

'I warn you, too, most gravely and solemnly, that your obstinacy will entail *very serious consequences* for yourself. I shall regret the steps I contemplate taking, but I have the interest of our family to consider, and I have your uncle's entire approval.

'I am very deeply indebted to M. Stavridis, who, while unable to neglect his duty as the first citizen of Herakleion, has given me every proof of his personal friendship and confidence.

W. DAVENANT'

Julian showed this letter to Eve.

'What answer shall you send?'

'This,' he replied, tearing it into pieces.

'You are angry. Oh, Julian, I love you for being reckless.'

'I see red. He threatens me with disinheriting me. He takes good care to remain in Stavridis' good books himself. Do you want to go back?'

'No, Julian.'

'Of course, father is quite right: I am insane, and so are you. But, after all, you will run no danger, and as for compromising you, that is absurd: we have often been alone together before now. Besides,' he added brutally, 'you said yourself you belonged to the Islands no less than I; you can suffer for them a little if necessary.'

'I make no complaint,' she said with an enigmatic smile.

They dined together near the fountain in the courtyard, and overhead the sky grew dark, and the servant brought lighted candles for the table. Julian spoke very little; he allowed himself the supreme luxury of being spoilt by a woman who made it her business to please him; observing her critically, appreciatively; acknowledging her art; noting with admiration how the instinct of the born courtesan filled in the gaps in the experience of the child. He was, as yet, more mystified by her than he cared to admit.

But he yielded himself to her charm. The intimacy of this meal, their first alone together, enveloped him more and more with the gradual sinking of night, and his observant silence, which had originated with the deliberate desire to test her skill and also to indulge his own masculine enjoyment, insensibly altered into a shield against the emotion which was gaining him. The servant had left them. The water still plashed into the marble basin. The candles on the table burned steadily in the unruffled evening, and under their light gleamed the wine—rough, native wine, red and golden—in the long-necked, transparent bottles, and the bowl of fruit: grapes, a cut melon, and bursting figs, heaped with the lavishness of plenty. The table was a pool of light, but around it the court and cloisters were full of dim, mysterious shadows.

Opposite Julian, Eve leaned forward, propping her bare elbows on the table, disdainfully picking at the fruit, and talking. He looked at her smooth, beautiful arms, and little white hands that he had always loved. He knew that he preferred her company to any in the world. Her humour, her audacity, the width of her range, the picturesqueness of her phraseology, her endless inventiveness, her subtle undercurrent of the personal, though 'you' or 'I' might be entirely absent from her lips all seemed to him wholly enchanting. She was a sybarite of life, an artist; but the glow and recklessness of her saved her from all taint of intellectual sterility. He knew that his life had been enriched and coloured by her presence in it; that it would, at any moment, have become a poorer, a grayer, a less magical thing through the loss of her. He shut his eyes for a second as he realised that she could be, if he chose, his own possession, she the elusive and unattainable; he might claim the redemption of all her infinite promise; might discover her in the rôle for which she was so obviously created; might violate the sanctuary and tear the veils from the wealth of treasure hitherto denied to all; might exact for himself the first secrets of her unplundered passion. He knew her already as the perfect companion, he divined her as the perfect mistress; he reeled and shrank before the unadmitted thought, then looked across at her where she sat with an open fig halfway to her lips, and knew fantastically that they were alone upon an island of which he was all but king.

'A deserted city,' she was saying, 'a city of Portuguese settlers; pink marble palaces upon the edge of the water; almost crowded into the water by the encroaching jungle; monkeys peering through their ruined windows; on the sand, great sleepy tortoises; and, twining in and out of the broken doorways of the palaces, orchids and hibiscus—that is Trincomali! Would you like the tropics, I wonder, Julian? their exuberance, their vulgarity? . . . One buys little sacks of precious stones; one puts in one's hand, and lets the sapphires and the rubies and the emeralds run through one's fingers.'

Their eyes met; and her slight, infrequent confusion overcame her. . . .

'You aren't listening,' she murmured.

'You were only fifteen when you went to Ceylon,' he said, gazing at the blue smoke of his cigarette. 'You used to write to me from there. You had scarlet writing-paper. You were a deplorably affected child.'

'Yes,' she said, 'the only natural thing about me was my affectation.'

They laughed, closely, intimately.

'It began when you were three,' he said, 'and insisted upon always wearing brown kid gloves; your voice was even deeper then than it is now, and you always called your father Robert.'

'You were five; you used to push me into the prickly pear.'

'And you tried to kill me with a dagger; do you remember?'

'Oh, yes,' she said quite gravely, 'there was a period when I always carried a dagger.'

'When you came back from Ceylon you had a tiger's claw.'

'With which I once cut my initials on your arm.'

'You were very theatrical.'

'You were very stoical.'

Again they laughed.

'When you went to Ceylon,' he said, 'one of the ship's officers fell in love with you; you were very much amused.'

'The only occasion, I think, Julian, when I ever boasted to you of such a thing? You must forgive me—*il ne faut pas m'en vouloir*—remember I was only fifteen.'

'Such things amuse you still,' he said jealously.

'*C'est possible,*' she replied.

He insisted,—

'When did you really become aware of your own heartlessness?'

She sparkled with laughter.

'I think it began life as a sense of humour,' she said, 'and degenerated gradually into its present state of spasmodic infamy.'

He had smiled, but she saw his face suddenly darken, and he got up abruptly, and stood by the fountain, turning his back on her.

'My God,' she thought to herself in terror, 'he has remembered Paul.'

She rose also, and went close to him, slipping her hand through his arm, endeavouring to use, perhaps unconsciously, the powerful weapon of her physical nearness. He did not shake away her hand, but he remained unresponsive, lost in contemplation of the water. She hesitated as to whether she should boldly attack the subject—she knew her danger; he would be difficult to acquire, easy to lose, no more tractable than a young colt—then in the stillness of the night she faintly heard the music of the gramophone playing in the village café.

'Come into the drawing-room and listen to the music, Julian,' she said, pulling at his arm.

He came morosely; then exchanged the court with its pool of light for the darkness of the drawing-room; she felt her way, holding his hand, towards a window seat, sat down, and pulled him down beside her; through the rusty iron grating they saw the sea, lit up by the rising moon.

'We can just hear the music,' she whispered.

Her heart was beating hard and fast: they had been as under a spell, so close were they to one another, but now she was bitterly conscious of having lost him. She knew that he had slipped from the fairyland of Aphros back to the world of principles, of morals both conventional and essential. In fairyland, whither she had enticed him, all things were feasible, permissible, even imperative. He had accompanied her, she thought, very willingly, and they had strayed together down enchanted paths, abstaining, it is true, from adventuring into the perilous woods that surrounded them, but hand in hand, nevertheless, their departure from the path potential at any rate, if not imminent. They had been alone; she had been so happy, so triumphant. Now he had fled her, back to another world inhabited by all the enemies she would have had him forget: her cruelties, her vanities—her vanities! he could never reconcile her vanities and her splendour; he was incapable of seeing them both at the same time; the one excluded the other, turn and turn about, in his young eyes; her deceptions, her evasions of the truth, the men she had misled, the man, above all, that she had killed and whose death she had accepted with comparative indifference. These things rose in a bristling phalanx against her, and she faced them, small, afraid, and at a loss. For she was bound to admit their existence, and the very vivid, the very crushing, reality of their existence, all-important to her, in Julian's eyes; although she herself might be too completely devoid of moral sense, in the ordinary acceptance of the word, to admit any justification for his indignation. She knew with sorrow that they would remain for ever as a threat in the background, and that she would be fortunate indeed if in that background she could succeed in keeping them more or less permanently. Her imagination sighed for a potion of forgetfulness. Failing that, never for an instant must she neglect her rôle of Calypso. She knew that on the slightest impulse to anger on Julian's part—and his impulses to anger, were alas, both violent and frequent—all those enemies in their phalanx would instantly rise and range themselves on his side against her. Coaxed into abeyance, they would revive with fatal ease.

She knew him well in his present mood of gloom. She was afraid, and a desperate anxiety to regain him possessed her. Argument, she divined, would be futile. She whispered his name.

He turned on her a face of granite.

'Why have you changed?' she said helplessly. 'I was so happy, and you are making me so miserable.'

'I have no pity for you,' he said, 'you are too pitiless yourself to deserve any.'

'You break my heart when you speak to me like that.'

'I should like to break it,' he replied, unmoved.

She did not answer, but presently he heard her sobbing. Full of suspicion, he put out his hand and felt the tears running between her fingers.

'I have made you cry,' he said.

'Not for the first time,' she answered.

She knew that he was disconcerted, shaken in his harshness, and added,—

'I know what you think of me sometimes, Julian. I have nothing to say in my own defence. Perhaps there is only one good thing in me, but that you must promise me never to attack.'

'What is it?'

'You sound very sceptical,' she answered wistfully. 'My love for you; let us leave it at that.'

'I wonder!' he said; and again, 'I wonder! . . .'

She moved a little closer to him, and leaned against him, so that her hair brushed his cheek. Awkwardly and absently-mindedly, he put his arms around her; he could feel her heart beating through her thin muslin shirt, and lifting her bare arm in his hand he weighed it pensively; she lay against him, allowing him to do as he pleased; physically he held her nearer, but morally he was far away. Humiliating herself, she lay silent, willing to sacrifice the pride of her body if therewith she might purchase his return. But he, awaking with a start from his brooding grievances, put her away from him. If temptation was to overcome him, it must rush him by assault; not thus, sordid and unlit. . . . He rose, saying,—

'It is very late; you must go to bed; good-night.'

Two

PANAIOANNOU attempted a landing before sunrise on the following day.

A few stars were still visible, but the moon was paling, low in the heavens, and along the eastern horizon the sky was turning rosy and yellow above the sea. Earth, air, and water were alike bathed in purity and loveliness. Julian, hastily aroused, remembered the Islands as he had seen them from the mainland on the day of Madame Lafarge's picnic. In such beauty they were lying now, dependent on his defence. . . . Excited beyond measure, he dressed rapidly, and as he dressed he heard the loud clanging of the school bell summoning the men to arms; he heard the village waking, the clatter of banging doors, of wooden soles upon the cobbles, and excited voices. He rushed from his room into the passage, where he met Eve.

She was very pale, and her hair was streaming round her shoulders. She clung to him.

'Oh, Julian, what is it? why are they ringing the bells? why are you dressed? where are you going?

He explained, holding her, stroking her hair.

'Boats have been sighted, setting out from Herakleion; I suppose they think they will take us by surprise. You know, I have told two men to look after you; you are to go into the little hut which is prepared for you in the very centre of the island. They will never land, and you will be perfectly safe there. I will let you know directly they are driven off. You must let me go, darling.'

'Oh, but you? but you?' she cried desperately.

'They won't come near me,' he replied laughing.

'Julian, Julian,' she said, holding on to his coat as he tried to loosen her fingers, 'Julian, I want you to know: you're all my life, I give you myself, on whatever terms you like, for ever if you like, for a week if you like; you can do with me whatever you choose; throw me away when you've done with me; you think me worthless; I care only for you in the world.'

He was astonished at the starkness and violence of the passion in her eyes and voice.

'But I am not going into any danger,' he said, trying to soothe her.

'For God's sake, kiss me,' she said, distraught, and seeing that he was impatient to go.

'I'll kiss you to-night,' he answered tempestuously, with a ring of triumph as one who takes a decision.

'No, no: now.'

He kissed her hair, burying his face in its thickness.

'This attack is a comedy, not a tragedy,' he called back to her as he ran down the stairs.

The sentry who had first sighted the fleet of boats was still standing upon his headland, leaning on his rifle, and straining his eyes over the sea. Julian saw him thus silhouetted against the morning sky. Day was breaking as Julian came up the mule-path, a score of islanders behind him, walking with the soft, characteristic swishing of their white woollen skirts, and the slight rattle of slung rifles. All paused at the headland, which was above a little rocky creek; the green and white water foamed gently below. Out to sea the boats were distinctly visible, dotted about the sea, carrying each a load of men; there might be twenty or thirty, with ten or fifteen men in each.

'They must be out of their senses,' Tsigaridis growled; 'their only hope would have lain in a surprise attack at night—which by the present moonlight would indeed have proved equally idle—but at present they but expose themselves to our butchery.'

'The men are all at their posts?' Julian asked.

'Malista, Kyrie, malista.' They remained for a little watching the boats as the daylight grew. The colours of the dawn were shifting, stretching, widening, and the water, turning from iron-gray to violet, began along the horizon to reflect the transparency of the sky. The long, low, gray clouds caught upon their edges an orange flush; a sudden bar of gold fell along the line where sky and water met; a drift of tiny clouds turned red like a flight of flamingoes; and the blue began insensibly to spread, pale at first, then deepening as the sun rose out of the melting clouds and flooded over the full expanse of sea. To the left, the coast of the mainland, with Mount Mylassa soaring, and Herakleion at its base, broke the curve until it turned at an angle to run northward. Smoke began to rise in steady threads of blue from the houses of Herakleion. The red light died away at the tip of the pier. The gulls circled screaming, flashes of white and gray, marbled birds; and beyond the thin line of foam breaking against the island the water was green in the shallows.

All round Aphros the islanders were lying in pickets behind defences, the naturally rocky and shelving coast affording them the command of every approach. The port, which was the only really suitable landing-place, was secure, dominated as it was by the village; no boat could hope to live for five minutes under concentrated rifle fire from the windows of the houses. The other possible landing-places—the creeks and little beaches—could be held with equal easy by half a dozen men with rifles lying under shelter upon the headlands or on the ledges of the rocks. Julian was full of confidence. The danger of shelling he discounted, firstly because Herakleion possessed no man-of-war, or, indeed, any craft more formidable than the police motor-launch, and secondly because the authorities in Herakleion knew well enough that Italy, for reasons of her own, neither wholly idealistic nor disinterested, would never tolerate the complete destruction of Aphros. Moreover, it would be hopeless to attempt to starve out an island whose population lived almost entirely upon the fish caught round their own shores, the vegetables and fruit grown upon their own hillsides, the milk and cheeses from their own rough-feeding goats, and the occasional but sufficient meat from their own sheep and bullocks.

'Kyrie,' said Tsigaridis, 'should we not move into shelter?'

Julian abandoned the headland regretfully. For his own post he had chosen the Davenant house in the village. He calculated that Panaïoannou, unaware of the existence of a number of rifles on the island, would make his first and principal attempt upon the port, expecting there to encounter a hand to hand fight with a crowd diversely armed with knives, stones, pitch-forks, and a few revolvers—a brief, bloody, desperate resistance, whose term could be but a matter of time, after which the village would fall into the hands of the invaders and the rebellion would be at an end. At most, Panaïoannou would argue, the fighting would be continued up into the main street of the village, the horizontal street that was its backbone, terminating at one end by the market-place above the port, and at the other by the Davenants' house; and ramifications of fighting—a couple of soldiers here and there pursuing a fleeing islander—up the sloping, narrow, stepped streets running between the houses, at right angles from the main street, up the hill. Julian sat with his rifle cocked across his knees in one of the window recesses of his own house, and grinned as he anticipated Panaïoannou's surprise. He did not want a massacre of the fat, well-meaning soldiers of Herakleion—the casino, he reflected, must be closed to-day, much to the annoyance of the gambling dagos; however, they would have excitement enough, of another kind, to console them—he did not want a massacre of the benevolent croupier-soldiers he had seen parading the *platia* only two days before, but he wanted them taught that Aphros was a hornets' nest out of which they had better keep their fingers. He thought it extremely probable that after a first repulse they would refuse to renew the attack. They liked well enough defiling across the *platia* on Independence Day, and recognising their friends amongst the admiring crowd, but he doubted whether they would appreciate being shot down in open boats by an enemy they could not even see.

In the distance, from the windows of his own house, he heard firing, and from the advancing boats he could see spurts of smoke. He discerned a commotion in one boat; men got up and changed places, and the boat turned round and began to row in the opposite direction. Young Zapantiotis called to him from another window,—

'You see them, Kyrie? Some one has been hit.'

Julian laughed exultantly. On a table near him lay a crumpled handkerchief of Eve's, and a gardenia; he put the flower into his buttonhole. Behind all his practical plans and his excitement lay the memory of his few words with her in the passage; under the stress of her emotion she had revealed a depth and vehemence of truth that he hitherto scarcely dared to imagine. To-day would be given to him surely more than his fair share for any mortal man: a fight, and the most desirable of women! He rejoiced in his youth and his leaping blood. Yet he continued sorry for the kindly croupier-soldiers.

The boats came on, encouraged by the comparative silence on the island. Julian was glad it was not the fashion among the young men of Herakleion, his friends, to belong to the army. He wondered what Grbits was thinking of him. He was probably on the quay, watching through a telescope. Or had the expedition been kept a secret from the still sleeping Herakleion? Surely! for he could distinguish no crowd upon the distant quays across the bay.

A shot rang out close at hand, from some window of the village, and in one of the foremost boats he saw a man throw up his hands and fall over backwards.

He sickened slightly. This was inevitable, he knew, but he had no lust for killing in this cold-blooded fashion. Kneeling on the window-seat he took aim between the bars of the grating, and fired a quantity of shots all round the boat; they splashed harmlessly into the water, but had the effect he desired; the boat turned round in retreat.

Firing crackled now from all parts of the island. The casualties in the boats increased. In rage and panic the soldiers fired wildly back at the island, especially at the village; bullets ping-ed through the air and rattled on the roofs; occasionally there came a crash of broken glass. Once Julian heard a cry, and, craning his head to look down the street, he saw an islander lying on his face on the ground between the houses with his arms outstretched, blood running freely from his shoulder, and staining his white clothes.

'My people!' Julian cried in a passion, and shot deliberately into a boat-load of men.

'God!' he said to himself a moment later, 'I've killed him.'

He laid down his rifle with a gesture of horror, and went out into the courtyard where the fountain still played and the pigeons prinked and preened. He opened the door into the street, went down the steps and along the street to where the islander lay groaning, lifted him carefully, and dragged him into the shelter of the house. Zapantiotis met him in the court.

'Kyrie,' he said, scared and reproachful, 'you should have sent me.'

Julian left him to look after the wounded man, and returned to the window; the firing had slackened, for the boats were now widely dispersed over the sea, offering only isolated targets at a considerable distance. Time had passed rapidly, and the sun had climbed high overhead. He looked at the little dotted boats, bearing their burden of astonishment, death, and pain. Was it possible that the attack had finally drawn away?

At that thought, he regretted that the fighting had not given an opportunity of a closer, a more personal struggle.

An hour passed. He went out into the village, where life was beginning to flow once more into the street and market-place; the villagers came out to look at their broken windows, and their chipped houses; they were all laughing and in high good-humour, pointing proudly to the damage, and laughing like children to see that in the school-house, which faced the sea and in which the remaining Greek officials were still imprisoned, nearly all the windows were broken. Julian, shaking off the people, men and women, who were trying to kiss his hands or his clothes, appeared briefly in the class-room to reassure the occupants. They were all huddled into a corner, behind a barricade of desks and benches. The one guard who had been left with them had spent his time inventing terrible stories for their distress. The wooden wall opposite the windows was pocked in two or three places by bullets.

As Julian came out again into the market-place he saw old Tsigaridis riding down on his great white mule from the direction of the hills, accompanied by two runners on foot. He waited while the mule picked its way carefully and delicately down the stepped path that led from the other side of the market-place up into the interior of the island.

'They are beaten off, Tsantilas.'

'No imprudences,' said the grave old man, and recommended to the people, who came crowding round his mule, to keep within the shelter of their houses.

'But, Tsantilas, we have the boats within our sight; they cannot return without our knowledge in ample time to seek shelter.'

'There is one boat for which we cannot account—the

198

motor-boat—it is swift and may yet take us by surprise,' Tsigaridis replied pessimistically.

He dismounted from his mule, and walked up the street with Julian by his side, while the people, crest-fallen, dispersed with lagging footsteps to their respective doorways. The motor-launch, it would appear, had been heard in the far distance, 'over there,' said Tsigaridis, extending his left arm; the pickets upon the eastern coasts of the island had distinctly heard the echo of its engines—it was, fortunately, old and noisy—but early in the morning the sound had ceased, and since then had not once been renewed. Tsigaridis inferred that the launch was lying somewhere in concealment amongst the tiny islands, from where it would emerge, unexpectedly and in an unexpected place, to attack.

'It must carry at least fifty men,' he added.

Julian revelled in the news. A motor-launch with such a crew would provide worthier game than little cockle-shell rowing-boats. Panaïoannou himself might be of the party. Julian saw the general already as his prisoner.

He remembered Eve. So long as the launch lay in hiding he could not allow her to return to the village. It was even possible that they might have a small gun on board. He wanted to see her, he ached with the desire to see her, but, an instinctive Epicurean, he welcomed the circumstances that forced him to defer their meeting until nightfall. . . .

He wrote her a note on a leaf of his pocket-book, and dispatched it to her by one of Tsigaridis' runners.

The hours of waiting fretted him, and to ease his impatience he started on a tour of the island with Tsigaridis. They rode on mules, nose to tail along the winding paths, not climbing into the interior, but keeping to the lower track that ran above the sea, upon the first flat ledge of the rock, all around the island. In some places the path was so narrow and so close to the edge that Julian could, by leaning side-ways in his saddle, look straight down the cliff into the water swirling and foaming below. He was familiar with almost every creek, so often had he bathed there as a boy. Looking at the foam, he murmured to himself,—

'Aphros. . . .'

There were no houses here among the rocks, and no

trees, save for an occasional group of pines, whose little cones clustered among the silvery branches, quite black against the sky. Here and there, above creeks or the little sandy beaches where a landing for a small boat would have been possible, the picket of islanders had come out from their shelter behind the boulders, and were sitting talking on the rocks, holding their rifles upright between their knees, while a solitary sentinel kept watch at the extremity of the point, his kilted figure white as the circling seagulls or as the foam. A sense of lull and of siesta lay over the afternoon. At every picket Julian asked the same question, and at every picket the same answer was returned,—

"We have heard no engines since earliest morning, Kyrie.'

Round the curve of the island, the first tiny, uninhabited islands came into view. Some of them were mere rocks sticking up out of the sea; others, a little larger, grew a few trees, and a boat could have hidden, invisible from Aphros, on their farther side. Julian looked longingly at the narrow stretches of water which separated them. He even suggested starting to look for the launch.

'It would be madness, Kyrie.'

Above a little bay, where the ground sloped down less abruptly, and where the sand ran gently down under the thin wavelets, they halted with the picket of that particular spot. Their mules were led away by a runner. Julian enjoyed sitting amongst these men, hearing them talk, and watching them roll cigarette after cigarette with the practised skill of their knotty fingers. Through the sharp lines of their professional talk, and the dignity of their peasant trades—for they were all fishermen, vintagers, or sheep- and goat-herds—he smiled to the hidden secret of Eve, and fancied that the soft muslin of her garments brushed, as at the passage of a ghost, against the rude woollen garments of the men; that her hands, little and white and idle, fluttered over their hardened hands; that he alone could see her pass amongst their group, smile to him, and vanish down the path. He was drowsy in the drowsy afternoon; he felt that he had fought and had earned his rest, and, moreover, was prepared to rise from his sleep with new strength to fight again. Rest between a battle and a battle. Strife, sleep, and love; love, sleep, and strife; a worthy plan of life!

He slept.

When he woke the men still sat around him, talking still of their perennial trades, and without opening his eyes he lay listening to them, and thought that in such a simple world the coming and going of generations was indeed of slight moment, since in the talk of crops and harvests, of the waxing and waning of moons, of the treachery of the sea or the fidelity of the land, the words of the ancestor might slip unchanged as an inheritance to grandson and great-grandson. Of such kindred were they with nature, that he in his half-wakefulness barely distinguished the voices of the men from the wash of waves on the shore. He opened his eyes. The sun, which he had seen rising out of the sea in the dawn, after sweeping in its great flaming arc across the sky, had sunk again under the horizon. Heavy purple clouds like outpoured wine stained the orange of the west. The colour of the sea was like the flesh of a fig.

Unmistakably, the throb of an engine woke the echoes between the islands.

All eyes met, all voices hushed; tense, they listened. The sound grew; from a continuous purr it changed into separate beats. By mutual consent, and acting under no word of command, the men sought the cover of the boulders, clambering over the rocks, carrying their rifles with them, white, noiseless, and swift. Julian found himself with three others in a species of little cave the opening of which commanded the beach; the cave was low, and they were obliged to crouch; one man knelt down at the mouth with his rifle ready to put to his shoulder. Julian could smell, in that restricted place, the rough smell of their woollen clothes, and the tang of the goat which clung about one man, who must be a goat-herd.

Then before their crouching position could begin to weary them, the beat of the engines became insistent, imminent; and the launch shot round the curve, loaded with standing men, and heading directly for the beach. A volley of fire greeted them, but the soldiers were already overboard, waist-deep in water, plunging towards the shore with their rifles held high over their heads, while the crew of the launch violently reversed the engines and drove themselves off the sand by means of long poles, to save the launch from an irrevocable grounding. The attack was well planned, and executed by men who knew intimately the lie of the coast. With loud shouts, they emerged dripping from the water on to the beach.

They were at least forty strong; the island picket numbered only a score, but they had the advantage of concealment. A few of the soldiers dropped while yet in the water; others fell forward on to their faces with their legs in the water and their heads and shoulders on dry land; many gained a footing but were shot down a few yards from the edge of the sea; the survivors flung themselves flat behind hummocks of rock and fired in the direction of the defending fire. Everything seemed to have taken place within the compass of two or three minutes. Julian had himself picked off three of the invaders; his blood was up, and he had lost all the sickening sense of massacre he had felt during the early part of the day.

He never knew how the hand to hand fight actually began; he only knew that suddenly he was out of the cave, in the open, without a rifle, but with his revolver in his grasp, backed and surrounded by his own shouting men, and confronted by the soldiers of Herakleion, heavily impeded by their wet trousers, but fighting sheerly for their lives, striving to get at him, losing their heads and aiming wildly, throwing aside their rifles and grappling at last bodily with their enemies, struggling not be driven back into the sea, cursing the islanders, and calling to one another to rally, stumbling over the dead and the wounded. Julian scarcely recognised his own voice in the shout of, 'Aphros!' He was full of the lust of fighting; he had seen men roll over before the shot of his revolver, and had driven them down before the weight of his fist. He was fighting joyously, striking among the waves of his enemies as a swimmer striking out against a current. All his thought was to kill, and to rid his island of these invaders; already the tide had turned, and that subtle sense of defeat and victory that comes upon the crest of battle was infusing respectively despair and triumph. There was now no doubt in the minds of either the attackers or the defenders in whose favour the attack would end. There remained but three alternatives: surrender, death, or the sea.

Already many were choosing the first, and those that turned in the hope of regaining the launch were shot down or captured before they reached the water. The prisoners, disarmed, stood aside in a little sulky group under the guard of one islander, watching, resignedly, and with a certain indifference born of their own secession from activity, the swaying clump of men, shouting, swearing, and stumbling, and the feeble efforts of the wounded to drag themselves out of the way of the trampling feet. The sand of the beach was in some places, where blood had been spilt, stamped into a dark mud. A wounded soldier, lying half in and half out of the water, cried out pitiably as the salt water lapped over his wounds.

The decision was hastened by the crew of the launch, who, seeing a bare dozen of their companions rapidly overpowered by a superior number of islanders, and having themselves no fancy to be picked off at leisure from the shore, started their engines and made off to sea. At that a cry of dismay went up; retreat, as an alternative, was entirely withdrawn; death an empty and unnecessary display of heroism; surrender remained; they chose it thankfully.

Three

JULIAN never knew, nor did he stop to inquire, why Eve
had returned to the village without his sanction. He only
knew that as he came up the street, escorted by all the
population, singing, pressing around him, taking his hands,
throwing flowers and even fruit in his path, holding up
their children for him to touch, he saw her standing in the
doorway of their house, the lighted courtyard yellow behind her. She stood there on the highest of the three steps,
her hands held out towards him. He knew, too, although
no word was spoken, that the village recognised them as
lovers. He felt again the triumphant completeness of life;
a fulfilment, beyond the possibility of that staid world
that, somewhere, moved upon its confused, mercenary,
mistaken, and restricted way. Here, the indignities of
hypocrisy were indeed remote. There, men shorn of candour entangled the original impulse of their motives until
in a sea of perplexity they abandoned even to the ultimate
grace of self-honesty; here, in an island of enchantment,
he had fought for his dearest and most constituent beliefs—O honourable privilege! unhindered and rare
avowal!—fought, not with secret weapons, but with the
manhood of his body; and here, under the eyes of fellow-
creatures, their presence no more obtrusive then the
presence of the sea or the evening breeze, under their unquestioning eyes he claimed the just reward, the consum-
mation, the right of youth, which in that pharisaical world
would have been denied him.

Eve herself was familiar with his mood. Whereas he
had noted, marvelled, and rejoiced at the simplicity with
which they came together, before that friendly concourse
of people, she had stretched out her hands to him with an
unthinking gesture of possession. She had kept her counsel
during the unpropitious years, with a secrecy beyond the

determination of a child; but here, having gained him for her own; having enticed him into the magical country where the standards drew near to her own standards; where she, on the one hand, no less than he upon the other, might fight with the naked weapons of nature for her desires and beliefs—here she walked at home and without surprise in the perfect liberty; that liberty which he accepted with gratitude, but she as a right out of which man elsewhere was cheated. He had always been surprised, on the rare occasions when a hint of her philosophy, a fragment of her creed, had dropped from her lips unawares. From these fragments he had been incapable of reconstructing the whole. He had judged her harshly, too young and too ignorant to query whether the falseness of convention cannot drive those, temperamentally direct and uncontrolled, into the self-defence of a superlative falseness. . . . He had seen her vanity; he had not seen what she was now, because himself in sympathy, beginning to apprehend, her whole-heartedness that was, in its way, so magnificent. Very, very dimly he apprehended; his apprehension, indeed, limited chiefly to the recognition of a certain correlation in her to the vibrant demands alive in him: he asked from her, weakness to fling his strength into relief; submission to entice his tyranny; yet at the same time, passion to match his passion, and mettle to exalt his conquest in his own eyes; she must be nothing less than the whole grace and rarity of life for his pleasure; flattery, in short, at once subtle and blatant, supreme and meticulous, was what he demanded, and what she was, he knew, so instinctively ready to accord.

As she put her hand into his, he felt the current of her pride as definitely as though he had seen a glance of understanding pass between her and the women of the village. He looked up at her, smiling. She had contrived for herself a garment out of some strip of dark red silk, which she had wound round her body after the fashion of an Indian sari; in the opening of that sombre colour her throat gleamed more than usually white, and above her swathed slenderness her lips were red in the pallor of her face, and her waving hair held glints of burnish as the leaves of autumn. She was not inadequate in her anticipation of his unspoken demands: the exploitation of her sensuous delicacy was all for him—for him!

He had expected, perhaps, that after her proud, frank welcome before the people, she would turn to him when they were alone; but he found her manner full of a deliberate indifference. She abstained even from any allusion to her day's anxiety. He was reminded of all their meetings when, after months, she betrayed no pleasure at his return, but rather avoided him, and coldly disregarded his unthinking friendliness. Many a time, as a boy, he had been hurt and puzzled by this caprice, which, ever meeting him unprepared, was ever renewed by her. To-night he was neither hurt nor puzzled, but with a grim amusement accepted the pattern she set; he could allow her the luxury of a superficial control. With the harmony between them, they could play the game of pretence. He delighted in her unexpectedness. Her reticence stirred him, in its disconcerting contrast with his recollection of her as he had left her that morning. She moved from the court into the drawing-room, and from the drawing-room back into the court, and he followed her, impersonal as she herself, battening down all outward sign of his triumph, granting her the grace of that Epicurean and ironic chivalry. He knew their quietness was ominous. They moved and spoke like people in the near, unescapable neighbourhood of a wild beast, whose attention they must on no account arouse, whose presence they must not mention, while each intensely aware of the peril, and each alive to the other's knowledge of it. She spoke and laughed, and he, in response to her laughter, smiled gravely; silence fell, and she broke it; she thought that he took peasure in testing her power of reviving their protective talk; the effort increased in difficulty; he seemed to her strangely and paralysingly sinister.

Harmony between them! if such harmony existed, it was surely the harmony of hostility. They were enemies that evening, not friends. If an understanding existed, it was, on her part, the understanding that he was mocking her; on his part, the understanding that she, in her fear, must preserve the veneer of self-assurance, and that some fundamental convention—if the term was not too inherently contradictory—demanded his co-operation. He granted it. On other occasions his manner towards her might be rough, violent, uncontrolled; this evening it was of an irreproachable civility. For the first time in her life she felt herself at a disadvantage. She invented pretext after pretext for prolonging their evening. She knew that if she could once bring a forgetful laugh to Julian's lips, she would fear him less; but he continued to smile gravely at her sallies, and to watch her with that same unbending intent. In the midst of her phrase she would look up, meet his eyes bent upon her, and forget her words in confusion. Once he rose, and stretched his limbs luxuriously against the back-ground of the open roof and the stars; she thought he would speak, but to her relief he sat down again in his place, removed his eyes from her, and fell to the dissection, grain by grain, of a bunch of grapes.

She continued to speak; she talked of Kato, even of Alexander Christopoulos; she scarcely knew he was not listening to her until he broke with her name into the heart of her sentence, unaware that he interrupted. He stood up, came round to her chair, and put his hand upon her shoulder; she could not control her trembling. He said briefly, but with all the repressed triumph ringing in his voice, 'Eve, come'; and without a word she obeyed, her eyes fastened to his, her breath shortened, deceit fallen from her, nothing but naked honesty remaining. She had lost even her fear of him. In their stark desire for each other they were equals. He put out his hand and extinguished the candles; dimness fell over the court.

'Eve,' he said, still in that contained voice, 'you know we are alone in this house.'

She acquiesced, 'I know,' not meaning to speak in a whisper, but involuntarily letting the words glide out with her breath.

As he paused, she felt his hand convulsive upon her shoulder; her lids lay shut upon her eyes like heavy petals. Presently he said wonderingly,—

'I have not kissed you.'

'No,' she replied, faint, yet marvellously strong.

He put his arm around her, and half carried her towards the stairs.

'Let me go,' she whispered, for the sake of his contradiction.

'No,' he answered, holding her more closely to him.

'Where are you taking me, Julian?'

He did not reply, but together they began to mount the stairs, she failing and drooping against his arm, her eyes still closed and her lips apart. They reached her room, bare, full of shadows, whitewashed, with the windows open upon the black moonlit sea.

'Eve!' he murmured exultantly, 'Aphros! . . .'

Four

THE LYRIC of their early days of love piped clear and sweet upon the terraces of Aphros.

Their surroundings entered into a joyous conspiracy with their youth. Between halcyon sky and sea the island lay radiantly; as it were suspended, unattached, coloured like a rainbow, and magic with the enchantment of its isolation. The very foam which broke around its rocks served to define, by its lacy fringe of white, the compass of the magic circle. To them were granted solitude and beauty beyond all dreams of lovers. They dwelt in the certainty that no intruder could disturb them—save those intruders to be beatan off in frank fight—no visitor from the outside world but those that came on wings, swooping down out of the sky, poising for an instant upon the island, that halting place in the heart of the sea, and flying again with restless cries, sea-birds, the only disturbers of their peace. From the shadow of the olives, or of the stunted pines whose little cones hung like black velvet balls in the transparent tracery of the branches against the sky, they lay idly watching the gulls, and the tiny white clouds by which the blue was almost always flaked. The population of the island melted into a harmony with nature like the trees, the rocks and boulders, or the roving flocks of sheep and herds of goats. Eve and Julian met with neither curiosity nor surprise; only with acquiescence. Daily as they passed down the village street, to wander up the mule-tracks into the interior of Aphros, they were greeted by smiles and devotion that were as unquestioning and comfortable as the shade of the trees or the cool splash of the water; and nightly as they remained alone together in their house, dark, roofed over with stars, and silent but for the ripple of the fountain, they could believe that they had been tended by invisible hands in the island over which they reigned in isolated sovereignty.

They abandoned themselves to the unbelievable romance. He, indeed, had striven half-heartedly; but she, with all the strength of her nature, had run gratefully, nay, clamantly, forward, exacting the reward of her patience, demanding her due. She rejoiced in the casting aside of shackles which, although she had resolutely ignored them in so far as was possible, had always irked her by their latent presence. At last she might gratify to the full her creed of living for and by the beloved, in a world of beauty where the material was denied admittance. In such a dream, such an ecstasy of solitude, they gained marvellously in one another's eyes. She revealed to Julian the full extent of her difference and singularity. For all their nearness in the human sense, he received sometimes with a joyful terror the impression that he was living in the companionship of a changeling, a being strayed by accident from another plane. The small moralities and tendernesses of mankind contained no meaning for her. They were burnt away by the devastating flame of her own ideals. He knew now, irrefutably, that she had lived her life withdrawn from all but external contact with her surroundings.

Her sensuality, which betrayed itself even in the selection of the arts she loved, had marked her out for human passion. He had observed her instinct to deck herself for his pleasure; he had learnt the fastidious refinement with which she surrounded her body. He had marked her further instinct to turn the conduct of their love into a fine art. She had taught him the value of her reserve, her evasions, and of her sudden recklessness. He never discovered, and, no less Epicurean than she, never sought to discover, how far her principles were innate, unconscious, or how far deliberate. They both tacitly esteemed the veil of some slight mystery to soften the harshness of their self-revelation.

He dared not invoke the aid of unshrinking honesty to apportion the values between their physical and their mental affinity.

What was it, this bond of flesh? so material, yet so imperative, so compelling, as to become almost a spiritual, not a bodily, necessity? so transitory, yet so recurrent?

dying down like a flame, to revive again? so unimportant, so grossly commonplace, yet creating so close and tremulous an intimacy? this magic that drew together their hands like fluttering butterflies in the hours of sunlight, and linked them in the abandonment of mastery and surrender in the hours of night? that swept aside the careful training, individual and hereditary, replacing pride by another pride? this unique and mutual secret? this fallacious yet fundamental and dominating bond? this force, hurling them together with such cosmic power that within the circle of frail human entity rushed furiously the tempest of an inexorable law of nature?

They had no tenderness for one another. Such tenderness as might have crept into the relationship they collaborated in destroying, choosing to dwell in the strong clean air of mountain-tops, shunning the ease of the valleys. Violence was never far out of sight. They loved proudly, with a flame that purged all from their love but the essential, the ideal passion.

'I live with a Mænad,' he said, putting out his hand and bathing his fingers in her loosened hair.

From the rough shelter of reeds and matting where they stood then among the terraced vineyards, the festoons of vines and the bright reds and yellows of the splay leaves, brilliant against the sun, framed her consonant grace. The beautiful shadows of lacing vines dappled the ground, and the quick lizards darted upon the rough terrace walls.

He said, pursuing his thought,—

'You have never the wish of other women—permanency? a house with me? never the inkling of such a wish?'

'Trammels!' she replied, 'I've always hated possessions.'

He considered her at great length, playing with her hair, fitting his fingers into its waving thicknesses, putting his cheek against the softness of her cheek, and laughing.

'My changeling. My nymph,' he said.

She lay silent, her arms folded behind her head, and her eyes on him as he continued to utter his disconnected sentences.

'Where is the Eve of Herakleion? The mask you wore! I dwelt only upon your insignificant vanity, and in your pride you made no defence. Most secret pride! Incredible chastity of mind! Inviolate of soul, to all alike. Inviolate.

211

Most rare restraint! The expansive vulgarity of the crowd!
My Eve . . .'

He began again,—

'So rarely, so stainlessly mine. Beyond mortal hopes.
You allowed all to misjudge you, myself included. You
smiled, not even wistfully, lest that betray you, and said
nothing. You held yourself withdrawn. You perfected your
superficial life. That profound humour . . . I could not
think you shallow—not all your pretence could disguise
your mystery—but, may I be forgiven, I have thought you
shallow in all but mischief. I prophesied for you'—he
laughed—'a great career as a destroyer of men. A great
courtesan. But instead I find you a great lover. *Une
grande amoureuse.*'

'If that is mischievous,' she said, 'my love for you goes
beyond mischief; it would stop short of no crime.'

He put his face between his hands for a second.

'I believe you; I know it.'

'I understand love in no other way,' she said, sitting up
and shaking her hair out of her eyes; 'I am single-hearted.
It is selfish love: I would die for you, gladly, without a
thought, but I would sacrifice my claim on you to no one
and to nothing. It is all-exorbitant. I make enormous demands. I must have you exclusively for myself.'

He teased her,—

'You refuse to marry me.'

She was serious.

'Freedom, Julian! romance! The world before us, to
roam at will; fairs to dance at; strange people to consort
with, to see the smile in their eyes, and the tolerant "Lovers!" forming on their lips. To tweak the nose of Propri-
ety, to snatch away the chair on which she would sit
down! Who in their senses would harness the divine courser
to a mail-cart?'

She seemed to him lit by an inner radiance, that shone
through her eyes and glowed richly in her smile.

'Vagabond!' he said. 'Is life to be one long carnival?'

'And one long honesty. I'll own you before the world—
and court its disapproval. I'll release you—no, I'll leave
you—when you tire of me. I wouldn't clip love's golden
wings. I wouldn't irk you with promises, blackmail you
into perjury, wring from you an oath we both should
know was made only to be broken. We'll leave that to

212

middle-age. Middle-age——I have been told there is such a thing? Sometimes it is fat, sometimes it is wan, surely it is always dreary! It may be wise and successful and contented. Sometimes, I'm told, it even loves. We are young. Youth!' she said, sinking her voice, 'the winged and the divine.'

When he talked to her about the Islands, she did not listen, although she dared not check him. He talked, striving to interest her, to fire her enthusiasm. He talked, with his eyes always upon the sea, since some obscure instinct warned him not to keep them bent upon her face; sometimes they were amongst the vines, which in the glow of their September bronze and amber resembled the wind flowing from their fruits, and from here the sea shimmered, crudely and cruelly blue between those flaming leaves, undulating into smooth, nacreous folds; sometimes they were amongst the rocks on the lower levels, on a windier day, when white crests spurted from the waves, and the foam broke with a lacy violence against the island at the edge of the green shallows; and sometimes, after dusk, they climbed to the olive terraces beneath the moon that rose through the trees in a world strangely gray and silver, strangely and contrastingly deprived of colour. He talked, lying on the ground, with his hands pressed close against the soil of Aphros. Its contact gave him the courage he needed. . . . He talked doggedly; in the first week with the fire of inspiration, after that with the perseverance of loyalty. These monologues ended always in the same way. He would bring his glance from the sea to her face, would break off his phrase in the middle, and, coming suddenly to her, would cover her hair, her throat, her mouth, with kisses. Then she would turn gladly and luxuriously towards him, curving in his arms, and presently the grace of her murmured speech would again bewitch him, until upon her lips he forgot the plea of Aphros.

There were times when he struggled to escape her, his physical and mental activity rebelling against the subjection in which she held him. He protested that the affairs of the Islands claimed him; that Herakleion had granted but a month for negotiations; precautions must be taken, and the scheme of government amplified and consolidated. Then the angry look came over her face, and all the bitterness of her resentment broke loose. Having captured him, much of her precocious wisdom seemed to have abandoned her.

'I have waited for you ten years, yet you want to leave me. Do I mean less to you than the Islands? I wish the Islands were at the bottom of the sea instead of on the top of it.'

'Be careful, Eve.'

'I resent everything which takes you from me,' she said recklessly.

Another time she cried, murky with passion,—

'Always these councils with Tsigaridis and the rest! always these secret messages passing between you and Kato! Give me that letter.'

He refused, shredding Kato's letter and scattering the pieces into the sea.

'What secrets have you with Kato, that you must keep from me?'

'They would have no interest for you,' he replied, remembering that she was untrustworthy—that canker in his confidence.

The breeze fanned slightly up the creek where they were lying on the sand under the shadow of a pine, and out in the dazzling sea a porpoise leapt, turning its slow black curve in the water. The heat simmered over the rocks.

'We share our love,' he said morosely, 'but no other aspect of life. The Islands are nothing to you. An obstacle, not a link.' It was a truth that he rarely confronted.

'You are wrong: a background, a setting for you, which I appreciate.'

'You appreciate the picturesque. I know. You are an artist in appreciation of the suitable stage-setting. But as for the rest ...' he made a gesture full of sarcasm and renunciation.

'Give me up, Julian, and all my shortcomings. I have always told you I had but one virtue. I am the first to admit the insufficiency of its claim. Give yourself wholly to your Islands. Let me go.' She spoke sadly, as though conscious of her own irremediable difference and perversity.

'Yet you yourself—what were your words?—said you believed in me; you even wrote to me, I remember still, "conquer, shatter, demolish!" But I must always struggle

214

against you, against your obstructions. What is it you want? Liberty and irresponsibility, to an insatiable degree!'

'Because I love you insatiably.'

'You are too unreasonable sometimes' ('Reason!' she interrupted with scorn, 'what has reason got to do with love?') 'you are unreasonable to grudge me every moment I spend away from you. Won't you realise that I am responsible for five thousand lives? You must let me go now; only for an hour. I promise to come back to you in an hour.'

'Are you tired of me already?'

'Eve. . . .'

'When we were in Herakleion, you were always saying you must go to Kato; now you are always going to some council; am I never to have you to myself?'

'I will go only for an hour. I *must* go, Eve, my darling.'

'Stay with me, Julian. I'll kiss you. I'll tell you a story.' She stretched out her hands. He shook his head, laughing, and ran off in the direction of the village.

When he returned, she refused to speak to him.

But at other times they grew marvellously close, passing hours and days in unbroken union, until the very fact of their two separate personalities became an exasperation. Then, silent as two souls tortured, before a furnace, they struggled for the expression that ever eludes; the complete, the satisfying expression that shall lay bare one soul to another soul, but that, ever failing, mockingly preserves the unwanted boon of essential mystery.

That dumb frenzy outworn, they attained, nevertheless, to a nearer comradeship, the days, perhaps, of their greatest happiness, when with her reckless fancy she charmed his mind; he thought of her then as a vagrant nymph, straying from land to land, from age to age, decking her spirit with any flower she met growing by the way, chastely concerned with the quest of beauty, strangely childlike always, pure as the fiercest, tallest flame. He could not but bow to that audacity, that elemental purity, of spirit. Untainted by worldliness, greed, or malice. . . . The facts of her life became clearer to him, startling in their consistency. He could not associate her with possessions, or a fixed abode, she who was free and elusive as a swallow, to whom the slightest responsibility was an intolerable and inadmissible yoke from beneath which, without commotion but also without compunction she slipped. On no material point could she be touched—save her own personal luxury, and that seemed to grow with her, as innocent of effort as the colour on a flower; she kindled only in response to music, poetry, love, or laughter, but then with what a kindling! she flamed, she glowed; she ranged over spacious and fabulous realms; her feet never touched earth, they were sandal-shod and carried her in the clean path of breezes, and towards the sun, exalted and ecstatic, breathing as the common air the rarity of the upper spaces, At such times she seemed a creature blown from legend, deriving from no parentage; single, individual, and lawless.

He found that he had come gradually to regard her with a superstitious reverence.

He evolved a theory, constructed around her, dim and nebulous, yet persistent; perforce nebulous, since he was dealing with a matter too fine, too subtle, too unexplored to lend itself to the gross imperfect imprisonment of words. He never spoke of it, even to her, but staring at her sometimes with a reeling head he felt himself transported, by her medium, beyond the matter-of-fact veils that shroud the limit of human vision. He felt illuminated, on the verge of a new truth; as though by stretching out his hand he might touch something no hand of man had ever touched before, something of unimaginable consistency, neither matter nor the negation of matter; as though he might brush the wings of truth, handle the very substance of a thought. . . .

He felt at these times like a man who passes through a genuine physical experience. Yes, it was as definite as that; he had the glimpse of a possible revelation. He returned from his vision—call it what he would, vision would serve as well as any other word—he returned with that sense of benefit by which alone such an excursion—or was it incursion?—could be justified. He brought back a benefit. He had beheld, as in a distant prospect, a novel balance and proportion of certain values. That alone would have left him enriched forever.

Practical as he could be, theories and explorations were yet dear to him: he was an inquisitive adventurer of the mind no less than an active adventurer of the world. He sought eagerly for underlying truths. His apparently inactive moods were most accurately his fallow moods. His thought was an ardent plough, turning and shifting the loam of his mind. Yet he would not allow his fancy to outrun his conviction; if fancy at any moment seemed to lead, he checked it until more lumbering conviction could catch up. They must travel ever abreast, whip and reins alike in his control.

Youth—were the years of youth the intuitive years of perception? Were the most radiant moments the moments in which one stepped farthest from the ordered acceptance of the world? Moments of danger, moments of inspiration, moments of self-sacrifice, moments of perceiving beauty, moments of love, all the drunken moments! Eve moved, he knew, permanently upon that plane. She led an exalted, high-keyed inner life. The normal mood to her was the mood of a sensitive person caught at the highest pitch of sensibility. Was she unsuited to the world and to the necessities of the world because she belonged, not here, but to another sphere apprehended by man only in those rare, keen moments that Julian called the drunken moments? apprehended by poet or artist—the elect, the aristocracy, the true path-finders among the race of man!—in moments when sobriety left them and they passed beyond?

Was she to blame for her cruelty, her selfishness, her disregard for truth? was she, not evil, but only alien? to be forgiven all for the sake of the rarer, more distant flame? Was the standard of cardinal virtues set by the world the true, the ultimate standard? Was it possible that Eve made part of a limited brotherhood? was indeed a citizen of some advanced state of such perfection that this world's measures and ideals were left behind and meaningless? meaningless because unnecessary in such a realm of serenity?

Aphros, then—the liberty of Aphros—and Aphros meant to him far more than merely Aphros—that was surely a lovely and desirable thing, a worthy aim, a high beacon? If Eve cared nothing for the liberty of Aphros, was it because in *her* world (he was now convinced of its existence) there was no longer any necessity to trouble over such aims, liberty being as natural and unmeditated as the air in the nostrils?

(Not that this would ever turn him from his devotion;

at most he could look upon Aphros as a stage upon the journey towards that higher aim—the stage to which he and his like, who were nearly of the elect, yet not of them, might aspire. And if the day should ever come when disillusion drove him down; when, far from becoming a citizen of Eve's far sphere, he should cease to be a citizen even of Aphros and should become a citizen merely of the world, no longer young, no longer blinded by ideals, no longer nearly a poet, but merely a grown, sober man—then he would still keep Aphros as a bright memory of what might have been, of the best he had grasped, the possibility which in the days of youth had not seemed too extravagantly unattainable.)

But in order to keep his hold upon this world of Eve's, which in his inner consciousness he already recognised as the most valuable rift of insight ever vouchsafed to him, it was necessary that he should revolutionise every ancient gospel and reputable creed. The worth of Eve was to him an article of faith. His intimacy with her was a privilege infinitely beyond the ordinary privilege of love. Whatever she might do, whatever crime she might commit, whatever baseness she might perpetrate, her ultimate worth, the core, the kernel, would remain to him unsullied and inviolate. This he knew blindly, seeing it as the mystic sees God; and knew it the more profoundly that he could have defended it with no argument of reason.

What then? the poet, the creator, the woman, the mystic, the man skirting the fringes of death—were they kin with one another and free of some realm unknown, towards which all, consciously or unconsciously, were journeying? Where the extremes of passion (he did not mean only the passion of love), of exaltation, of danger, of courage and vision—where all these extremes met—was it there, the great crossways where the moral ended, and the divine began? Was it for Eve supremely, and to a certain extent for all women and artists—the visionaries, the lovely, the graceful, the irresponsible, the useless!—was it reserved for them to show the beginning of the road?

Youth! youth and illusion! to love Eve and Aphros! when those two slipped from him he would return sobered to the path designated by the sign-posts and milestones of man, hoping no more than to keep as a gleam within him the light glowing in the sky above that unattainable but remembered city.

He returned to earth; Eve was kneading and tormenting a lump of putty, and singing to herself meanwhile; he watched her delicate, able hands, took one of them, and held it up between his eyes and the sun.

'Your fingers are transparent, they're like cornelian against the light,' he said.

She left her hand within his grasp, and smiled down at him.

'How you play with me, Julian,' she said idly.

'You're such a delicious toy.'

'Only a toy?'

He remembered the intricate, untranslatable thoughts he had been thinking about her five minutes earlier, and began to laugh to himself.

'A great deal more than a toy. Once I thought of you only as a child, a helpless, irritating, adorable child, always looking for trouble, and turning to me for help when the trouble came.'

'And then?'

'Then you made me think of you as a woman,' he replied gravely.

'You seemed to hesitate a good deal before deciding to think of me as that.'

'Yes, I tried to judge our position by ordinary codes; you must have thought me ridiculous.'

'I did, darling.' Her mouth twisted drolly as she said it.

'I wonder now how I could have insulted you by applying them to you,' he said with real wonderment; everything seemed so clear and obvious to him now.

'Why, how do you think of me now?'

'Oh, God knows!' he replied. 'I've called you changeling sometimes, haven't I?' He decided to question her. 'Tell me, Eve, how do you explain your difference? you outrage every accepted code, you see, and yet one retains one's belief in you. Is one simply deluded by your charm? or is there a deeper truth? can you explain?' He had spoken in a bantering tone, but he knew that he was trying an experiment of great import to him.

'I don't think I'm different, Julian; I think I feel things strongly, no more.'

'Or else you don't feel them at all.'

'What do you mean?'

'Well—Paul,' he said reluctantly.

'You have never got over that, have you?'

'Exactly!' he exclaimed. 'It seems to you extraordinary that I should still remember Paul, or that his death should have made any impression upon me. I ought to hate you for your indifference. Sometimes I have come very near to hating you. But now—perhaps my mind is getting broader—I blame you for nothing because I believe you are simply not capable of understanding. But evidently you can't explain yourself. I love you!' he said, 'I love you!'

He knew that her own inability to explain herself—her unself-consciousness—had done much to strengthen his new theories. The flower does not know why or how it blossoms. . . .

On the day that he told her, with many misgivings, that Kato was coming to Aphros, she uttered no word of anger, but wept despairingly, at first without speaking, then with short, reiterated sentences that wrung his heart for all their unreason,—

'We were alone. I was happy as never in my life. I had you utterly. We were alone. Alone! Alone!'

'We will tell Kato the truth,' he soothed her; 'she will leave us alone still.'

But it was not in her nature to cling to straws of comfort. For her, the sunshine had been unutterably radiant; and for her it was not proportionately blackened out.

'We were alone,' she repeated, shaking her head with unspeakable mournfulness, the tears running between her fingers.

For the first time he spoke to her with a moved, a tender compassion, full of reverence.

'Your joy . . . your sorrow . . . equally over-whelming and tempestuous. How you feel—you tragic child! Yesterday you laughed and made yourself a crown of myrtle.'

She refused to accompany him when he went to meet Kato, who, after a devious journey from Athens, was to land at the rear of the island away from the curiosity of Herakleion. She remained in the cool house, sunk in idleness, her pen and pencil alike neglected. She thought

220

only of Julian, absorbingly, concentratedly. Her past life appeared to her, when she thought of it at all, merely as a period in which Julian had not loved her, a period of waiting, of expectancy, of anguish sometimes, of incredible reticence supported only by the certainty which had been her faith and her inspiration. . . .

To her surprise, he returned, not only with Kato but with Grbits.

Every word and gesture of the giant demonstrated his enormous pleasure. His oddly Mongolian face wore a perpetual grin of triumphant truancy. His good-humour was not to be withstood. He wrung Eve's hands, inarticulate with delight. Kato, her head covered with a spangled veil—Julian had never seen her in a hat—stood by, looking on, her hands on her hips, as though Grbits were her exhibit. Her little eyes sparkled with mischief.

'He is no longer an officer in the Serbian army,' she said at last, 'only a free-lance, at Julian's disposal. Is it not magnificent? He has sent in his resignation. His career is ruined. The military representative of Serbia in Herakleion!'

'A free-lance,' Grbits repeated, beaming down at Julian. (It annoyed Eve that he should be so much the taller of the two).

'We sent you no word, not to lessen your surprise,' said Kato.

They stood, all four, in the courtyard by the fountain.

'I told you on the day of the elections that when you needed me I should come,' Grbits continued, his grin widening.

'Of course, you are a supreme fool, Grbits,' said Kato to him.

'Yes,' he replied, 'thank Heaven for it.'

'In Athens the sympathy is all with the Islands,' said Kato. She had taken off her veil, and they could see that she wore the gold wheat-ears in her hair. Her arms were, as usual, covered with bangles, nor had she indeed made any concessions to the necessities of travelling, save that on her feet, instead of her habitual square-toed slippers, she wore long, hideous, heelless, elastic-sided boots. Eve reflected that she had grown fatter and more stumpy, but she was, as ever, eager, kindly, enthusiastic, vital; they brought with them a breath of confidence and efficiency, those disproportionately assorted travelling companions; Julian felt a slight shame that he had neglected the Islands for Eve; and Eve stood by, listening to their respective recitals, to Grbits' startling explosions of laughter, and Kato's exuberant joy, tempered with wisdom. They both talked at once, voluble and excited; the wheat-ears trembled in Kato's hair, Grbits' white regular teeth flashed in his broad face, and Julian, a little bewildered, turned from one to the other with his unsmiling gravity.

'I mistrust the forbearance of Herakleion,' Kato said, a great weight of meditated action pressing on behind her words; 'a month's forbearance! In Athens innumerable rumours were current: of armed ships purchased from the Turks, even of a gun mounted on Mylassa—but that I do not believe. They have given you, you say, a month in which to come to your senses. But they are giving themselves also a month in which to prepare their attack,' and she plied him with practical questions that demonstrated her clear familiarity with detail and tactic, while Grbits contributed nothing but the cavernous laugh and ejaculations of his own unquestioning optimism.

Five

THE SECOND ATTACK on Aphros was delivered within a week of their arrival.

Eve and Kato, refusing the retreat in the heart of the island, spent the morning together in the Davenant house. In the distance the noise of the fighting alternately increased and waned; now crackling sharply, as it seemed, from all parts of the sea, now dropping into a disquieting silence. At such times Eve looked mutely at the singer. Kato gave her no comfort, but, shaking her head and shrugging her shoulders, expressed only her ignorance. She found that she could speak to Julian sympathetically of Eve, but not to Eve sympathetically of Julian. She had made the attempt, but after the pang of its effort, had renounced it. Their hostility smouldered dully under the shelter of their former friendship. Now, alone in the house, they might indeed have remained for the most time apart in separate rooms, but the common anxiety which linked them drew them together, so that when Kato moved Eve followed her, unwillingly, querulously; and expressions of affection were even forced from them, of which they instantly repented, and by some phrase of veiled cruelty sought to counteract.

No news reached them from outside. Every man was at his post, and Julian had forbidden all movement about the village. By his orders also the heavy shutters had been closed over the windows of the Davenant drawing-room, where Eve and Kato sat, with the door open on to the courtyard for the sake of light, talking spasmodically, and listening to the sounds of the firing. At the first quick rattle Kato had said, 'Machine-guns,' and Eve had replied, 'Yes; the first time—when we were here alone—he told me they had a machine-gun on the police-launch;' then

Kato said, after a pause of firing, 'This time they have more than one.'

Eve raised tormented eyes.

'Anastasia, he said he would be in shelter.'

'Would he remain in shelter for long?' Kato replied scornfully.

Eve said,—

'He has Grbits with him.'

Kato, crushing down the personal preoccupation, dwelt ardently on the fate of her country. She must abandon to Eve the thought of Julian, but of the Islands at least she might think possessively, diverting to their dear though inanimate claim all the need of passion and protection humanly denied her. From a woman of always intense patriotism, she had become a fanatic. Starved in one direction, she had doubled her energy in the other, realising, moreover, the power of that bond between herself and Julian. She could have said with thorough truthfulness that her principal cause of resentment against Eve was Eve's indifference toward the Islands—a loftier motive than the more human jealousy. She had noticed Julian's reluctance to mention the Islands in Eve's presence. Alone with herself and Grbits, he had never ceased to pour forth the flood of his scheme, both practical and utopian, so that Kato could not be mistaken as to the direction of his true preoccupations. She had seen the vigour he brought to his governing. She had observed with a delighted grin to Grbits that, despite his Socialistic theories, Julian had in point of fact instituted a complete and very thinly-veiled autocracy in Hagios Zacharie. She had seen him in the village assembly, when in spite of his deferential appeals to the superior experience of the older men, he steered blankly past any piece of advice that ran contrary to the course of his own ideas. She knew that, ahead of him, when he should have freed himself finally of Herakleion (and that he would free himself he did not for a moment doubt), he kept always the dream of his tiny, ideal state. She revered his faith, his energy, and his youth, as the essence in him most worthy of reverence. And she knew that Eve, if she loved these things in him, loved them only in theory, but in practice regarded them with impatient indifference. They stole him away, came between him and her. . . . Kato knew well Eve's own ideals. Courage she exacted. Talents she esteemed. Genius, freedom, and beauty she passionately worshipped as her gods upon earth. But she could tolerate nothing material, nor any occupation that removed her or the other from the blind absorption of love.

Kato sighed. Far otherwise would she have cared for Julian! She caught sight of herself in a mirror, thick, squat, black, with little sparkling eyes; she glanced at Eve, glowing with warmth, sleek and graceful as a little animal, idle and seductive. Outside a crash of firing shook the solid house, and bullets rattled upon the roofs of the village.

It was intolerable to sit unoccupied, working out bitter speculations, while such activity raged around the island. To know the present peril neither of Julian nor of Aphros! To wait indefinitely, probably all day, possibly all night!

'Anastasia, sing.'

Kato complied, as much for her own sake as for Eve's. She sang some of her own native songs, then, breaking off, she played, and Eve drew near to her, lost and transfigured by the music; she clasped and unclasped her hands, beautified by her ecstasy, and Kato's harsh thoughts vanished; Eve was, after all, a child, an all too loving and passionate child, and not, as Kato sometimes thought her, a pernicious force of idleness and waste. Wrong-headed, tragically bringing sorrow upon herself in the train of her too intense emotions. . . . Continuing to play, Kato observed her, and felt the light eager fingers upon her arm.

'Ah, Kato, you make me forget. Like some drug of forgetfulness that admits me to caves of treasure. Underground caves heaped with jewels. Caves of the winds; zephyrs that come and go. I'm carried away into oblivion.'

'Tell me,' Kato said.

Obedient to the lead of the music, Eve wandered into a story,—

'Riding on a winged horse, he swept from east to west; he looked down upon the sea, crossed by the wake of ships, splashed here and there with islands, washing on narrow brown stretches of sand, or dashing against the foot of cliffs—you hear the waves breaking?—and he saw how the moon drew the tides, and how ships came to rest for a little while in harbours, but were homeless and restless and free; he passed over the land, swooping low, and he saw the straight streets of cities, and the gleam of fires, the neat fields and guarded frontiers, the wider plains; he saw the gods throned on Ida, wearing the clouds like mantles and like crowns, divinely strong or divinely beautiful; he saw things mean and magnificent; he saw the triumphal procession of a conqueror, with prisoners walking chained to the back of his chariot, and before him white bulls with gilded horns driven to the sacrifice, and children running with garlands of flowers; he saw giants hammering red iron in northern mountains; he saw all the wanderers of the earth; Io the tormented, and all gipsies, vagabonds, and wastrels: all jongleurs, poets, and mountebanks; he saw these wandering, but all the staid and solemn people lived in the cities and counted the neat fields, saying, "This shall be mine and this shall be yours." And sometimes, as he passed above a forest, he heard a scurry of startled feet among crisp leaves, and sometimes he heard, which made him sad, the cry of stricken trees beneath the axe.'

She broke off, as Kato ceased playing.

'They are still firing,' she said.

'Things mean and magnificent,' quoted Kato slowly. 'Why, then, withhold Julian from the Islands?'

She had spoken inadvertently. Consciousness of the present had jerked her back from remembrance of the past, when Eve had come almost daily to her flat in Herakleion, bathing herself in the music, wrapped up in beauty; when their friendship had hovered on the boundaries of the emotional, in spite of—or perhaps because of?—the thirty years that lay between them.

'I heard the voice of my fantastic Eve, of whom I once thought,' she added, fixing her eyes on Eve, 'as the purest of beings, utterly removed from the sordid and the ugly.'

Eve suddenly flung herself on her knees beside her.

'Ah, Kato,' she said, 'you throw me off my guard when you play to me. I'm not always hard and calculating, and your music melts me. It hurts me to be, as I constantly am, on the defensive. I'm too suspicious by nature to be very happy, Kato. There are always shadows, and . . . and tragedy. Please don't judge me too harshly. Tell me what you mean by sordid and ugly—what is there sordid and ugly in love?'

Kato dared much: she replied in a level voice,—

'Jealousy. Waste. Exorbitance. Suspicion. I am sometimes afraid of your turning Julian into another of those men who hoped to find their inspiration in a woman, but found only a hindrance.'

She nodded sagely at Eve, and the gold wheat-ears trembled in her hair.

Eve darkened at Julian's name; she got up and stood by the door looking into the court. Kato went on,—

'You are so much of a woman, Eve, that it becomes a responsibility. It is a gift, like genius. And a great gift without a great soul is a curse, because such a gift is too strong to be disregarded. It's a force, a danger. You think I am preaching to you'—Eve would never know what the words were costing her—'but I preach only because of my belief in Julian—and in you,' she hastened to add, and caught Eve's hand; 'don't frown, you child. Look at me; I have no illusions and no sensitiveness on the score of my own appearance; look at me hard, and let me speak to you as a sexless creature.'

Eve was touched in spite of her hostility. She was also shocked and distressed. There was to her, so young herself, so insolently vivid in her sex-pride, something wrong and painful in Kato's renouncement of her right. She had a sense of betrayal.

'Hush, Anastasia,' she whispered. They were both extremely moved, and the constant volleys of firing played upon their nerves and stripped reserve from them.

'You don't realise,' said Kato, who had, upon impulse, sacrificed her pride, and beaten down the feminine weakness she branded as unworthy, 'how finely the balance, in love, falters between good and ill. You, Eve, are created for love; any one who saw you, even without speaking to you, across a room, could tell you that.' She smiled affectionately; she had, at that moment, risen so far above all personal vanity that she could bring herself to smile affectionately at Eve. 'You said, just now, with truth I am sure, that shadows and tragedy were never far away from you; you're too *rare* to be philosophical. I wish there were a word to express the antithesis of a philosopher; if I could call you by it, I should have said all that I could wish to say about you, Eve. I'm so much afraid of sorrow for you and Julian. . . .'

'Yes, yes,' said Eve, forgetting to be resentful, 'I am afraid, too; it overcomes me sometimes; it's a presentiment.' She looked really haunted, and Kato was filled with an immense pity for her.

'You mustn't be weak,' she said gently. 'Presentiment is only a high-sounding word for a weak thought.'

'You are so strong and sane, Kato; it is easy for you to be—strong and sane.'

They broke off, and listened in silence to an outburst of firing and shouts that rose from the village.

Grbits burst into the room early in the afternoon, his flat sallow face tinged with colour, his clothes torn, and his limbs swinging like the sails of a windmill. In one enormous hand he still brandished a revolver. He was triumphantly out of breath.

'Driven off!' he cried. 'They ran up a white flag. Not one succeeded in landing. Not one.' He panted between every phrase. 'Julian—here in a moment. I ran. Negotiations now, we hope. Sea bobbing with dead.'

'Our losses?' said Kato sharply.

'Few. All under cover,' Grbits replied. He sat down, swinging his revolver loosely between his knees, and ran his fingers through his oily black hair, so that it separated into straight wisps across his forehead. He was hugely pleased and good-humoured, and grinned widely upon Eve and Kato. 'Good fighting—though too much at a distance. Julian was grazed on the temple—told me to tell you,' he added, with the tardy haste of a child who has forgotten to deliver a message. 'We tied up his head, and it will be nothing of a scratch.—Driven off! They have tried and failed. The defence was excellent. They will scarcely try force again. I am sorry I missed the first fight. I could have thrown those little fat soldiers into the sea with one hand, two at a time.'

Kato rushed up to Grbits and kissed him; they were like children in their large, clumsy excitement.

Julian came in, his head bandaged; his unconcern deserted him as he saw Kato hanging over the giant's chair. He laughed out loud.

'A miscellaneous fleet!' he cried. 'Coastal steamers, fort tugs, old chirkets from the Bosphorous—who was the admiral, I wonder?'

'Panaïoannou,' cried Grbits, 'his uniform military down one side, and naval down the other.'

'Their white flag!' said Julian.

'Sterghiou's handkerchief!' said Grbits.

'Coaling steamers, mounting machine-guns,' Julian continued.

'Stavridis must have imagined that,' said Kato.

'Play us a triumphal march, Anastasia!' said Grbits.

Kato crashed some chords on the piano; they all laughed and sang, but Eve, who had taken no part at all, remained in the window-seat staring at the ground and her lips trembling. She heard Julian's voice calling her, but she obstinately shook her head. He was lost to her between Kato and Grbits. She heard them eagerly talking now, all three, of the negotiations likely to follow. She heard the occasional shout with which Grbits recalled some incident in the fighting, and Julian's response. She felt that her ardent hatred of the Islands rose in proportion to their ardent love. 'He cares nothing for me,' she kept repeating to herself, 'he cares for me as a toy, a pastime, nothing more; he forgets me for Kato and the Islands. The Islands hold his true heart. I am the ornament to his life, not life itself. And he is all my life. He forgets me. . . .' Pride alone conquered her tears.

Later, under cover of a white flag, the ex-Premier Malteios was landed at the port of Aphros, and was conducted—since he insisted that his visit was unofficial—to the Davenant house.

Peace and silence reigned. Grbits and Kato had gone together to look at the wreckage, and Eve, having watched their extraordinary progress down the street until they turned into the market-place, was alone in the drawing-room. Julian slept heavily, his arms flung wide, on his bed upstairs. Zapantiotis, who had expected to find him in the court or in the drawing-room, paused perplexed. He spoke to Eve in a low voice.

'No,' she said, 'do not wake Mr Davenant,' and, raising her voice, she added, 'His Excellency can remain with me.'

She was alone in the room with Malteios, as she had desired.

'But why remain thus, as it were, at bay?' he said pleasantly, observing her attitude, shrunk against the wall, her hand pressed to her heart. 'You and I were friends once, mademoiselle. Madame?' he substituted.

'Mademoiselle,' she replied levelly.

'Ah? Other rumours, perhaps—no matter. Here upon your island, no doubt, different codes obtain. Far be it from me to suggest. . . . An agreeable room,' he said, looking round, linking his fingers behind his back, and humming a little tune; 'you have a piano, I see; have you played much during your leisure? But, of course, I was forgetting: Madame Kato is your companion here, is she not? and to her skill a piano is a grateful ornament. Ah, I could envy you your evenings, with Kato to make your music. Paris cries for her; but no, she is upon a revolutionary island in the heart of the Ægean! Paris cries the more. Her portrait appears in every paper. Madame Kato, when she emerges, will find her fame carried to its summit. And you, Mademoiselle Eve, likewise something of a heroine.'

'I am here in the place of my cousin,' Eve said, looking across at the ex-Premier.

He raised his eyebrows, and in a familiar gesture, smoothed away his beard from his rosy lips with the tips of his fingers.

'Is that indeed so? A surprising race, you English. Very surprising. You assume or bequeath very lightly the mantle of government, do you not? Am I to understand that you have permanently replaced your cousin in the—ah!—presidency of Hagios Zacharie?'

'My cousin is asleep; there is no reason why you should not speak to me in his absence.'

'Asleep? but I must see him, mademoiselle.'

'If you will wait until he wakes.'

'Hours, possibly!'

'We will send to wake him in an hour's time. Can I not entertain you until then?' she suggested, her natural coquetry returning.

She left the wall against which she had been leaning, and, coming across to Malteios, gave him her fingers with a smile. The ex-Premier had always figured picturesquely in her world.

'Mademoiselle,' he said, kissing the fingers she gave him, 'you are as delightful as ever, I am assured.'

They sat, Malteios impatient and ill at ease, unwilling to forego his urbanity, yet tenacious of his purpose. In the midst of the compliments he perfunctorily proffered, he broke out,—

'Children! *Ces gosses. . . . Mais il est fou, voyons, votre cousin.* What is he thinking about? He has created a ridiculous disturbance; well, let that pass; we overlook it, but this persistence. . . . Where is it all to end? Obstinacy feeds and grows fat upon obstinacy; submission grows daily more impossible, more remote. His pride is at stake. A threat, well and good; let him make his threat; he might then have arrived at some compromise. I, possibly, might myself have acted as mediator between him and my friend and rival, Gregori Stavridis. In fact, I am here to-day in the hope that my effort will not come too late. But after so much fighting! Tempers run high no doubt in the Islands, and I can testify that they run high in Herakleion. Anastasia—probably you know this already—Madame Kato's flat is wrecked. Yes, the mob. We are obliged to keep a cordon of police always before your uncle's house. Neither he nor your father and mother dare to show themselves at the windows. It is a truly terrible state of affairs.'

He reverted to the deeper cause of his resentment,—

'I could have mediated, in the early days, so well between your cousin and Gregori Stavridis. Pity, pity, pity!' he said, shaking his head and smiling his benign, regretful smile that to-day was tinged with a barely concealed bitterness, 'a thousand pities, mademoiselle.'

He began again, his mind on Herakleion,—

'I have seen your father and mother, also your uncle. They are very angry and impotent. Because the people threw stones at their windows and even, I regret to say, fired shots into the house from the *platia*, the windows are all boarded over and they live by artificial light. I have seen them breakfasting by candles. Yes. Your father, your mother, and your uncle, breakfasting together in the drawing-room with lighted candles on the table. I entered the house from the back. Your father said to me apprehensively, "I am told Madame Kato's flat was wrecked last night?" and your mother said, "Outrageous! She is infatuated, either with those Islands or with that boy. She will not care. All her possessions, littering the quays! An outrage." Your uncle said to me, "See the boy, Malteios! Talk to him. We are hopeless." Indeed they appeared hopeless, although not resigned, and sat with their hands hanging by their sides instead of eating their eggs; your mother, even, had lost her determination.

'I tried to reassure them, but a rattle of stones on the boarded windows interrupted me. Your uncle got up and flung away his napkin. "One cannot breakfast in peace," he said petulantly, as though that constituted his most serious grievance. He went out of the room, but the door had scarcely closed behind him before it reopened and he came back. He was quite altered, very irritable, and all his courteous gravity gone from him. "See the inconvenience," he said to me, jerking his hands, "all the servants have gone with my son, all damned islanders." I found nothing to say.'

'Kato may return to Herakleion with you?' Eve suggested after a pause during which Malteios recollected himself, and tried to indicate by shrugs and rueful smiles that he considered the bewilderment of the Davenants a deplorable but nevertheless entertaining joke. At the name of Kato, a change came over his face.

'A fanatic, that woman,' he replied; 'a martyr who will rejoice in her martyrdom. She will never leave Aphros while the cause remains.—A heroic woman,' he said, with unexpected reverence.

He looked at Eve, his manner veering again to the insinuating and the crafty; his worse and his better natures were perpetually betraying themselves.

'Would she leave Aphros? no! Would your cousin leave Aphros? no! They have between them the bond of a common cause. I know your cousin. He is young enough to be an idealist. I know Madame Kato. She is old enough to applaud skilfully. Hou!' He spread his hands. 'I have said enough.'

Eve revealed but little interest, though for the first time during their interview her interest was passionately aroused. Malteios watched her, new schemes germinating in his brain; they played against one another, their hands undeclared, a blind, tentative game. This conversation, which had begun as it were accidentally, fortuitously, turned to a grave significance along a road whose end lay hidden far behind the hills of the future. It led, perhaps, nowhere. It led, perhaps . . .

Eve said lightly,—

'I am outdistanced by Kato and my cousin; I don't understand politics, or those impersonal friendships.'

'Mademoiselle,' Malteios replied, choosing his words and infusing into them an air of confidence, 'I tell you an open secret, but one to which I would never refer save with a sympathetic listener like yourself, when I tell you that for many years a friendship existed between myself and Madame Kato, political indeed, but not impersonal. Madame Kato,' he said, drawing his chair a little nearer and lowering his voice, 'is not of the impersonal type.'

Eve violently rebelled from his nearness; fastidious, she loathed his goatish smile, his beard, his rosy lips, but she continued to smile to him, a man who held, perhaps, one of Julian's secrets. She was aware of the necessity of obtaining that secret. Of the dishonour towards Julian, sleeping away his hurts and his fatigue in the room above, she was blindly unaware. Love to her was a battle, not a fellowship. She must know! Already her soul, eagerly receptive and bared to the dreaded blow, had adopted the theory of betrayal. In the chaos of her resentments and suspicions, she remembered how Kato had spoken to her in the morning, and without further reflection branded that conversation as a blind. She even felt a passing admiration for the other woman's superior cleverness. She, Eve, had been completely taken in. . . . So she must contend, not only against the Islands, but against Kato also? Anguish and terror rushed over her. She scarcely knew what she believed or did not believe, only that her mind was one seething and surging tumult of mistrust and all-devouring jealousy. She was on the point of abandoning her temperamentally indirect methods, of stretching out her hands to Malteios, and crying to him for the agonising, the fiercely welcome truth, when he said,—

'Impersonal? Do you, mademoiselle, know anything of your sex? Ah, charming! disturbing, precious, indispensable, even heroic, *tant que vous voudrez,* but impersonal, no! Man, yes, sometimes. Woman, never. Never.' He took her hand, patted it, kissed the wrist, and murmured, 'Chère enfant, these are not ideas for your pretty head.'

She knew from experience that his preoccupation with such theories, if no more sinister motive, would urge him towards a resumption of the subject, and after a pause full of cogitation he continued,—

'Follow my advice, mademoiselle: never give your heart to a man concerned in other affairs. You may love, both of you, but you will strive in opposite directions. Your cousin, for example. . . . And yet,' he mused, 'you are a woman to charm the leisure of a man of action. The toy of a conqueror.' He laughed. 'Fortunately, conquerors are rare.' But she knew he hovered round the image of Julian. 'Believe me, leave such men to such women as Kato; they are more truly kin. You—I discover you—are too exorbitant; love would play too absorbing a rôle. You would tolerate no rival, neither a person nor a fact. Your eyes smoulder; I am near the truth?'

'One could steal a man from his affairs,' she said almost inaudibly.

'The only hope,' he replied.

A long silence fell, and his evil benevolence gained on her; on her aroused sensitiveness his unspoken suggestions fell one by one as definitely as the formulated word. He watched her; she trembled, half compelled by his gaze. At length, under the necessity of breaking the silence, she said,—

'Kato is not such a woman; she would resent no obstacle.'

'Wiser,' he added, 'she would identify herself with it.'

He began to banter horribly,—

'Ah, child, Eve, child made for love, daily bless your cousinship! Bless its contemptuous security. Smile over the confabulations of Kato and your cousin. Smile to think that he, she, and the Islands are bound in an indissoluble triology. If there be jealousy to suffer, rejoice in that it falls, not to your share, but to mine, who am old and sufficiently philosophical. Age and experience harden, you know. Else, I could not see Anastasia Kato pass to another with so negligible a pang. Yet the imagination makes its own trouble. A jealous imagination. . . . Very vivid. Pictures of Anastasia Kato in your cousin's arms—ah, crude, crude, I know, but the crudity of the jealous imagination is unequalled. Not a detail escapes. That is why I say, bless your cousinship and its security.' He glanced up and met her tortured eyes. 'As I bless my philosophy of the inevitable,' he finished softly, caressing her hand which he had retained all the while.

No effort at 'Impossible!' escaped her; almost from the

first she had blindly adopted his insinuations. She even felt a perverse gratitude towards him, and a certain fellowship. They were allies. Her mind was now set solely upon one object. That self-destruction might be involved did not occur to her, nor would she have been deterred thereby. Like Samson, she had her hands upon the columns. . . .

'Madame Kato lives in this house?' asked Malteios, as one who has been following a train of thought.

She shook her head, and he noticed that her eyes were turned slightly inwards, as with the effort of an immense concentration.

'You have power,' he said with admiration.

Bending towards her, he began to speak in a very low, rapid voice; she sat listening to him, by no word betraying her passionate attention, nodding only from time to time, and keeping her hands very still, linked in her lap. Only once she spoke, to ask a question, 'He would leave Herakleion?' and Malteios replied, 'Inevitably; the question of the Islands would be for ever closed for him'; then she said, producing the words from afar off, 'He would be free,' and Malteios, working in the dark, following only one of the two processes of her thought, reverted to Kato; his skill could have been greater in playing upon the instrument, but even so it sufficed, so taut was the stringing of the cords. When he had finished speaking, she asked him another question, 'He could never trace the thing to me?' and he reassured her with a laugh so natural and contemptuous that she, in her ingenuity, was convinced. All the while she had kept her eyes fastened on his face, on his rosy lips moving amongst his beard, that she might lose no detail of his meaning or his instructions, and at one moment he had thought, 'There is something terrible in this child,' but immediately he had crushed the qualm, thinking 'By this recovery, if indeed it is to be, I am a made man,' and thanking the fate that had cast this unforeseen chance across his path. Finally she heard his voice change from its earnest undertone to its customary platitudinous flattery, and turning round she saw that Julian had come into the room, his eyes already bent with brooding scorn upon the emissary.

Six

SHE WAS SILENT that evening, so silent that Grbits, the unobservant, commented to Kato; but after they had dined, all four, by the fountain in the court, she flung aside her preoccupation, laughed and sang, forced Kato to the piano, and danced with reckless inspiration to the accompaniment of Kato's songs. Julian, leaning against a column, watched her bewildering gaiety. She had galvanised Grbits into movement—he who was usually bashful with women especially with Eve, reserving his enthusiasm for Julian—and as she passed and re-passed before Julian in the grasp of the giant she flung at him provocative glances charged with a special meaning he could not interpret; in the turn of her dance he caught her smile and the flash of her eyes, and smiled in response, but his smile was grave, for his mind ran now upon the crisis with Herakleion, and, moreover, he suffered to see Eve so held by Grbits, her turbulent head below the giant's shoulder, and regretted that her gaiety should not be reserved for him alone. Across the court, through the open door of the drawing-room, he could see Kato at the piano, full of delight, her broad little fat hands and wrists racing above the keyboard, her short torso swaying to the rhythm, her rich voice humming, and the gold wheat-ears shaking in her hair. She called to him, and, drawing a chair close to the piano, he sat beside her, but through the door he continued to stare at Eve dancing in the court. Kato said as she played, her perception sharpened by the tormented watch she kept on him,—

'Eve celebrates your victory of yesterday,' to which he replied, deceived by the kindly sympathy in her eyes,—

'Eve celebrates her own high spirits and the enjoyment of a new partner; my doings are of the least indifference to her.'

Kato played louder; she bent towards him,—

'You love her so much, Julian?'

He made an unexpected answer,—

'I believe in her.'

Kato, a shrewd woman, observed him, thinking,—'He does not; he wants to convince himself.'

She said aloud, conscientiously wrenching out the truth as she saw it,—

'She loves you; she is capable of love such as is granted to few; that is the sublime in her.'

He seized upon this, hungrily, missing meanwhile the sublime in the honesty of the singer,—

'Since I am given so much, I should not exact more. The Islands. . . . She gives all to me. I ought not to force the Islands upon her.'

'Grapes of thistles,' Kato said softly.

'You understand,' he murmured with gratitude. 'But why should she hamper me, Anastasia? are all women so irrational? What am I to believe?'

'We are not so irrational as we appear,' Kato said, 'because our wildest sophistry has always its roots in the truth of instinct.'

Eve was near them, crying out,—

'A tarantella, Anastasia!'

Julian sprang up; he caught her by the wrist,—

'Gipsy!'

'Come with the gipsy?' she whispered.

Her scented hair blew near him, and her face was upturned, with its soft, sweet mouth.

'Away from Aphros?' he said, losing his head.

'All over the world!'

He was suddenly swept away by the full force of her wild, irresponsible seduction.

'Anywhere you choose, Eve.'

She triumphed, close to him, and wanton.

'You'd sacrifice Aphros to me?'

'Anything you asked for,' he said desperately.

She laughed, and danced away, stretching out her hands towards him,—

'Join in the saraband, Julian?'

She was alone in her room. Her emotions and excitement were so intense that they drained her of physical strength, leaving her faint and cold; her eyes closed now and then as under the pressure of pain; she yawned, and her breath came shortly between her lips; she sat by the open window, rose to move about the room, sat again, rose again, passed her hand constantly over her forehead, or pressed it against the base of her throat. The room was in darkness; there was no moon, only the stars hung over the black gulf of the sea. She could see the long, low lights of Herakleion, and the bright red light of the pier. She could hear distant shouting, and an occasional shot. In the room behind her, her bed was disordered. She wore only her Spanish shawl thrown over her long nightgown; her hair hung in its thick plait. Sometimes she formed, in a whisper, the single word, 'Julian!'

She thought of Julian. Julian's rough head and angry eyes. Julian when he said, 'I shall break you,' like a man speaking to a wild young supple tree. (Her laugh of derision, and her rejoicing in her secret fear!) Julian in his lazy ownership of her beauty. Julian when he allowed her to coax him from his moroseness. Julian when she was afraid of him and of the storm she had herself aroused: Julian passionate. . . .

Julian whom she blindly wanted for herself alone.

That desire had risen to its climax. The light of no other consideration filtered through into her closely shuttered heart. She had waited for Julian, schemed for Julian, battled for Julian; this was the final battle. She had not foreseen it. She had tolerated and even welcomed the existence of the Islands until she began to realise that they took part of Julian from her. Then she hated them insanely, implacably; including Kato, whom Julian had called their tutelary deity, in that hatred. Had Julian possessed a dog, she would have hated that too.

The ambitions she had vaguely cherished for him had not survived the test of surrendering a portion of her own inordinate claim.

She had joined battle with the Islands as with a malignant personality. She was fighting them for the possession of Julian as she might have fought a woman she thought more beautiful, more unscrupulous, more appealing than herself, but with very little doubt of ultimate victory. Julian would be hers, at last; more completely hers than he had been even in those ideal, uninterrupted days before

Grbits and Kato came, the days when he forgot his obligations, almost his life's dream for her. Love all-eclipsing. . . . She stood at the window, oppressed and tense, but in the soft silken swaying of her loose garments against her limbs she still found a delicately luxurious comfort.

Julian had been called away, called by the violent hammering on the house-door; it had then been after midnight. Two hours had passed since then. No one had come to her, but she had heard the tumult of many voices in the streets, and by leaning far out of the window she could see a great flare burning up from the market-place. She had thought a house might be on fire. She could not look back over her dispositions; they had been completed in a dream, as though under direct dictation. It did not occur to her to be concerned as to their possible miscarriage; she was too ignorant of such matters, too unpractical, to be troubled by any such anxiety. She had carried out Malteios' instructions with intense concentration; there her part had ended. The fuse which she had fired was burning. . . . If Julian would return, to put an end to her impatience!

(Down in the market-place the wooden school-buildings flamed and crackled, redly lighting up the night, and fountains of sparks flew upward against the sky. The lurid market-place was thronged with sullen groups of islanders, under the guard of the soldiers of Herakleion. In the centre, on the cobbles, lay the body of Tsigaridis, on his back, arms flung open, still, in the enormous pool of blood that crept and stained the edges of his spread white fustanelle. Many of the islanders were not fully dressed, but had run out half-naked from their houses, only to be captured and disarmed by the troops; the weapons which had been taken from them lay heaped near the body of Tsigaridis, the light of the flames gleaming along the blades of knives and the barrels of rifles, and on the bare bronzed chests of men, and limbs streaked with tricklets of bright red blood. They stood proudly, contemptuous of their wounds, arms folded, some with rough bandages about their heads. Panaïoannou, leaning both hands on the hilt of his sword, and grinning sardonically beneath his fierce moustaches, surveyed the place from the steps of the assembly-room).

Eve in her now silent room realised that all sounds of tumult had died away. A shivering came over her, and, impelled by a suddenly understood necessity, she lit the candles on her dressing-table and, as the room sprang into light, began flinging the clothes out of the drawers into a heap in the middle of the floor. They fluttered softly from her hands, falling together in all their diverse loveliness of colour and fragility of texture. She paused to smile to them, friends and allies. She remembered now, with the fidelity of a child over a well-learnt lesson, the final words of Malteios, 'A boat ready for you both to-night, secret and without delay,' as earlier in the evening she had remembered his other words, 'Midnight, at the creek at the back of the islands . . .'; she had acted upon her lesson mechanically, and in its due sequence, conscientious, trustful.

She stood amongst her clothes, the long red sari which she had worn on the evening of Julian's first triumph drooping from her hand. They foamed about her feet as she stood doubtfully above them, strangely brilliant herself in her Spanish shawl. They lay in a pool of rich delicacy upon the floor. They hung over the backs of chairs, and across the tumbled bed. They pleased her; she thought them pretty. Stooping, she raised them one by one, and allowed them to drop back on to the heap, aware that she must pack them and must also dress herself. But she liked their butterfly colours and gentle rustle, and, remembering that Julian liked them too, smiled to them again. He found her standing there amongst them when after a knock at her door he came slowly into her room.

He remained by the door for a long while looking at her in silence. She had made a sudden, happy movement towards him, but inexplicably had stopped, and with the sari still in her hand gazed back at him, waiting for him to speak. He looked above all, mortally tired. She discovered no anger in his face, not even sorrow; only that mortal weariness. She was touched; she to whom those gentler emotions were usually foreign.

'Julian?' she said, seized with doubt.

'It is all over,' he began, quite quietly, and he put his hand against his forehead, which was still bandaged, raising his arm with the same lassitude; 'they landed where young Zapantiotis was on guard, and he let them through; they were almost at the village before they were discovered. There was very little fighting. They have allowed me to come here. They are waiting for me downstairs. I am to leave.'

'Yes,' she said, and looked down at her heap of clothes.

He did not speak again, and gradually she realised the implications of his words.

'Zapantiotis. . . .' she said.

'Yes,' he said, raising his eyes again to her face, 'yes, you see, Zapantiotis confessed it all to me when he saw me. He was standing amongst a group of prisoners, in the market-place, but when I came by he broke away from the guards and screamed out to me that he had betrayed us. Betrayed us. He said he was tempted, bribed. He said he would cut his own throat. But I told him not to do that.'

She began to tremble, wondering how much he knew. He added, in the saddest voice she had ever heard,—

'Zapantiotis, an islander, could not be faithful.'

Then she was terrified; she did not know what was coming next, what would be the outcome of this quietness. She wanted to come towards him, but she could only remain motionless, holding the sari up to her breast as a means of protection.

'At least,' he said, 'old Zapantiotis is dead, and will never know about his son. Where can one look for fidelity? Tsigaridis is dead too, and Grbits. I am ashamed of being alive.'

She noticed then that he was disarmed.

'Why do you stand over there, Julian?' she said timidly.

'I wonder how much your promised Zapantiotis?' he said in a speculative voice; and next, stating a fact, 'You were, of course, acting on Malteios' suggestion.'

'You know?' she breathed. She was quite sure now that he was going to kill her.

'Zapantiotis tried to tell me that too—in a strange jumble of confessions. But they dragged him away before he could say more than your bare name. That was enough for me. So I know, Eve.'

'Is that all you were going to say?'

He raised his arms and let them fall.

'What is there to say?'

Knowing him very well, she saw that his quietness was dropping from him; she was aware of it perhaps before he was aware of it himself. His eyes were losing their dead apathy, and were travelling round the room; they rested on the heap of clothes, on her own drawing of himself hanging on the wall, on the disordered bed. They flamed suddenly, and he made a step towards her.

'Why? why? why?' he cried out with the utmost anguish and vehemence, but stopped himself, and stood with clenched fists. She shrank away. 'All gone—in an hour!' he said, and striding towards her he stood over her, shaken with a tempest of passion. She shrank farther from him, retreating against the wall, but first she stooped and gathered her clothes around her again, pressing her back against the wall and cowering with the clothes as a rampart round her feet. But as yet full realisation was denied her; she knew that he was angry, she thought indeed that he might kill her, but to other thoughts of finality she was, in all innocence, a stranger.

He spoke incoherently, saying, 'All gone! All gone!' in accents of blind pain, and once he said, 'I thought you loved me,' putting his hands to his head as though walls were crumbling. He made no further reproach, save to repeat, 'I thought the men were faithful, and that you loved me,' and all the while he trembled with the effort of his self-control, and his twitching hands reached out towards her once or twice, but he forced them back. She thought, 'How angry he is! but he will forget, and I shall make up to him for what he has lost.' So, between them, they remained almost silent, breathing hard, and staring at one another.

'Come, put up your clothes quickly,' he said at last, pointing; 'they want us off the island, and if we do not go of our own accord they will tie our hands and feet and carry us to the boat. Let us spare ourselves that ludicrous scene. We can marry in Athens to-morrow.'

'Marry?' she repeated.

'Naturally. What else did you suppose? That I should leave you? now? Put up your clothes. Shall I help you? Come!'

'But—marry, Julian?'

'Clearly: marry,' he replied, in a harsh voice and added, 'Let us go. For God's sake, let us go now! I feel stunned, I mustn't begin to think. Let us go.' He urged her towards the door.

'But we had nothing to do with marriage,' she whispered.

He cried, so loudly and so bitterly that she was startled,—

'No, we had to do only with love—love and rebellion! And both have failed me. Now, instead of love, we must have marriage; and instead of rebellion, law. I shall help on authority, instead of opposing it.' He broke down and buried his face in his hands.

'You no longer love me,' she said slowly, and her eyes narrowed and turned slightly inwards in the way Malteios had noticed. 'Then the Islands . . .'

He pressed both hands against his temples and screamed like one possessed, 'But they were all in all in all! It isn't the thing, it's the soul behind the thing. In robbing me of them you've robbed me of more than them—you've robbed me of all the meaning that lay behind them.' He retained just sufficient self-possession to realise this. 'I knew you were hostile, how could I fail to know it? but I persuaded myself that you were part of Aphros, part of all my beliefs, even something beyond all my beliefs. I loved you, so you and they had to be reconciled. I reconciled you in secret. I gave up mentioning the Islands to you because it stabbed me to see your indifference. It destroyed the illusion I was cherishing. So I built up fresh, separate illusions about you. I have been living on illusions, now I have nothing left but facts. I owe this to you, to you, to you!'

'You no longer love me,' she said again. She could think of nothing else. She had not listened to his bitter and broken phrases. 'You no longer love me, Julian.'

'I was so determined that I would be deceived by no woman, and like every one else I have fallen into the trap. Because you were you, I ceased to be on my guard. Oh, you never pretended to care for Aphros; I grant you that honesty; but I wanted to delude myself and so I was deluded. I told myself marvellous tales of your rarity; I thought you were above even Aphros. I am punished for my weakness in bringing you here. Why hadn't I the strength to remain solitary? I reproach myself; I had not the right to expose my Islands to such a danger. But how could I have known? how could I have known?'

'Clearly you no longer love me,' she said for the third time.

'Zapantiotis sold his soul for money—was it money you promised him?' he went on. 'So easily—just for a little money! His soul, and all of us, for money. Money, father's god; he's a wise man, father, to serve the only remunerative god. Was it money you promised Zapantiotis?' he shouted at her, seizing her by the arm, 'or was he, perhaps, like Paul, in love with you? Did you perhaps promise him yourself? How am I to know? There may still be depths in you—you woman—that I know nothing about. Did you give yourself to Zapantiotis? Or is he coming tonight for his reward? Did you mean to ship me off to Athens, you and your accomplices, while you waited here in this room—*our* room—for your lover?'

'Julian!' she cried—he had forced her on to her knees—'you are saying monstrous things.'

'You drive me to them,' he replied; 'when I think that while the troops were landing you lay in my arms, here, knowing all the while that you had betrayed me—I could believe anything of you. Monstrous things! Do you know what monstrous things I am thinking? That you shall not belong to Zapantiotis, but to me. Yes, to me. You destroy love, but desire revives, without love; horrible, but sufficient. That's what I am thinking. I dare say I could kiss you still, and forget. Come!'

He was beside himself.

'Your accusations are so outrageous,' she said, half-fainting, 'your suggestions are obscene, Julian; I would rather you killed me at once.'

'Then answer me about Zapantiotis. How am I to know?' he repeated, already slightly ashamed of his outburst, 'I'm readjusting my ideas. Tell me the truth; I scarcely care.'

'Believe what you choose,' she replied, although he still held her, terrified, on the ground at his feet, 'I have more pride than you credit me with—too much to answer you.'

'It was money,' he said after a pause, releasing her. She stood up; reaction overcame her, and she wept.

'Julian, that you should believe that of me! You cut me to the quick—and I gave myself to you with such pride and gladness,' she added almost inaudibly.

'Forgive me; I suppose you, also, have your own moral

code; I have speculated sufficiently about it, Heaven known, but that means very little to me now,' he said, more quietly, and with even a spark of detached interest and curiosity. But he did not pursue the subject. 'What do you want done with your clothes? We have wasted quite enough time.'

'You want me to come with you?'

'You sound incredulous; why?'

'I know you have ceased to love me. You spoke of marrying me. Your love must have been a poor flimsy thing, to topple over as it has toppled! Mine is more tenacious, alas. It would not depend on outside happenings.'

'How dare you accuse me?' he said, 'You destroy and take from me all that I care for' ('Yes,' she interpolated, as much bitterness in her voice as in his own—but all the time they were talking against one another—'you cared for everything but me'), 'then you brand my love for you as a poor flimsy thing. If you have killed it, you have done so by taking away the one thing . . .'

'That you cared for more than for me,' she completed.

'With which I would have associated you. You yourself made that association impossible. You hated the things I loved. Now you've killed those things, and my love for you with them. You've killed everything I cherished and possessed.'

'Dead? Irretrievably?' she whispered.

'Dead.'

He saw her widened and swimming eyes and added, too much stunned for personal malice, yet angry because of the pain he was suffering,—

'You shall never be jealous of me again. I think I've loved all women, loved you—gone through the whole of love, and now washed my hands of it; I've tested and plumbed your vanity, your hideous egotism'—she was crying like a child, unreservedly, her face hidden against her arm—'your lack of breadth in everything that was not love.'

As he spoke, she raised her face and he saw light breaking on her—although it was not, and never would be, precisely the light he desired. It was illumination and horror; agonised horror, incredulous dismay. Her eyes were streaming with tears, but they searched him imploringly, despairingly, as in a new voice she said,—

245

'I've hurt you, Julian . . . how I've hurt you! Hurt you! I would have died for you. Can't I put it right? oh, tell me! Will you kill me?' and she put her hand up to her throat, offering it. 'Julian, I've hurt you . . . my own, my Julian. What have I done? What madness made me do it? Oh, what is there now for me to do? only tell me; I do beseech you only to tell me. Shall I go—to whom?—to Malteios? I understand nothing; you must tell me. I wanted you so greedily; you must believe that. Anything, anything you want me to do. . . . It wasn't sufficient, to love you, to want you; I gave you all I had, but it wasn't sufficient. I loved you wrongly, I suppose; but I loved you, I loved you!'

He had been angry, but now he was seized with a strange pity; pity of her childish bewilderment: the thing that she had perpetrated was a thing she could not understand. She would never fully understand. . . . He looked at her as she stood crying, and remembered her other aspects, in the flood-time of her joy, careless, radiant, irresponsible; they had shared hours of illimitable happiness.

'Eve! Eve!' he cried, and through the wrenching despair of his cry he heard the funeral note, the tear of cleavage like the downfall of a tree.

He took her in his arms and made her sit upon the bed; she continued to weep, and he sat beside her, stroking her hair. He used terms of endearment towards her, such as he had never used in the whole course of their passionate union, 'Eve, my little Eve'; and he kept on repeating, 'my little Eve,' and pressing her head against his shoulder.

They sat together like two children. Presently she looked up, pushing back her hair with a gesture he knew well.

'We both lose the thing we cared most for upon earth, Julian: you lose the Islands, and I lose you.'

She stood up, and gazed out of the window towards Herakleion. She stood there for some time without speaking, and a fatal clearness spread over her mind, leaving her quite strong, quite resolute, and coldly armoured against every shaft of hope.

'You want me to marry you,' she said at length.

'You must marry me in Athens to-morrow, if possible, and as soon as we are married we can go to England.'

'I utterly refuse,' she said, turning round towards him.

He stared at her; she looked frail and tired, and with one small white hand held together the edges of her Spanish shawl. She was no longer crying.

'Do you suppose,' she went on, 'that not content with having ruined the beginning of your life for you—I realise it now, you see—I shall ruin the rest of it as well? You may believe me or not, I speak the truth like a dying person when I tell you I love you to the point of sin; yes, it's a sin to love as I love you. It's blind, it's criminal. It's my curse, the curse of Eve, to love so well that one loves badly. I didn't see. I wanted you too blindly. Even now I scarcely understand how you can have ceased to love me.—No, don't speak. I do understand it—in a way; and yet I don't understand it. I don't understand that an idea can be dearer to one than the person one loves. . . . I don't understand responsibilities; when you've talked about responsibilities I've sometimes felt that I was made of other elements than you. . . . But you're a man and I'm a woman; that's the rift. Perhaps it's a rift that can never be bridged. Never mind that. Julian, you must find some more civilised woman than myself; find a woman who will be a friend, not an enemy. Love makes me into an enemy, you see. Find somebody more tolerant, more unselfish. More maternal. Yes, that's it,' she said, illuminated, 'more maternal; I'm only a lover, not a mother. You told me once that I was of the sort that sapped and destroyed. I'll admit that, and let you go. You mustn't waste yourself on me. But, oh, Julian,' she said, coming close to him, 'if I give you up—because in giving you up I utterly break myself—grant me one justice: never doubt that I loved you. Promise me, Julian. I shan't love again. But don't doubt that I loved you; don't argue to yourself, "She broke my illusions, therefore she never loved me," let me make amends for what I did, by sending you away now without me.'

'I was angry; I was lying; I wanted to hurt you as you had hurt me,' he said desperately. 'How can I tell what I have been saying to you? I've been dazed, struck. . . . It's untrue that I no longer love you. I love you, in spite, in spite . . . Love can't die in an hour.'

'Bless you,' she said, putting her hand for a moment on his head, 'but you can't deceive me. Oh,' she hurried on, 'you might deceive yourself; you might persuade yourself that you still loved me and wanted me to go with you; but I know better. I'm not for you. I'm not for your happiness, or for any man's happiness. You've said it yourself: I am different. I let you go because you are strong and useful—oh, yes, useful! so disinterested and strong, all that I am not—too good for me to spoil. You have nothing in common with me. Who has? I think I haven't any kindred. I love you! I love you better than myself!'

He stood up; he stammered in his terror and earnestness, but she only shook her head.

'No, Julian.'

'You're too strong,' he cried, 'you little weak thing; stronger than I.'

She smiled; he was unaware of the very small reserve of her strength.

'Stronger than you,' she repeated; 'yes.'

Again he implored her to go with him; he even threatened her, but she continued to shake her head and to say in a faint and tortured voice,—

'Go now, Julian; go, my darling; go now, Julian.'

'With you, or not at all.' He was at last seriously afraid that she meant what she said,

'Without me.'

'Eve, we were so happy. Remember! Only come; we shall be as happy again.'

'You mustn't tempt me; it's cruel,' she said, shivering. 'I'm human.'

'But I love you!' he said. He seized her hands, and tried to drag her towards the door.

'No,' she answered, putting him gently away from her. 'Don't tempt me, Julian, don't; let me make amends in my own way.'

Her gentleness and dignity were such that he now felt reproved, and, dimly, that the wrong done was by him towards her, not by her towards him.

'You are too strong—magnificent, and heartbreaking,' he said in despair.

'As strong as a rock,' she replied, looking straight at him and thinking that at any moment she must fall. But still she forced her lips to a smile of finality.

'Think better of it,' he was beginning, when they heard a stir of commotion in the court below.

'They are coming for you!' she cried out in sudden panic. 'Go; I can't face any one just now. . . .'

He opened the door on to the landing.

'Kato!' he said, falling back. Eve heard the note of fresh anguish in his voice.

Kato came in; even in that hour of horror they saw that she had merely dragged a quilt round her shoulders, and that her hair was down her back. In this guise her appearance was indescribably grotesque.

'Defeated, defeated,' she said in lost tones to Julian. She did not see that they had both involuntarily recoiled before her; she was beyond such considerations.

'Anastasia,' he said, taking her by the arm and shaking her slightly to recall her from her bemusement, 'here is something more urgent—thank God, you will be my ally—Eve must leave Aphros with me; tell her so, tell her so; she refuses.' He shook her more violently with the emphasis of his words.

'If he wants you. . . .' Kato said, looking at Eve, who had retreated into the shadows and stood there, half fainting, supporting herself against the back of a chair. 'If he wants you. . . .' she repeated, in a stupid voice, but her mind was far away.

'You don't understand, Anastasia,' Eve answered; 'it was I that betrayed him.' Again she thought she must fall.

'She is lying!' cried Julian.

'No,' said Eve. She and Kato stared at one another, so preposterously different, yet with currents of truth rushing between them.

'You!' Kato said at last, awaking.

'I am sending him away,' said Eve, speaking as before to the other woman.

'You!' said Kato again. She turned wildly to Julian. 'Why didn't you trust yourself to me, Julian, my beloved?' she cried; 'I wouldn't have treated you so, Julian; why didn't you trust yourself to me?' She pointed at Eve, silent and brilliant in her coloured shawl; then, her glance falling upon her own person, so sordid, so unkempt, she gave a dreadful cry and looked around as though seeking for escape. The other two both turned their heads away; to look at Kato in that moment was more than they could bear.

Presently they heard her speaking again; her self-abandonment had been brief; she had mastered herself, and was making it a point of honour to speak with calmness.

'Julian, the officers have orders that you must leave the island before dawn; if you do not go to them, they will fetch you here. They are waiting below in the courtyard now. Eve,'—her face altered,—'Eve is right: if she has indeed done as she says, she cannot go with you. She is right; she is more right, probably, than she has ever been in her life before or ever will be again. Come, now; I will go with you.'

'Stay with Eve, if I go,' he said.

'Impossible!' replied Kato, instantly hardening, and casting upon Eve a look of hatred and scorn.

'How cruel you are, Anastasia!' said Julian, making a movement of pity towards Eve.

'Take him away, Anastasia,' Eve murmured, shrinking from him.

'See, she understands me better than you do, and understands herself better too,' said Kato, in a tone of cruel triumph; 'if you do not come, Julian, I shall send up the officers.' As she spoke she went out of the room, her quilt trailing, and her heel-less slippers clacking on the boards.

'Eve, for the last time. . . .'

A cry was wrenched from her,—

'Go! if you pity me!'

'I shall come back.'

'Oh, no, no!' she replied, 'you'll never come back. One doesn't live through such things twice.' She shook her head like a tortured animal that seeks to escape from pain. He gave an exclamation of despair, and, after one wild gesture towards her, which she weakly repudiated, he followed Kato. Eve heard their steps upon the stairs, then crossing the courtyard, and the tramp of soldiers; the house-door crashed massively. She stooped very slowly and mechanically, and began to pick up the gay and fragile tissue of her clothes.

Seven

SHE LAID THEM all in orderly fashion across the bed, smoothing out the folds with a care that was strongly opposed to her usual impatience. Then she stood for some time drawing the thin silk of the sari through her fingers and listening for sounds in the house; there were none. The silence impressed her with the fact that she was alone.

'Gone!' she thought, but she made no movement.

Her eyes narrowed and her mouth became contracted with pain.

'Julian . . .' she murmured, and, finding some slippers, she thrust her bare feet into them with sudden haste and threw the corner of her shawl over her shoulder.

She moved now with feverish speed; any one seeing her face would have exclaimed that she was not in conscious possession of her will, but would have shrunk before the force of her determination. She opened the door upon the dark staircase and went rapidly down; the courtyard was lit by a torch the soldiers had left stuck and flaring in a bracket. She had some trouble with the door, tearing her hands and breaking her nails upon the great latch, but she felt nothing, dragged it open, and found herself in the street. At the end of the street she could see the glare from the burning buildings of the market-place, and could hear the shout of military orders.

She knew she must take the opposite road; Malteios had told her that. 'Go by the mule-path over the hill; it will lead you straight to the creek where the boat will be waiting, he had said. 'The boat for Julian and me,' she kept muttering to herself as she speeded up the path stumbling over the shallow steps and bruising her feet upon the cobbles. It was very dark. Once or twice as she put out her hand to save herself from falling she encountered only a prickly bush of aloe or gorse, and the pain stung her, causing a momentary relief.

'I mustn't hurry too much,' she said to herself, 'I mustn't arrive at the creek before they have pushed off the boat. I mustn't call out . . .'

She tried to compare her pace with that of Julian, Kato, and the officers, and ended by sitting down for a few minutes at the highest point of the path, where it had climbed over the shoulder of the island, and was about to curve down upon the other side. From this small height, under the magnificent vault studded with stars, she could hear the sigh of the sea and feel the slight breeze ruffling her hair. 'Without Julian, without Julian—no never,' she said to herself, and that one thought revolved in her brain. 'I'm alone,' she thought, 'I've always been alone. . . . I'm an outcast, I don't belong here. . . .' She did not really know what she meant by this, but she repeated it with a blind conviction, and a terrible loneliness overcame her. 'Oh, stars!' she said aloud, putting up her hands to them, and again she did not know what she meant, either by the words or the gesture. Then she realised that it was dark, and standing up she thought, 'I'm frightened,' but there was no reply to the appeal for Julian that followed immediately upon the thought. She clasped her shawl round her, and tried to stare through the night; then she thought 'People on the edge of death have no need to be frightened,' but for all that she continued to look fearfully about her, to listen for sounds, and to wish that Julian would come to take care of her.

She went down the opposite side of the hill less rapidly than she had come up. She knew she must not overtake Julian and his escort. She did not really know why she had chosen to follow them, when any other part of the coast would have been equally suitable for what she had determined to do. But she kept thinking, as though it brought some consolation, 'He passed along this path five—ten—minutes ago; he is there somewhere, not far in front of me.' And she remembered how he had begged her to go with him. '. . . But I couldn't have gone!' she cried, half in apology to the dazzling happiness she had renounced, 'I was a curse to him—to everything I touch. I could never have controlled my jealousy, my exorbitance. . . . He asked me to go, to be with him always,' she thought, sobbing and hurrying on; and she sobbed his name, like a child, 'Julian! Julian! Julian!'

Presently the path ceased to lead downhill and became flat, running along the top of the rocky cliff about twenty feet above the sea. She moved more cautiously, knowing that it would bring her to the little creek where the boat was to be waiting; as she moved she blundered constantly against boulders, for the path was winding and in the starlight very difficult to follow. She was still fighting with herself, 'No, I could not go with him; I am not fit. . . . I don't belong here. . . .' that reiterated cry. 'But without him—no, no, no! This is quite simple. Will he think me bad? I hope not; I shall have done what I could. . . .' Her complexity had entirely deserted her, and she thought in broad, childish lines. 'Poor Eve!' she thought suddenly, viewing herself as a separate person, 'she was very young' (in her eyes youth amounted to a moral virtue), 'Julian, Julian, be a little sorry for her,—I was cursed, I was surely cursed,' she added, and at that moment she found herself just above the creek.

The path descended to it in rough steps, and with a beating heart she crept down, helping herself by her hands, until she stood upon the sand, hidden in the shadow of a boulder. The shadows were very black and hunched, like the shadows of great beasts. She listened, the softness of her limbs pressed against the harshness of the rocks. She heard faint voices, and, creeping forward, still keeping in the shadows, she made out the shape of a rowing-boat filled with men about twenty yards from the shore.

'Kato has gone with him!' was her first idea, and at that all her jealousy flamed again—the jealousy that, at the bottom of her heart, she knew was groundless, but could not keep in check. Anger revived her—'Am I to waste myself on him?' she thought, but immediately she remembered the blank that that one word 'Never!' could conjure up, and her purpose became fixed again. 'Not life without him, she thought firmly and unchangeably, and moved forward until her feet were covered by the thin waves lapping the sandy edge of the creek. She had thrown off her shoes, standing barefoot on the soft wet sand.

Here she paused to allow the boat to draw farther away. She knew that she would cry out, however strong her will, and she must guard against all chance of rescue. She waited at the edge of the creek, shivering and drawing her silk garments about her, and forcing herself to endure the cold horror of the water washing round her ankles. How immense was the night, how immense the sea!—The oars in the boat dipped regularly; by now it was almost undistinguishable in the darkness.

'What must I do?' she thought wildly, knowing the moment had come. 'I must run out as far as I can. . . .' She sent an unuttered cry of 'Julian!' after the boat, and plunged forward; the coldness of the water stopped her as it reached her waist, and the long silk folds became entangled around her limbs, but she recovered herself and fought her way forward. Instinctively she kept her hands pressed against her mouth and nostrils, and her staring eyes tried to fathom this cruelly deliberate death. Then the shelving coast failed her beneath her feet; she had lost the shallows and was taken by the swell and rhythm of the deep. A thought flashed through her brain, 'This is where the water ceases to be green and becomes blue'; then in her terror she lost all self-control and tried to scream; it was incredible that Julian, who was so near at hand, should not hear and come to save her; she felt herself tiny and helpless in that great surge of water; even as she tried to scream she was carried forward and under, in spite of her wild terrified battle against the sea, beneath the profound serenity of the night that witnessed and received her expiation.

THE BIG BESTSELLERS
ARE AVON BOOKS!

Available at better bookstores everywhere, or order direct from the publisher.

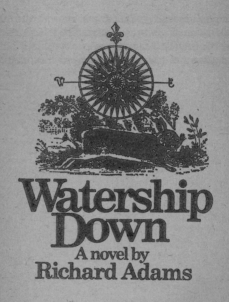

Watership Down

A novel by
Richard Adams